IMPERFECT GODS

A DARKLY FUNNY SUPERNATURAL SUSPENSE MYSTERY - BOOK 6 OF THE IMPERFECT CATHAR SERIES
C.N. ROWAN

CONTENTS

GLOSSARY

Mec – Modern French slang for a male friend.

Cadorna – Ancient Languedoc insult, literal meaning old cow.

Saabi – Arabic slang for friend

Laguna – Old Occitan/Basque slang for friend

Ami – Modern French word for friend.

To Mum & Dad.

For never giving up on me. Not even when I gave up on myself.

FOREWORD

Welcome to this, book 6 in the 'imPerfect Cathar' series. The culmination of all that's been so far. The end of the first story arc.

Which is a nice way of saying, I really do recommend you read the other five books before you get into this one!

If not, please be aware that excessive amounts of swearing — including the C word — abound in the following pages. And —a greater mortal sin in the eyes of some— British English spellings! Grab your safety Z's and hold on tight, cos those suckers are getting S'd in here.

To all who've walked this strange path with me so far. Who've trusted the process. Thank you.

Let's make it all worthwhile, shall we?

PROLOGUE

T here's always a price to pay for the choices we make, the paths we walk. In blood. In tears. In bones.

In those people lost, sacrificed, willingly or otherwise. In the parts of ourselves consumed just as utterly as those who've fallen in our stead.

The higher the stakes, the higher the bill when it comes due. There's no avoiding it, no ducking out at the last minute. Once you start down the path, unsure where the twists and turns will take you, there's one certainty you can carry with you every step of the way.

There's always a price to pay.

CHAPTER ONE
TOULOUSE, 9 JUNE, PRESENT DAY

Someone fetch me a pair of overly baggy trousers. I want to do the Hammered Dance.

By the Good God, I want to get drunk.

Let me be clear, I'm not about to crawl off into the gutter again. My days of drowning my miseries face-down in puddles of booze until they stop shrieking constantly in my face are done. For the time being at least. When your miseries swoop down on you like disease-ridden harpies to upset your banquet as often as mine do, the temptation is always going to linger.

No, I'm not about to do a booze cruise of the nearest alleyways and park benches. But I'd love to fall right into the nearest comfortable chair with a bottle of single malt, enough ice to sink a mid-sized ocean liner, and maybe even — wonder of wonders — a decent book. To have room to escape reality without it kicking my front door in and smacking me in the teeth.

But that's just a pipe dream. We're a long way from such hobbit-like reveries of quiet and calm.

The storm is arriving, and I feel like I'm standing in the middle of a field. On top of a metal ladder. Dressed in a suit of fucking armour. Holding a sign saying "Zeus is a right twat".

Of course, there's another good reason why I won't go off into a self-pitying pile of dejected spirits, both alcoholic and personal. Two good reasons actually. And they're both attached to the arms of the woman sitting next to me, who won't hesitate to wield her hands like the utterly deadly weapons they are, cracking me round the back of the skull if I decide to duck my responsibilities again. Those, I won't be able to duck.

While we might be waiting metaphorically for the storm to arrive, physically, it's already here. The night-time sky is split regularly on all sides by electrical flashes, like the gods have decided to have a disco. Having not been invited, we're just hanging around on the outside looking in while they get their rave on. Sheet lightning cracks off to the west; to the south, forks dance between the bubbled-up cloud mountains that dominate the horizon, blotting out the Pyrenees — the sky mocking the earth, replacing its mightiest features with terrible, deadly imitations of its own.

The rain sheets down, sluicing the streets of my city, washing them clean. I can't help thinking of a slaughterhouse getting sprayed down, ready for the next arriving cattle. Can't help wondering if these won't run red with blood before we get to the end of this story.

Except it's not really my city anymore. I'm still fed by the connection, still linked in. But just like I'm in a moving vehicle right now and I'm only a passenger, so it is with Toulouse. Isaac — well, Isaac and Jakob and Nithael and Nanael, because why settle for one person in a body when you can have two Kabbalah masters and two *freaking angels* — took over the wards when my own magic got eaten. I have *talent* again now, but it's only the *talent* I get from wearing the body of a dead fae queen. Next time I die, I'll be back at shizzard levels all over again. Isaac and the others had no choice but to take the strain. Not only that, they've pushed the wards out a lot farther — like a hundred kilometres farther in each direction, giving us all a better early warning system for whenever De Montfort comes calling. And he will because he needs Almeric's first original skull to complete his creepy sets. Someone really should get him into stamp-collecting or something instead.

So they hold the wards, meaning they hold the city. They're only doing what I asked them to do, what I told them needed to be done, but it still hurts in a way. Toulouse has always been mine, my one constant in a world changing at breakneck speed. Sure, I ended up co-habiting it with Franc, but somehow I always felt like the owner leasing out a granny flat to the local weirdo. I don't think Franc would have agreed, but it allowed me to sell it to myself. Plus, he was a scum-sucking shit heel. And now he's dead. Good. Fuck him.

'Any fresh ideas?' I don't have to spell out what I'm talking about. The same thing we've talked about every time we started up conversation the whole of the seven or so hours we've been travelling back from Paris. Discussed as we sat in the uncomfortable train seats. As we walked to the car park next door. While we stole a pretentious penis extension in the form of a Audi Spyder R8 from therein to get us to where Isaac is waiting. There's nothing else worth talking about, nothing else that's occupying a single braincell apart from the ones necessary to keep us safe on the road, moving in a straight line home.

The only other thing occupying our thoughts is Simon De Montfort. Him and his macabre ossuary. And how that all ties into the apparently alive Arnaud Almeric.

'None.' A short, sharp answer. Not surprising. Short and sharp are two words you could use to describe Aicha Kandicha anyhow. If you were feeling suicidal enough to make cracks about her height. Even I'm not that stupid. Most of the time. She has plenty of short, sharp objects she'd introduce into your various cracks were you to do so.

I sigh, a sound that has been as much the soundtrack to our drive as the eclectic blend of songs from the radio. Our station selection has been as unsettled as our minds have been, our fingers constantly jabbing out to try a different sound, searching for that elusive something that might allow us to relax, might bring us some peace.

My hyper-vigilant, utterly unsettled state of mind means I feel it — the moment the thought strikes Aich. Her body language changes at the wheel, her hands tightening, her frame stiffening. 'Could Almeric be behind it all?'

I'm about to dismiss it, but I stop, consider it. We know that all the bones are from previous times Almeric's been alive, bodies he's reincarnated in throughout the ages, starting with his own skull from his first life as the Butcher of Beziers. The one that Jakob and Nanael spent centuries trapped in. The life that I ended the first time I willingly killed anyone.

I rub my chin. 'I mean, he was certainly enough of an arsehole.' There's no question of that. Slaughtering twenty thousand people to kill a handful of Perfects, wiping out the town of Beziers with the now famous quote, "kill them all, God will know his own"? Not exactly sainthood material. Not that he would agree with that. 'He was a religious extremist though. Simon doesn't strike me as thinking he's on a mission from God. Jake and Elwood would think him as much of a cockgoblin as we do.'

Aicha shrugs. 'People change over centuries. Especially when reincarnating. Look at Ben.'

It's a fair point, albeit a painful one. Reincarnating broke my once-friend. Ruined him. Tore all the goodness from his soul and left him twisted, bitter, and ready to do anything to achieve his own ends. Of course, it's not true of everyone. 'Demon Fart hasn't changed.'

She nods acquiescence at the point. 'True. Neither have you. You're still a twat. Always have been, always will be.'

And on those pearls of wisdom, we both fall silent once more, lost in the same thoughts that haven't stopped swirling around and around in our minds since we left Paris. Where is De Montfort? What does he want with the skeletons? What horrors will be unleashed if he completes both sets? And where does Almeric fit into all of this?

By the time we turn onto the dirt path, my mood isn't so much soured as pickled, wrapped in slices of lemon and then painted with tamarind. Because every time I feel like we're getting closer to an answer, another hundred questions seem to pop up like the world's most unfair game of whack-a-mole. The reassuringly familiar crunch of the gravel chips under the tyres brings with it a touch of upliftment, of returning positivity. Because if there are any individuals in the world capable of answering a hundred impossible questions simultaneously without breaking a sweat, it's the geniuses waiting for me inside the farmhouse folly that becomes visible through the parting forest boughs.

I walk into the comfortably familiar country-farm kitchen area. The warmth outside is mitigated instantly by the cool tiles underfoot, and it's a relief. After having visited Paris and the middle of England, the temperature on dismounting the train at Matabiau felt oppressively hot, and I'm still struggling to reacclimatise. Isaac stands and sweeps me up into a manly hug, and now I'm crushing the breasts currently attached to me into my father figure, which is precisely as weird and as uncomfortable for me as it sounds. I quite like this current body, apart from the gender dysmorphia it causes me. It'd be a shame if I ended up killing it trying to snort bleach powder to cleanse my brain of such terribly disturbing memories later.

Once we get past the entirely normal hug that I just succeeded in making unnecessarily weird, we all grab a seat. Different seats, obviously; otherwise, it'd just get weird again.

At Isaac's insistence, we fill him in on what happened during our time in Paris. Because I love him dearly, I do so instead of punching him repeatedly in the face and screaming in his ear until he tells me who Almeric is at this precise moment. It's a level of self-restraint that I think deserves a written commendation — possibly an actual medal. For resisting violence in the face of extreme provocation or something. I'm basically Gandhi and Isaac, the rapacious British colonialists, here. And I'm definitely not exaggerating with that particular metaphor in the slightest.

Once we get Isaac caught up on our hi-jinks — and our low jinks and all the jinks in between — I'm ready to do my impression of Hiroshima if I don't get the answers I want. So, of course, Isaac changes subject.

'I said on the phone I have another surprise for you,' he says.

Now I'm in a quandary. I want answers regarding Almeric. Let's be honest, most of my mental capacity —which is fairly limited at the best of times— has been focused on the Grail-infused bone sets De Montfort has been collecting like Panini stickers. But there's a gleam in his eye that is tickling my brain. He mentioned he had a surprise for us before Paris, but frankly, under the weight of exhaustion and terror and terrified exhaustion, I clean forgot. Plus, he's clearly having to work damn hard not to bounce up and down in excitement, to hold on to his scholarly poise. This is Isaac being a kid at Christmas.

'Go for it, man. Knock our socks off.'

Boy, does he. Does he ever.

Off to the right, from out of the doorway that leads to his workshop, comes what, I assume for a moment, is a robot sent from Skynet in order to stop me leading the human rebellion. Who am I kidding? The target would clearly be Aicha. That's beside the point though.

The point is, it's not every day a seven-foot gleaming chrome monstrosity, all burnished metal and walking death, strolls into your kitchen. If you're reading this and that isn't the case, then my sincerest apologies to the future. We fucked it up even worse than it looked like we had. Or if this is being read by a seven-foot gleaming chrome monstrosity and I'm still alive, please let me say how glad I am to have handed over control to our clearly superior robotic overlords.

The automaton definitely resembles that skeletal badass underneath Arnie's fake flesh like in the original *Terminator*. I suppose "metallic murder skeleton" is a pretty go-to design strategy if you're creating a deadly robot. It's a fabulous feat of engineering, and I'd applaud rapturously if I wasn't currently tensing all the muscles in my body simultaneously in order to stop from wetting myself.

This isn't made any easier when it strides directly towards me, wraps its arms around me, and pulls me inexorably towards it. I manage a *meep* of dismay as it crushes me into what, I realise after a good few seconds of waiting for my head to pop like a grape, is a warm embrace.

'Hello, my dear boy!' The warm, almost plummy intonations are clearly identifiable, even warped by the harsh grate of the speaker apparently embedded in its throat. Or rather, his throat if it's who I think it is. Or even their throat, actually. I suspect both of them have gone along for the ride.

'Jakob?' I ask, blinking, trying to calm down my fight-or-flight instincts, which keep going into overdrive every time I catch the reflection of my own eyelids blinking in the metallic carapace. 'Is that you and Nanael? Really?'

'It is indeed! What do you think of my rather marvellous new body?'

I pull away to give myself the space to look more appreciatively now I'm not on the edge of gibbering in terror at its very presence. 'Very impressive,

Jak! Far better than the beaten-up old rust bucket you've had to ride around in until now.'

Isaac swats at my arm. 'Watch it, lad. None of your lip now. I'm ready to bask in all the praise for the miraculous creation I've made.'

I have to admit, this is beyond extra. This is master craftsmanship that'd make Hephaestus snuff out his forge and hang up his blacksmith apron for good. It's the kind of design work that would have haunted Steve Jobs' dreams and would make any government's military wing cream their pants in excitement. Still, one thing concerns me with the whole setup.

'Zac, it's amazing. Like, seriously incredible. But it's a bit...' I search for the right term. '"Exterminate all in my path. I have become Death, Destroyer of Worlds" for a pacifist researcher and a committedly non-violent angel, isn't it?' And there's another part of this that doesn't make sense for me as well. 'Also, how did you manage it? I thought you ruled out golems as an option for getting Jak his independence back?'

Isaac goes that delightful shade of glowing pink I always aim to make him turn when setting out to embarrass him. 'Well, yes. Admittedly, I may have gone a bit OTT with the design aesthetics. Still, we are effectively at war, are we not? And Jak and Nan need to be able to defend themselves. Especially considering they're now a major target — the major target, presumably — for De Montfort.'

I'm about to ask him what he means about them being a major target when a sneaking suspicion slides into my mind.

'You used Almeric's skull, haven't you? Put it inside the golem?' I almost whisper the words, as if saying them too loud will make them irrevocably real. It seems inconceivable that after centuries of emasculated imprisonment where Jakob and Nanael were helpless and out of control of their own power that they would willingly re-enter their prison cell. I can't help thinking about my own recent stint of captivity. Three weeks, give or take, and I'll never go willingly back into that dark hole. Hell, going near anywhere like it is going to be hard work for a damn long time. I can't imagine how much courage it must have taken for them to step back into the skull, to take up residence in it all over again, especially since the first time they had, they'd also had someone they'd trusted. Love had led them to centuries of suffering. Ben's trickery had cost them everything. That they can trust anyone again, that they can risk everything to go back into that skull? It shows two things. The unwavering faith they have in Isaac. And the incorruptible love they have for us all.

Jakob pats me reassuringly on the shoulder. This tells me just how recently they've made the transfer because he clearly hasn't even come close to learning his own strength yet. Were I not in the considerably tougher-than-human frame of a daoine sidhe, I suspect my shoulder blade would have just snapped in two. As is, I can feel some very pretty bruises blooming like flower petals where his heavy-duty fingers made contact.

'It was my choice, my dear boy,' he says as I step as tactfully as possible out of range of any more sympathetic gestures. 'We worked out the details together. Of course, obtaining this much titanium wasn't easy, but it was worth it.'

Bloody hell. Titanium might be cheaper and easier to get hold of than gold, but still. I can only imagine how many tonnes of the material they had to obtain. Fuck-tonnes would be my educated guess.

Of course, articulating and animating a structure based on modern robotics would be precisely zero problem for these two prodigies. Considering they are capable of making articulated clay, like the Golem of Prague, this must have been a doddle for them. It's also a lot easier when you can probably replace some of the trickier wiring components with Kabbalist runes and sigils. Still, to achieve this? To take the skull and all it must symbolise for Jak and Nan and transform it into a form of freedom for them, to give them back their independence and liberty? Not to mention giving us an even more formidable weapon than the mage and angel combination already were...

'Absolute fucking genius. The pair of you. Top marks. Seriously. Colour me impressed.'

Aicha's been quiet throughout most of this. I catch her eye, and note the furrow of her brow. She sees the moment when I work out what she's already worked out though. Before, we had an easily transportable skull, a chess piece we could use and — if needs be sacrifice — in this fucked-up game we're apparently playing with Demon Fart. Now? Well now, it's infinitely more valuable and, considering who now lives inside it again, there's not one of us who would be prepared to sacrifice it. And that makes it both more vulnerable, as well as more valuable.

She gives a shake of her head though, a subtle no. It's too late to start upsetting Isaac with those details now. All it'll do is make him worry more, second-guess himself harder, and we need him on his a-game. Instead she starts to applaud, and for once, it's not even sarcastic. 'Bravo, both of you. I think you should work out a song and dance routine to "Puttin' On The Ritz" for when you debut this to the Talented community at large.'

Jakob peers at her. At least, I think that's what the camera-lens-style optics he has in place of eyes mean when they whirr and narrow. 'Are you suggesting I'm Frankenstein's monster here, young lady?'

Well, well. Isaac's introduced Jak to the works of Mel Brooks. I'm surprised and impressed for the second time. Aicha, though, returns his look so impassively, it's a toss up which is the automaton. 'Tell me, in all honesty, there wasn't an operating table with restraints and plasma globes and probably even a thunderstorm. Also, 'Zac, if you didn't shout, "It's alive!" after it worked, I'm revoking your mad scientist card.'

Isaac blushes that deeply satisfying colour again. 'I may have mumbled it,' he says, shuffling his feet.

Jak leans forward, a hand cupped to the side of his mouth. 'He screamed it to the heavens as I sat up. You'd have been very proud, my girl.'

Isaac coughs and harrumphs. 'Right, well, quite enough of that. We have other fish to fry. Let's get to the matter at hand, shall we? Quite enough of Paul's meanderings. We all know how incapable he is of focusing on getting to the heart of the matter.'

Now, look. There may be some small truth in the suggestion that I can get side-tracked at times, especially when telling stories. That I might, occasionally, end up going off on a tangent or straying into some slightly elaborate flight of fancy that can keep me from reaching the point quite as quickly as some might like. Now and then.

But this time, it definitely isn't my fault. I've been raring to go since we got here, desperate to know the answer to the questions steadily burning a hole through my cerebellum. Sadly, by the time I consider this and reach that conclusion, the conversation has moved on, and my rebuttal is no longer timely. Good God damn it.

I'm still going to interrupt with it though. 'I know you are, but what am I?'

'A complete and utter dickhead.' No prizes for guessing who that one comes from.

'Anyhow,' Isaac says, 'we should get to the matter at hand.'

Finally, I think, finally we're going to find out who Almeric is in this life, and we can start making a plan to move forward. Then I see Isaac's eyes widen slightly. I have a brief moment to wonder why. Then I feel it too.

I'm still tied to the wards. I created them, after all. And I can still tell precisely the moment they're breached.

We're under attack.

CHAPTER TWO

TOULOUSE, 9 JUNE, PRESENT DAY

Of course we're under attack. The Good God forbid I get a little down time and A FUCKING ANSWER AS TO WHO ALMERIC IS NOW.

I leap to my feet, sending the chair skittering backwards. Jak shoots across, catching it before it falls, and gently puts it back on four feet. Damn, he's fast. That, though, isn't the overriding concern at the moment.

'I thought you said the new super-charged wards could keep people out!' I shout at Isaac.

'They should! I don't get it. Hold on. I'll ju...' He cuts off, and I can tell he's communing with Nithael, the Bene Elohim from the higher dimensions he shares his body with. Nith won't go on the offensive, but he'll play a good defence game, such as helping Isaac soup up my wards.

Isaac blinks back to us. 'Ah, bugger it. Apparently the individuals in question? They threw themselves against the wards with such reckless abandonment that the wards would've killed them.'

'Not seeing a problem here.' Aicha unsheaths her swords even though we should have time, theoretically, before they reach us. Isaac pushed the wards' thresholds back to nearly an hour drive from here. Still, anyone who can get through them may be able to close the distance quicker than we expect.

Isaac indicates us to sit again. Apparently, he's confident they're not arriving any time soon. 'Unfortunately, Nith does see one. They're not in their right minds. It's not a choice for them to be attacking.'

'You're saying they're possessed?'

'*I'm* not saying that. Nith is. Or something very much bloody like it.'

Fucknuggets. That's not good news. Basically, we're down our two most powerful weapons in that case.

Nithael and Nanael are awesome in the "make your jaw drop and your eyes bleed" sense of the word. They're from a higher plane of existence. One where violence is frowned upon and seen as a sign of barbarity. Which is, of course, absolutely true, but it also means they're not ready to rumble even if Michael Buffer himself is screaming at them down a ring-side microphone. They won't go on the offensive. They'll keep Isaac and Jakob safe and do everything they can to protect the innocent. Problem is, in this case, innocent includes the people pouring over our boundaries to attack us. Pouring over because Nithael isn't prepared to let them fry against his wards, so he's letting them through.

And they are pouring in. This isn't a little posse, like the werewolves Ben sent against us to test our resolve and demonstrate his. This is a full-on platoon, maybe even a company. All coming to kick our asses and take back the skull. Unless some other megalomaniac has somehow possessed a load of innocents and turned them into an invading army with us as their targets. Which ventures off into the realms of implausibility, considering the timing.

Even though they're in vehicles, we still have time before they arrive. Every moment they run over our territory, we're gaining more info about them, the territory giving us what it can gather, a literal home field advantage. Plus, here, the land itself is like an oversized battery, ready to keep us topped up to the brim with *talent* no matter how much we burn through.

And that worries me enormously.

De Montfort's never been stupid or sloppy. He's never rushed to action without carefully laid plans. He's been fucking with me for hundreds of years, and I've now caught him out twice. Once by Aicha rescuing me from the cave he trapped me in before my sanity snapped, and the other day when we tracked him to Kenilworth Castle and burst in on his inner sanctuary. I suppose you could add the time I smashed the Grail onto that too, but he was just a grunt for Papa Nicetas then rather than a Talented threat all of his own.

So hurling cannon fodder at us on home turf doesn't really feel like his sort of play. It's a real hit-and-hope kind of strategy, like he thinks he can outgun us by sheer weight of numbers. Throw enough bodies at a problem until it goes away. Which is the sort of thing I might do but doesn't seem to correlate with the level of fox-like cunning De Montfort has shown so far.

'This doesn't make sense!' Considering everyone here in this room, up to and including Hubert, the short-toed snake eagle currently roosting in the rafters, is considerably smarter than me, it's worth verbalising. Throw it out there for public debate.

'Nope. Trap. Gotta be.' Aicha's in war mode.

It's a transition that'd make the God of War, Kratos, himself think twice before tangling with her. Actually, there are quite a lot of similarities between the two of them, outside of the penchant for face tattoos. Except I'd choose to have Aicha by my side every time even if Kratos were real.

Which he's not. He's just a video game character spin on Greek mythology. As far as I know, anyhow. Stranger things in heaven and earth, Horatio, and all that jazz.

'What do you mean?' Jakob's voice carries a measure of his uncertainty even through the slight distortion of his speakers. Which, by the way, is mental. How did they build what is effectively a robot that even the chief demons running Google would sell their immortal souls to even more evil demons to own, but they couldn't install a decent quality speaker? My burner phone has more bass and mids in it than Jakob's.

I sigh. I love Jakob like the uncle he sort of is to me, but there are times when his naivety plunges off the edge of "charming" and into the depths of "painfully oblivious". 'Jak, even without your funky new body, even if Aicha and I didn't get back in time, you and 'Zac are serious heavyweights. You should be more than capable of protecting the skull, whether the two Bene boys insisted on sitting it out or not. Hoping to drown you in cannon fodder doesn't make sense unless it's part of a broader trap.'

Jakob rubs the back of his skull, which would be an infinitely more humanising gesture if it didn't produce a squealing metal-on-metal sound like a car tearing its bumper down a brick wall. Being a brilliant driver, I've obviously never heard that noise. Honest. 'They're not technically boys, Paul. They're really outside of such petty distinctions as gender and...' He pauses, looking around at our faces. 'And this isn't the time for this discussion, is it?'

'Not at all, but well done for realising it.' I can feel the minutes ticking away while we engage in off-the-point banter. I wonder if it's possible to get a Ritalin prescription for a band of immortal heretics, whether it might help us all to focus. Surely that's something Isaac or Jakob can knock up in their labs? A sudden thought hits me. Another off the fucking point one, but I have to share it. Have. To.

'Jak, you are capable of preparing tinctures and potions, right? One could say you meddle with esoteric forces? Hell, given the proper motivation, I bet you could turn lead into gold, even?'

Jak nods his skeletal metal head. 'You could say that, dear boy. What does that have to do with our situation?' His excitement is audible. 'Can you see a way we can dispel the poor souls inbound?'

'No, but...' Getting up, I walk forward and tap on his new body so it gives a satisfying ring. 'You're a *full metal alchemist*.'

Even with his whole immovable cyborg face, I can feel the blankness of Jakob's regard. Isaac looks equally confused. Luckily, Aicha is here...to clip me round the back of the head as she passes hard enough to make my ears ring.

'No. Way too obvious. Not the time, dickhead. Focus on the incoming hordes.'

Totally worth it.

I turn to Isaac. 'Can you tell anything at all about the spell or whatever's drained their free will away?'

I can see by the faraway look, he's back talking to Nithael. By the frown, it's not going well. 'Not really. Nith can't without damaging them, and he sees them as something to pity rather than to punish,' he says when rejoining us.

Damn it. I concentrate, reaching out again through the wards. It takes conscious effort now that they aren't really mine anymore. The intruders have covered about a third of the distance already. Shit, they're eating up the miles. I guess speed limits aren't a concern when you're not in your right mind. Or if you're in the backseat and someone or something else is doing the driving both mentally and physically.

I can tell more than I could before, but it's still not much. An impression of numbers — somewhere around thirty. It's hard to get an accurate read.

They're moving too fast, and these aren't really my wards anymore. Mine protected Toulouse city, stopping at the ring-road. And if Nith or Nan can't or won't do anything, all they are to me is an early warning system. Granted, that's all mine were too — and slightly porous ones at that, which I plugged with that slimeball Franc's help — but I felt overconfident in souped-up angel ones. Turns out they're just as porous but for different reasons.

I'm pacing now. Their invading presence feels like an egg-timer where they're jumping up and down on the sand in the top, making the granules tumble down faster. It's making me anxious. I want to go and meet them head-on, but it's not sensible. I made a vow to stop rushing straight into messy situations without thinking it through properly. Unfortunately, all the thinking has done so far is get the *Full Metal Alchemist* theme song running on loop in my head, an earworm I'm going to struggle to get rid of for hours. Assuming I don't get rid of my head by having it chopped off or blown up during the pending battle.

'What are we missing?' My frustration isn't faked. I can see the two boffin brothers are deep in thought — or else communing with their better halves. Aicha is by the door, her body pressed against the jamb. She's holding the net curtain of the nearby window aside to allow her a clear but protected view of the drive they're likely to arrive up. I don't see them suddenly hiking cross-country to try to come in any other way. Whatever's keeping them under control must know they've triggered the wards. They might as well just come gunning up the most easy path of ingress.

Isaac suddenly pipes up. 'Nithael says they believe they can break the spell individually. They say it seems most like an activated geas that has possessed each soul. If they can lay our hands on each one suffering, they can unbind them from its chains.'

Finally, some good news. There's only one problem. If they've come here to fight and die if necessary because whoever's controlling them doesn't care if they live or not...

Keeping ourselves alive, as well as them long enough for 'Zac and Jak to lay hands on them?

That's not going to be easy.

CHAPTER THREE
TOULOUSE, 9 JUNE, PRESENT DAY
Feeling slightly better to have something resembling a plan. It's more prepared than we are normally.

We get ourselves into position just before the first car comes bouncing up the potholed driveway like it's being driven by the fucking Dukes of Hazzard and they're aiming to jump a river. The amount of air they're getting on what looks like a Dacia Duster is insane, and were whoever or whatever is inside actually in control of themselves, I'm sure they'd be screaming in terror and readying themselves to launch whiplash compensation claims against the driver's insurance. Even if said driver were themselves.

This would be a wonderful moment to transform said Duster from a flying car into a flying fireball by making the gas tank explode. Sadly, Nith and Nan have both begged for mercy for the unwitting occupants, so the easy way out is off the table. Of course, fuel reserves aren't the only thing I can make explode.

As the wannabe 4x4 SUV touches back down with all the grace of a ballet-dancing hippo tripping over its own feet, it starts to skid to a stop. Not for long. Sitting up a tree I chose as an ambush vantage beside the access road, I call on the air inside the left front tyre and suggest it might like to expand dramatically. Right now.

Air is basically the definition of nature, seeing as how without it, the Earth would just be a lifeless ball of rock, so it responds well to my fae nature. The wheel shreds itself, sections of rubber flinging out wildly as the metal rim spins down onto nothing, gouging into the gravel of the drive. It can't push the vehicle forward, not like the other wheels can. So it transforms from forward momentum to a pivot point, and the car careens wildly off to the side, smashing into the trunk of a tree side-first. Probably not hard enough to kill anyone inside, but hopefully enough to put them out of operation for the time being.

Car number two is also arriving now at a speed of knots. Aicha deals with this one in a similar, albeit slightly flashier way. As this one slows down, anticipating the stop, plus seeing the wreckage of the first car, she flicks a tiny fireball at their front wheel. One very satisfying pop later, it also decides to wrap itself around one of the trunks lining the side of the driveway.

So far, so good. Isaac hurries across to the first car. We decided Jakob should stay inside, at least to start with. His new body armour or armour body, whichever way round it is, forms an ace in the hole for us. We don't know if De Montfort can see what our attackers can see. On the other hand, we don't know he can't, so better to play it safe unless we actually need him.

Isaac reaches the wreck just as the first body staggers out. I turn from him, my eyes peeled, waiting for the next car to arrive when I hear a noise I didn't expect. A *pop* like someone just cracked open a bottle of champagne.

Problem is, I doubt anyone's being so pre-emptive as to start celebrating our victory just yet.

I turn back around, and my heart sinks. Isaac is covered in blood. Arterial spray soaks his clothes; they're absolutely sodden, and his face is a red so entirely different from the embarrassed blush I enjoyed earlier. His expression breaks my heart. The pain, the horror at seeing someone die in his arms.

These days I can get soaked in more gore than Derek from *Bad Taste* and I'd still be able to make a witty quip or some sort of snarky put-down. Isaac isn't built that way. Never has been, and I honestly hope he never will be. I'm happy to take that bit of soul tarnish if it keeps him safe from it. There's guilt in his expression too. A shame that he's failed. I don't know how he has — and frankly, considering he's trying to keep the army turning up at his house to burn it and us to the ground alive, I don't see it as a failure. But I know it's something that's going to keep him up at night for a long time.

That last thought stirs something, a slight niggle, like worrying at a loose tooth and feeling that tiny snap that means it'll actually come out now. I don't have time to worry about that for the moment though. I need to move.

I cover the distance to Isaac at a pace that'd make Usain Bolt dab in appreciation. Arm round his shoulders, I shepherd him back inside. Aicha's just behind us, slamming the door and securing the locks. The moment we're in, Jak powers up the protective barrier he's been readying, using the outer walls of the house itself. These differ from the main wards, so should work better at repelling the invaders rather than frying them.

The next car's about to arrive, and the first bodies are already pulling themselves out of the wrecks, paying precisely bupkis attention to the corpse nearby.

Isaac sinks into a chair as I move from looking out the window, his pale face sweat-beaded. I want to wrap him up in a hug and tell him it'll be all right. I try not to lie to my friends though, and I don't have time to sugarcoat it because we need a new plan and fast. 'What happened, 'Zac?'

His eyes flick back to me, from wherever he went in his mind. 'Plastic explosives, lad. Implanted in the neck. The moment I broke the geas, they triggered. Nith absorbed the force so it did me no damage, but...' He looks outside again, and this time I know he's looking at the prone form on the driveway. 'But there was nothing we could do for him.'

I might not have sugarcoating time, but I'll damn well make enough time to get this point through. I grab his face with both hands so he has to look at me. 'No. There wasn't. You're doing your best, trying to save them. This is on whoever did this.'

Then it clicks. That wobbly tooth feeling. A moment of clarity when I get what this is all about. I swear loudly and prolifically but manage to avoid kicking anything and breaking any bones. My anger management is obviously improving with time.

Now it's Isaac's turn to look concerned despite having his own trauma to handle. 'What is it, lad?'

I slam my fist down on the kitchen work surface. 'Ben's werewolves.'

Aicha gets it immediately. She curses equally proficiently on her side of the room. Isaac flinches at another painful memory.

Jakob looks confused. 'What werewolves?' I realise I don't know if we ever told him about that.

I turn in his direction, but Aicha beats me to it. 'Bunch of wolves. Ben forced them to attack us. Threatened their family. Killed one when Nith protected 'Zac.'

It's an effective summary. 'The idea was to give us a motivating kick up the arse because apparently, Ben didn't know the power of the words "please" and "thank you". The whole point of it was that either he'd keep killing innocent people —'

'Or make us kill them.'

'Right, Aich, or make us kill them until we did what he wanted.' I snarl in frustration. 'This is the same thing. Oh, shit.' The next car whips up the drive and comes to a halt.

We'll have to discuss the rest of this later. Right now, there are more pressing matters. The people outside are approaching close enough that the outside security lights detect movement and flick on, illuminating what we're up against.

They're a motley bunch. It looks like De Montfort hijacked Bill and Ted's telephone booth and went searching for the most bogus dudes in all the timelines. The first two cars were full of knights in armour. They've mostly extracted themselves from the wreckage now, and the curves of their plate metal gleam and glint as they pull themselves completely free. The car that screeches to a halt is being driven by a fellow dressed like he's off to a Jack Sparrow costume contest, only without the whimsical drunkenness and flouncing. No, he actually looks like he drinks rum sitting on fifteen dead men's chests, straight from the bottle, skipping all the yo-ho-hoing. This is an actual pirate — or was once upon a time. He has a cutlass in his hand that reminds me of Franc's cursed blade. It looks just as sharp and deadly.

The people accompanying him make me rub my eyes to check I'm not day-dreaming. You might think that seeing a group of what look like Nazi SS officers getting out might not seem any stranger than a bunch of knights, but dressing up as a chevalier is a cool thing to do. Historical re-enactments and LARPing for the win. Dressing up as a Nazi? Still something only Nazis do, whatever the twat at some posh right-wing fancy dress party claims. There's nothing even ironically cool about fascists.

The eye-rub does nothing except grind a loose eyelash under the lid, making me wince and rub harder as my eye streams. Who needs enemies to attack when you can blind yourself with your own body hair? Truly, there is no terrible situation that I cannot make worse. What it doesn't do, sadly, is make the SS twatsicles disappear.

It does mean, though, between the rubbing and the wincing and the half-crying, that I miss them unloading the boot of the car. When I can see again properly, it's in time to look at what they brought as a present for us.

I'm staring straight down the barrel of a bazooka. They shouldn't have. They really shouldn't have.

Chapter Four
TOULOUSE, 9 JUNE, PRESENT DAY

When it comes to RPGs, I prefer the ones with the dice and imagination and little plastic figures rather than the ones that come shooting out of metal tubes to blow your day into little pieces. And you along with it.

If you've come this far with us on the twists and turns that have been my excuse for an existence in recent times, then perhaps you're wondering why the sight of an antiquated non-magical weapon would cause my heart to sink.

Two reasons. First, just because it wasn't made magically doesn't mean it isn't enhanced — see my own sword as a classic example of that. Two, because I have a really, really bad feeling about it.

The fascist wankbugle holding it doesn't hesitate to show me I should always listen to my feelings. I see the flicker of ignition behind whatever he has packed in the firing hole and then the rocket's sailing towards us. What

I can see of it doesn't make my heart sink further so much as summons up an emotional kraken to wrap slimy tentacles around it and drag it down to the deepest depths. Because it should be utterly impossible. Sadly, not something that's ever stopped De Montfort from fucking with us thus far.

The shell is infused with *talent*. Not human *talent* or fae *talent*. As time slows down in the approximate half a second prior to impact, that momentary pause as the brain overloads in preparation for the world of pain and chaos it realises is about to descend, I can *see* it. Black essence coats it, covering it like it's been dipped in the magical equivalent of treacle, viscous and in that strange semi-state between solid and liquid. It's demon *talent*. Demon essence if I had to hazard a guess.

Just before we get blown to smithereens, let's just pause so I can take a moment to clear up a few misconceptions concerning demons. Despite what you've heard, they're not actually interested in stealing your soul, except in the sense that they're mischievous fuckers, and it'd amuse the hell out of them (no pun intended) to watch you try to find it again afterwards. In the same way that the Bene Elohim aren't really angels, just more highly evolved beings, demons and devils are just creatures from dimensions further down below ours...or existing parallel in ways where directions like down and up don't mean anything.

Similarly, the whole angels versus demons thing is a bit of a misnomer. Sure, from the little I know, demons tend not to like angels very much. But honestly? Angels don't even really pay demons much attention. That's what Isaac told me, and as he has the inside scoop, I tend to believe him. It's a bit like that local sports team that always gets hammered by another much more successful one. For the beaten team, they believe the other one to be their mortal foes, their sworn enemies. While the successful one doesn't even pay them any attention because it's a guaranteed easy win every time. The Bene Elohim's real hard-on is for the fae due to their tendency to flip between dimensions fucking people up and taking slaves. Demons are very happy in their own homes, and only end up in our world when some eye-liner wearing spunkmonkey decides it's a cracking idea to summon one over, and even then only very, very briefly. With similar results to when anyone tries to summon up angels, reality tends to get a bit explodey, wiping out summoner and their surrounding environs fairly rapidly if the demons actually manifest even slightly. There's only ever been one exception — my friend, Faustus, and his bound demon companion Mephy.

I once asked Isaac if demon magic was any threat to Nithael, and from what I can gather, Nith spent the equivalent of the next half an hour killing himself laughing haughtily. So I really shouldn't be worried. Except this isn't magic. As I said, I reckon this is actual demon essence, which —again— should not be possible. There's only one demon manifested in this reality, and he's a close personal friend of mine. So either De Montfort has captured Mephistopheles or somehow swayed him to the dark side, or he's pulled off another feat no one thought possible and managed to get a demon to manifest up here without blowing himself across the Pyrenees until the hills are alive with the sound of mucus being scattered across a hundred-kilometre radius.

And there's something very, very wrong about that demonic shell. Nith won't be worried, Nan either, but alarm bells are screaming in my head that the angelic wards just aren't going to be enough. It's a bit like wearing a super-advanced bulletproof vest that'll stop a high-velocity sniper round, no problem. Still won't do fuck-all if someone drops a ten-tonne boulder on your head.

Thus why I'm so stressed out to see our own equivalent of said ten-tonne boulder hurtling towards us. If I'm right, Jak's barrier is going to do basically diddly squat against the impending strike. I throw my own *talent* out, latching onto the woods surrounding us, and pour that sense of solidity, of the impenetrable ancientness of the forest's roots, to Jak's working to keep us from getting blown sky-high.

It works. Sort of. Problem is, trees don't stand up too well to an explosive bazooka strike either. But Jak's barrier diffuses some of the blast, and the living essence of the trees diffuses a bit of the weird demonic energy, so between us, we stop the house getting reduced to a pile of rubble. Unfortunately, it doesn't stop a significant part of the front wall from crumbling, and the protective barrier pops out of existence along with it. Not because of the explosion. Because of that fucking impossible demonic essence that should not exist and shouldn't have any effect on the angelic magic even if it did. I need to have some serious words with Isaac — and Nith and Nan by proxy — once we survive this.

If we survive this.

Another car comes screaming up the drive, pulling to a stop with a handbrake turn that makes Vin Diesel look like he's driving Miss Daisy. Isaac's going to have a hell of a time relaying all the scree, but as he has a ginormous hole in the front of his house, he probably has bigger things to worry about.

Plus, the tell-tale rattle of automatic gunfire is always a cause for concern. I fling up a shield of raw power just to give me mental space to work out what's going on without my mental getting spaced out across the wall behind me. Someone's equipped the Nazis with modern warfare gear, which is just bad sportsmanship in my book. Bullets rattle into my defences, and I feel the judder passing through my connection each time they strike.

This, by the way, is why the Talented don't run the world. In films, superheroes fling up shields and block an entire army's worth of bullets or just freeze them in the air before flipping them over and flinging them back to take out the shooters. I could do that, maybe. For a bullet. Problem is, and this might surprise you, bullets move really quickly. So trying to grab hold of one in flight with your *talent* is tough work. Stopping them is easier, but they still pack a punch, what with all that explosive velocity. So when hundreds of them rattle off your protective shielding within seconds of each other, it takes a huge amount of power to maintain it upright and keep patching up holes. It's sort of like the reverse of those shields from *Dune*, which would be a nifty gadget for someone to invent and then pop in the mail to me as my Secret Santa present this year, by the way. Blocking a melee attack or catching a falling tree — hell, even grabbing hold of a moving car — those are fairly straight-forward actions. Magic's gonna react to your intentions and get it done. Stopping bullets? That takes a shitload of concentration and a whole host of power to back it up. Being on home turf, we've plenty of the latter, but it's damn hard to concentrate when your home-from-home has just exploded into a battlefield full of screams and smoke and the sort of noises that demand your attention however occupied you are. It's a stimuli overload for anyone, and I'm easily distracted at the best of times.

I need to do something about the guns. Especially as more people are arriving, and apart from the knights (who are charging at Aicha, their swords raised because they're clearly in a hurry to stop breathing), high velocity weaponry seems to be their choice of armament. The problem is, I'm getting absolutely clattered by bullets, and keeping them from turning me into a fleshy colander is taking all my mental effort.

Thankfully, the angels choose this moment to get their heads back in the game. I'm assuming the demonic essence explosion knocked them off kilter for a minute, but suddenly the gunfire ceases at last. I'm not sure what they've done, but now the gunmen might as well be waving sticks around, making *pew pew* noises. The fact that they are still running around, though, and not frozen in a halo of angelic light, tells me one of two things. Either they have some of that weird demon essence protecting them — unlikely but not impossible, although I'd have said differently prior to the bazooka incident — or the Bene Brothers think the fuckers' necks will play 'Pop Goes The Weasel' if they grab them. I reckon that's more likely.

Right now, it's time to get up in the mix. The invading troops drop their now defunct modern weaponry and draw various bladed instruments. Looks like De Monfort anticipated this might happen. Now it's time to get down and dirty. Just my style.

I leap forward. Aicha fences with the two knights as I rush past. Killing them would be a matter of seconds, but she loves Isaac and, by extension, Nith. She's trying her damnedest to debilitate them rather than straight up slaughter them, so it's taking more time. Hard to slice a tendon when they're wearing armour plate, and these two are no slouches in the whole "wave a sword at someone till they go ouch" department. Ripostes aplenty from what I see, but I don't have time to dally with that.

Jakob's trying to talk down what looks like a Jacobean soldier, kilt and all. The chap in question is also simultaneously getting a science lesson in what happens when steel hits titanium as the head of his Lochaber axe crumples while trying to decapitate Jakob. It looks like he's not in any immediate danger, so I leave him trying to talk the puzzled Highlander to death.

I draw my sword as I run and wrap it in my *talent*, vines glowing green and deadly. Just in time. A sword swings in an arc that would do a good job of splitting my skull in two. My blade-edge shears it in half instead, and the end of their weapon buries itself into the ground just behind me. I make a mental note of where it is, as otherwise, knowing me, I'm liable to come rushing back, probably once the fight is over, and step straight on it, impaling my foot. I punch the sour-faced soldier dressed like he's about to go over the top at the Somme hard enough to snap his head back. His eyes roll like a pair of dice in a crap shoot, and he's out like a light. I turn my next step into a half leap, my foot pressing off his stomach mid-air as he falls like a felled tree, and propel myself towards the Nazis.

There's more of them now. Looks like a good part of their contingent are goose-steppers, which suits me down to the ground. Killing Nazis always was one of my favourite pastimes. I might be a tad rusty, but I'm happy to put in some practice all over again.

I know the Bene Elohim want us to not kill the attackers because they're under mind control. Thing is, seems to me, we have warriors from different time periods involved in this assault. I don't see De Montfort taking the time to dress them up with periodically precise clothing just to give us something to look at while we take them out of action. Nope. I'll lay money that somehow, he's had these soldiers on ice, waiting for just such a moment. I remember the bodies in the cave, the stasis magic he used to keep them preserved. I'll bet he worked something similar here too.

Which means these fuckers were Nazis before they got press-ganged into Team Demon Fart.

Am I one hundred percent sure? Nope. Can't be. But I'm willing to take an educated guess and live with the consequences if I'm wrong. I have enough baggage that two more bad calls won't break my back. I'm not convinced any of the other poor bastards are getting out of here alive anyhow, however hard we try.

I rain down a diagonally slicing blow on the nearest *seigheiler*. It doesn't sever his head from his body, but I reckon he's probably still dead — his skull is flapping about like a flag on a windy day. My front leg doesn't land quite as cleanly as I want, so I transform the plant, rolling under a cleaving *enrendolch*, or honour dagger — an ironic name considering what a bunch of honourless fucks the SS were. Launching myself back up into a spring, I bury my fist into the next Nazi's chest hard enough to hear their sternum splinter. If he's not dead, he's going to be out of action for the foreseeable future.

He was the last man standing in this direction, so I whirl around, blade in guard. My sword catches another dagger, and with a twist of my wrist, I send it flying. The shitheel I've disarmed isn't slowing down though. He drops his shoulder and rams into my stomach, lifting me off my feet, driving me backwards.

I'm off balance, but I catch him a glancing blow with my sword-pommel to the right-side of the back of his head just before we crash into the solid trunk of a tree. Damn, we've covered some distance. The bastard must be made of metal himself or something based on how bruised and winded my midriff feels. I'm dazed, and this isn't a good time to lose track of what's going on.

Luckily, he's done me a favour with what he chose to smash me into. My connection to the tree allows me to draw some power in, to start healing. At the same time, I extend a little of my senses into it, diffusing them into the leaves. Now at least, any sudden movements in my direction will get picked up, the air currents acting as an early warning system.

A few seconds later, and I'm back in the game. The bastard who shoulder-barged me is coming to his senses, which considering he can't draw on Nature's healing power like the crystal-waving hippie I now am, shows just what a man-mountain he is. He's ready to go another round, and if he gets me with a right hook, he looks like he'll take my head off. It makes me think of the scene from *Indiana Jones*. Sadly, I don't have a conveniently turning plane propeller to knock him into. Luckily, I have a sword instead.

I'm still a little woozy, so I don't go for anything flashy. Just rake it straight across his chest. The surrounding magic means it cuts deep — not enough to kill him but enough to make him scream in a high-pitch that Minnie Riperton would be proud of. The momentum turns me to the side, so I follow through with a stomp to his kneecap, snapping it in the process. He goes down to one knee, still squealing, and the blow I drive into the back of his skull this time puts him out properly.

Pivoting back to the action, I see Aicha's cleared through her own canned fools and is now mowing her way through the shitheils with equal abandon. It's hard work keeping people alive, and these guys aren't worth it. Pretty shitty to have been preserved for a few decades only to get wiped out as cannon fodder immediately after. Even shittier to have been a fucking Nazi in the first place.

Talking of — I can see one of them hanging back to the side of one of the nondescript black station wagons they rolled up in. His SS uniform means I'm already swinging for the fences as I close the gap between us. It takes most of my strength to refocus the blow downwards, slicing through the nearest car's back wheel rather than the man's midriff.

He turns towards me, his eyes blank. I don't think he recognises me. There's no one home, nothing there but the geas he's under.

I recognise *him* though. He's not changed a day since I escorted him through the Alps and away from the grip of the SS.

Otto Rahn.

CHAPTER FIVE

TOULOUSE, 9 JUNE, PRESENT DAY

I don't think Rahn's in the driving seat. He's on Otto pilot.

That last-minute deflection pulls my body sideways, leaving me exposed. Otto's carrying a huge serrated bowie knife that looks sharp enough to gut me easily. His head turns at the unexpected sound of the tyre exploding though, and I use that to take a knee, following the sword's trajectory, then reverse the direction of travel to bring it back to a horizontal guard, blocking the knife as he plunges it towards my midriff.

The clang of metal on metal makes him wince. Otto's a scholar, not a warrior, and the vibrations ringing through his arm must be enough to make his fingers numb. He fumbles the knife but catches it just before it slips from his grasp. Damn. That would have made the whole thing a lot easier.

I push up, curving the blade, so he pivots with it. The moment his knife is no longer in contact with my sword, I push onto the leading toes of my left foot and bring my right foot round in a sweep, taking his legs out from under him.

I'm amazed he doesn't impale himself on his own knife. Instead, he just drops it and comes down hard on his back. He's winded, or at least I assume that's why he's making croaking noises and doing a sterling beached-whale impression. I take the momentary pause to check around, make sure I don't have some other luft-waffle sneaking up behind me.

Looks like most of the assailants are down, if not out, apart from the shitheils. Nith and Nan seem to have got their shit together; most of the non-Nazis are frozen in place, surrounded by white light halos. I guess the Bene Elohim have accepted we aren't going to go easy on the Nazis. None of them seem to be similarly restrained. That's practically bloodthirsty for angels. I guess everyone with any sense is anti-fascist, regardless of which dimension they come from.

It's all going really rather well. So, of course, that's when the popping starts.

It kicks off with those haloed individuals. The luminosity surrounding them might keep them from moving, but it doesn't stop the blood erupting from their throats when the miniature explosives kick off. I don't know why the angels can't or don't stop it — whether they don't understand the modern weaponry or whether maybe somehow it has a touch of demon essence mixed into it. Whatever the reason, the invading forces are catching it in the neck. Literally.

I'm straight back to Otto. He has seconds, and I need to do something fast. The only thing I can think of is Half-Marred Jack. The damage Maeve wrought on his face through her touch, melting through his flesh, yet somehow keeping it alive. I'm not Maeve despite the fact I'm wearing her body. I gave up the mantle of Winter and with it a large swathe of her power.

But Nature's my jam *talent*-wise in this body, and you don't get anything much more natural than flesh. I don't want to lose my fingers even to help

Otto, so I wrap them in a protective shield. Then I mentally cross them (as this is going to be difficult enough without actually hooking them round each other) before plunging my hand into his throat.

I'm effectively merging our flesh, pushing my way through without splitting his neck open or tearing out his trachea. Neither of those would help with his life expectancy, I suspect. It doesn't make breathing very easy for him though. He bucks underneath me, and I have to change position to hold him still. Kneeling on his shoulders, I pin him to the ground.

It's a weird feeling, rooting around in flesh. It feels a bit like one of those games people set up at Halloween for kids, where they dip their hands in some goop and feel around for brains made of cauliflower or a banana "tongue". Except here I might grab his actual tongue if I'm not careful and choke him to death with it.

Time isn't on my side. I can't afford to be cautious, so I'm sweeping my hand through his neck as fast as it'll go, desperately searching for a foreign object while trying not to mistake muscle or cartilage for the explosive.

It's hard to really tell what anything is between the bizarre sensation of flesh giving way like mashed potato and the energy protecting my fingers. As I sweep them back across, I feel it. The hard angular form is unnatural, undoubtedly foreign, and I recognise it as such instantly. I don't have time for finesse, so I push it against the side of his neck, forcing the skin to give way with my *talent*. Considering the Bene Brothers couldn't do anything to help them, I don't dare use magic to try to contain it. I just need to get it out of him as quickly as possible.

I almost make it. Sadly, almost isn't enough.

The one good thing about trying to push the explosive device out of his flesh as it explodes is that the shielding round my fingers protects his trachea. Unfortunately, it doesn't stop it from blowing a huge chunk out of his neck, taking at least one of his major arteries or veins with it.

Blood isn't just pissing out of the hole. It's like someone's hooked up his circulatory system to a high-powered pump, then stuck it into overdrive. I'm desperately trying to re-knit his flesh, but there's too much gone, too quickly. His blood vessels won't regrow through empty space, and I can't fill the gap considering how much is gone.

I feel a weak pressure round my wrist. Looking down, I see his fingers wrapped around it, pulling at me. It's like a soft tide when wading in the sea. Noticeable but not about to sweep you away. I guess having most of your blood supply dump out of the side of your neck in one fell swoop is enough to sap anyone's strength.

He looks up at me; his eyes have changed. The glaze in them, the mindlessness, is gone, replaced once more by that sharp, sardonic brightness I associate with the man. Otto's back in the driving seat. Just in time to crash at high speed into the Wall of Death.

'Stop.' His speech is more of a gargle than anything. Apparently, I didn't succeed in stopping any blood getting into his throat. He's not drowning, but he's still dying.

'I can fix this. I can...' I stop when he shakes his head. I'm lying to myself, really. I'm lying to him too. He doesn't deserve that. I keep my hand inside of him though, trying to block as much blood from escaping as I can. Although he's already dead, I can try to honour him, try to make his death mean something.

'How did De Montfort get his hands on you?' My own hands are trembling, slick with the viscera I pulled out of his ravaged throat.

'The grail... all hunters...' His eyes flicker, almost strobing. He doesn't have much left in the tank, but he manages one more last word. 'Sorry...'

Then his eyes go blank, and Otto Rahn, the real-life inspiration for Indiana Jones, hunter of the Grail and reluctant Nazi, is gone from the world once and for all.

I close his eyes, leaving red streaks like tribal war paint across them with my fingertips. I'm running out of space on my tally for scores to settle with De Montfort. The next time we have words, it'll go entirely differently. He'll not get the upper hand again. Good God damn him, I'm coming for revenge for every misery he's inflicted on me, on the world. Enough is enough.

It's a sombre group that gathers in the ruins of Isaac's house. Luckily it's June, so it's not cold even though night is arriving quickly. I think starting a fire on the floor in his kitchen would just be adding insult to injury. There's no way I'm trusting any of the gas heating or appliances. Would be pretty fucking ridiculous to survive an onslaught of century-spanning warriors only to blow ourselves up by sparking the hob.

I look at the weary faces around me. That wasn't a tough fight, not really. It was a bloody depressing one, though, with the emphasis on the bloody. Which is, of course, exactly what De Montfort wanted.

Getting out of here is the priority. 'Can you seal up the house, 'Zac? Perhaps set up a wide-scale *don't look here* too?' We're well away from any nearby neighbours, but even at a distance, rocket launchers and machine guns do tend to catch people's attention. The last thing we want is the police to come poking about or getting their hands on some of Isaac's grimoires. Gendarmes accidentally opening portals through to the hell dimensions would just top off a spectacularly bad day.

Isaac nods, grim-faced, grime-streaked, and I turn to look at the now-driverless cars blocking up the driveway. Getting rid of them all is going to be a job and a half, although the angels can probably do something about that. I have a cursory root about through the pockets of the dead and the vehicles — or the twisted remains of them — just to make sure there're no clues with big flashing arrows pointing at them. Signs spelled out in neon lights, saying 'directions to De Montfort's lair'. That kind of thing.

Sadly, albeit predictably, my search turns up diddly squat. The good news is the cars at the back were far enough away from the small-scale war zone as to be undamaged. Rather than dealing with anything else right now, I suggest decamping back to my house. Nobody disagrees. Nobody has the energy to, I think.

We grab the two cars at the back. Sure, squeezing into one would be possible, but we might as well start getting rid of them. Also, I don't know how much Jakob weighs now in his new Mecha-Jak form, so tearing out the suspension the first time we hit a bump half a mile down the road is only going to further piss on my parade.

Thankfully, we make the twenty-minute journey without incident, which is good news for my dental-care bill, already liable to be astronomical considering the amount of grinding and gnashing I've done recently.

It is genuinely good to be home. Surprisingly so. It seems like aeons since I walked through my own front door and collapsed in a heap into a settee that has arranged itself around my posterior *just so* thanks to careful training over the preceding years. Even if my bum is now considerably curvier than it used to be, somehow Old Faithful gets it right and provides succour to my rear. Sadly, I need to act as host at least slightly — make coffee and some snacks with whatever remnants are left in my store cupboard. Sitting around isn't an option. I guess it goes to show — never give a succour an even break.

With a bit of fussing around, I provide Irish coffee, going heavy on the Irish, and a couple of packs of smiley face jam biscuits. Considering how shit we all feel now, hindsight says they were probably a terrible choice at the supermarket. Nobody wants to feel like they're getting smirked at by their snacks. Although it makes savagely biting them in half all the more satisfying.

Unusually, Jakob kicks off the discussion. 'What on earth was that all about, my boy?' He sounds baffled. Well, he sounds buzzy, and I'm really going to have to have words with Isaac about superior audio engineering, but enough emotion carries through for me to pick up the bafflement.

I can understand he's taking this hard. It's ironic how much Jakob isn't built for war considering the body he's now wearing couldn't be more so. It's like if Wolverine was a committed pacifist. Wouldn't make for a very interesting read. Might just have made his world a better place though.

Sadly, I know exactly what it was about. So does Aicha, and she answers the question. 'Ben's wolves.' She sounds like the only reason she isn't spitting after saying that is because she's inside, and it'd be a gross thing to do.

'Exactly so.' I dunk my mocking snack viciously in my coffee, soaking it till it's close to disintegration, then swallow it quickly down. Serves it right. 'Fucking power play.'

Isaac looks confused. This just isn't his or his brother's area of expertise. They're not equipped to think the worst of people, to look for that malicious motivation that drives others to despicable courses of action.

'That attack wasn't meant to work. Was a message.' I appreciate Aicha spelling it out for them. It gives me space to torture another couple of smarmy biscuits. 'Just like the wolf attack at L'Astronef.'

That was a shitty move by Ben. Sending wolves to attack us who didn't stand a chance, holding their families hostage to motivate them, then making us kill them all. Just to give us a kick up the arse and keep us trundling along the timeline he'd set.

Isaac's still looking blank-faced, so I take up the narrative. 'De Montfort knew perfectly well that wasn't going to work. Just like he knows that trying to bring the fight to us on our home turf, particularly bringing it to your front door when Nith and Nan are riding shotgun, is only going to end badly for him.'

'But he wants the skull.' Aicha snaffles another biscuit, tapping it on the table to underline her point.

'Correct. So what does he do? Either he tries to bring a scorched earth tactic, throws everything he's got into a full frontal assault...'

'Not really his style.'

'Right, Aich. We've seen so far he likes sneaky, carefully laid plans. He's not the spray-and-pray type.'

Isaac's frowning now, trying to get ahead of our logic. Problem is it's dark, twisted logic, and his mind doesn't work that way. 'So why send them in at all? What was the point?'

'Because the whole thing is a message. He wasn't really trying to get the skull back, not this time.'

Isaac thumps his fist on the table. 'So *why?*'

I look at his face. At the grief for the unknown dead, at the suffering it's causing him. He doesn't even care about the damage to his beloved cottage or the invasion of his privacy, the disturbing of his tranquil little sanctuary. He's marked by the misery of people he never knew. It's why I love him. And why I try to protect him where I can. And also why De Montfort did what he did.

I wave my hand up and down to indicate his state, both physical and mental. 'This is why, 'Zac. The impact on us, on you.'

'Drawing us out. Cuntsponge.'

That's a grade-A insult. De Montfort fully deserves it, of course. I file it away for future use. 'Exactly so. That's the message. You can stay where you are, hidden away safely behind your wards. But if you do, I'll keep sending innocents to your door to die. How many more waves like that do you think you can handle, 'Zac? How many before you crack and go hunting him instead?'

'And he'll be waiting.'

Aicha's right, of course. He may undoubtedly be a cuntsponge, but one thing De Montfort is not is stupid. He's also been prepared for anything and everything so far. Considering that still inexplicable trick with the demon-infused bazooka round, I don't doubt he has something up his sleeve to nullify the angels if we walk into whatever trap he's trying to guide us into.

Talking of messages, I've not yet told them about Rahn. 'One of the Nazis wasn't one. Well, he was but under duress. He was...a friend. Of sorts, anyhow.'

Aicha clocks it straight away, of course. Mind you, there's not many Nazis, ex or otherwise, I've ever considered using that term for. 'Otto Rahn?'

'Exactly. I tried to save him.' My shoulders droop at the thought. 'Emphasis on tried.'

Jak goes to pat my shoulder again in sympathy. I see it coming this time and duck before he puts stress fractures in my shoulder blade.

'Sometimes, my dear boy, trying is all we can do. Whether for ourselves or for others.'

Wise platitudes but not helpful at this precise moment. I appreciate the sentiment though.

Isaac's still looking troubled. No surprise considering what we've been through, but I can see he's trying to work his way through it all. 'What about all the soldiers from different time periods? Especially the knights? I thought De Montfort's only had magic since your marriage?'

Good old Isaac. Choosing to mention the marriage rather than the slaughter in the matrimonial bed of my wife while I danced and drank. Murdered by the same twatbungle fucking with us right now.

I have the answer to Isaac's question though. Otto gave it to me just before he died. 'Grail hunters.'

Isaac's brow furrows deeper. 'What?'

'Grail hunters.' He still looks blank. 'Look, the Grail holds this peculiar place in the human imagination. It seems to fire something in us, to provoke a reaction in the collective imagination. If you don't believe me, just look at Dan Brown's bank balance. And some people get drawn in more than others. Some get obsessed by the idea of it, drawn to hunting for its final resting place till it consumes their every waking moment. Rahn was like that. Even when I told him I'd destroyed the Grail, he didn't believe me. He couldn't. It defined his life, his self-identity. He just couldn't let that go.'

'And the knights?' Realisation dawns on Isaac's face. Solving the mysteries one by one helps get his powerhouse of a brain turning cleanly. Hopefully, it'll churn out some answers to the more pressing questions afterwards.

'Hard to say, but either remnants of the Round Table and their failed attempt to locate the Grail or later-day imitators following on with the chivalric obsession. I'd guess either they were *talented* enough that their vows to find it kept them alive, long past the end of their own epoch...'

'Or they got frozen, and De Montfort found them.' Isaac's caught up now. Good.

'Precisely. As for the others? My guess is that being possessed by the hunt for the Grail made them easy prey for De Montfort. He used the Grail energy residual in his bone collection to take over their minds. Or it could just be he can do that to anyone, but he liked the image of sending the poor deluded fuckers to their deaths against us. There's a dark, twisted sort of poetry to that, I suppose. I can see it appealing to the twatmonkey.'

'Well,' Isaac says, grim-faced but resolute, 'that seems to bear out your train of thought about them being Grail hunters.' His eyes widen. 'Maybe that's it! They went hunting for the Grail and got trapped. Maybe that's where De Montfort is! Back where it all began. The location of the Holy Grail!'

'What?' Aicha doesn't look so convinced. 'Lavaur?'

'Aye, lass!' I can see Isaac's really getting into this idea. It's sad that I'm going to have to break in and disillusion him in a moment. 'Either there or back at Foix where Nicetas stole it from. That's a sort of poetical justice, isn't it? Force Paul to confront his past? A showdown at the site of his first triumph? De Montfort hates his reincarnating, and that is, after all, where it all began.'

'Except,' I say before they get any more carried away on this particular train of thought, 'those last words of Rahn's? They were a trap.'

Isaac's face drops, confusion taking pride of place. Good God damn it, he's just not cut out for this. I hate having to get him involved at all in any way. 'A dying man's last word, a trap?'

'Absolutely. When did all the throat bombs start performing tracheostomies on the attackers?'

He shrugs, helpless. I put him out of his misery. 'Once I recognised Otto. When I turned my blade aside from killing him. And whose neck went pop last?'

Now Isaac gets it. 'Rahn's.'

'Right. Giving me enough time to save him? Nope, but giving me enough time to keep him alive...'

'Just long enough to deliver his message.' Aicha gets it. There's no need to hold her hand and lead her through it. Mainly because I don't want her to chop my hand off for even considering it.

'Exactly. Plus, how did he know the others were Grail hunters? I suppose he might have found their bodies and then been put in stasis himself, but it seems like exactly the sort of move De Montfort would pull off — has pulled off. Send us gallivanting off in one direction, either away from where we want to be, or towards where he wants us.'

Isaac still looks doubtful. 'Are you sure?'

I shake my head. 'Nope. Not even vaguely. But it's certainly plausible. Treating it as likely is how we stay alive.'

Aicha wipes an imaginary tear away from her eye. 'Learning basic self-preservation at last. They grow up so quick. Unless they're Paul. In which case, it takes the twatfish eight centuries.'

'Right, thanks, Momma Aicha.'

She shrugs. 'No problem. No one will ever love you like your mother does. Especially not me.'

'Nice one, Vera Cosgrove.' She tips me a hat for the movie reference catch.

Funnily enough, it settles me down a little. It adds a trace of normality to proceedings, makes me feel like we're back in our stride. Like maybe we've actually got ahead of him on one thing. If I'm not mistaken, he wants us to go rushing off to Foix or Lavaur. It may well be that's where he is or where we need to go, but we're not going to go charging, heads down, into danger. I like this body. I want to keep hold of it for a while longer if at all possible.

'So,' I say carefully, slowly, tasting the words, 'if he wants us to go heading over there, the question is why?'

Isaac's hand creeps up like a shy kid scared to answer wrong and look stupid or to answer right and get called a swot. 'I might know the answer to that one.'

This was why I took the time to answer his questions, to get him back on track. 'Hit us, man.'

'Well, it comes back to the conversation we were having before we were so rudely interrupted back at my place.'

Shit, I completely forgot. Which may well have been the point of the attack in the first place. Distract us from what we were digging into, the direction we were heading in and send us haring after a red herring. Possibly a red herring laced with cyanide and surrounded by face-hugger eggs.

Which brings us full circle to the question that was eating its way through my cortex all the way back from Paris like alien drool. 'Who is Arnaud Almeric? Right now?'

'The question isn't just who he is right now, but where he is right now.' And of course Isaac answers my question with another question. Because, apparently, I must have spilled his beer at some point in the preceding centuries, and he's been nursing a grudge. He clearly wants me to suffer. The wrongs I must have done him. I think about that for a moment. Actually, the wrongs I *have* done him, with him having to live in close proximity to me for far longer than can be good for anyone's mental health. Perhaps I'll let him off after all.

'Okay, oh wise and sage master, your incisive questions have allowed me to level up my spiritual awareness like Mario munching down a fuckload of mushrooms. Now can you please tell us who and where the shitstain is?'

Isaac nods gravely, clearly relishing the title of sage master. 'Of course, young padawan.' Damn, he's been studying in his spare time. Clearly, he's sick of the in-jokes between Aicha and me going straight over his head. 'As to who, his name is Frank Phillips.'

The name rings the very vaguest of bells. It makes more sense when he clarifies. 'He's the leader of the Eastville Pentecostal Church.'

Now I remember. They're the bunch of arseholes who boycott soldiers' funerals with signs saying things like 'God Hates Fags' and who generally celebrate every bit of misery in the world as a sign of the Almighty's wrath at the sinful way humanity has gone, with equal rights and social inclusion and female liberation. Because, apparently, the Supreme Being is a petty-minded bigot. I think Frank Phillips believes it wasn't God who made Man in his own image but rather Frank Phillips who made God in his.

It makes sense though. An extremist religious bigot. I've not read deeply into them, except to get the impression they're an inbred cult of utter wankstains, but no doubt he's called for the execution of heretics and witches too. It matches. Definitely sounds like Almeric.

Which brings us to the second part of the question, the addition Isaac was desperate to throw in. 'So now tell us where.'

Isaac's grin is so wide, I'm surprised the top of his head doesn't fall off. 'Right now? About halfway across the Atlantic, I'd guess.'

My eyes pop so far out of my head at that, I must look like Marty Feldman. 'Heading where?'

'Here. To France.'

Well, ain't that just a coinky-dinky if ever I saw one. Now I can see why De Montfort wants us distracted.

Arnaud Almeric is about to make his return to French shores. I get the feeling it's going to be a dramatic homecoming.

Chapter Six

PARIS, 5 FEBRUARY 1806

T he stink of piss burns my nostrils. I don't know if it's the shady nar-row alleyway I'm huddled in that carries such a pungent odour or me. I don't remember the last time I took a bath. Mind you, remembering's not exactly my favourite thing these days. Actively forgetting is more my game.

The wind carries other trace scents — the loam-like smell of spoiled vegetables piled up at a shop's mould-pocked back door, the lifted half-masked rot of the Seine, the smell of the shit and filth dumped in the river only partially obscured by the running water, the heavy-handedly applied perfume of the half-broken street walker around the corner, acting as a mask for that sweet putrid taint that the pox pushes out from the flesh. That she doesn't even proposition me, pulling back and hiding her hard-worn face behind her wine-stained sleeve speaks volumes to the sorry state I'm in.

The wind brings other things too. It brings the last bite of winter's filed teeth. The days may be lengthening, and the Seine may be breaking from ice to sluggish movement, but still it's savage enough to slide through flesh and gnaw the bones beneath. Especially when there's little enough flesh on said bones to act as warming cover. And it carries the past. The opium's numbing haze has long evaporated, and underneath the itching, clamouring need, that feeling that makes my toes clench like they're cramping each second I'm not scampering back towards the den, is the thawing out of my dope-frozen heart. Moments and memories are skittering their way back towards the front of my thoughts, pretty-tied with chains of feelings so weighty that they seem heavy enough to tear my mind apart.

I wish they would.

The clawing need for oblivion both demands I turn and flee back to the comfort of my dark dazed hole and is the very reason why I'm here. It's a risky move to make myself known, to bring myself to the very attention I've aimed to slide beneath until now. I don't see any other choice.

That isn't true. There are always other choices. I'm just not prepared to make any. Whatever choices I make, they all spoil as much as the abandoned wastage that my stomach, half-cramped and eager to impose its desires now that my mind is clearing, keeps suggesting might be worth a root through, to search for some part not entirely rotten, not completely wasted. I'm not sure I believe that's true for anything in this miserable world anymore.

Waiting's never been my favourite pastime. Patience? Never been a strong suit. I stamp my feet, trying to choose spots on the cobbles where I'm not going to end up splashing unidentifiable brown liquid in through the holes I've worn in them. Warming my wasted muscles will do me no good if my feet get soaked. Although I'm not convinced I'll ever be warm again. Not convinced I want to be either despite my futile attempts to push heat into my limbs by moving.

I don't want to be here. Mind you, that's why I am.

Movement at the mouth of the alleyway. Finally. I step forward, but then shrink back when an elongated shape steps around the corner.

'You're not Leandre.' My brain may be a long way from functioning at a hundred percent capacity — hell, it's not even producing enough steam power to push up half the pistons — but even I can tell this isn't the Lutin Prince.

The figure in front of me's too tall for starters. Not that I believe the Prince is necessarily tiny, but if he were half the size of me again, I'd have heard about it. Also, the Lutin Prince isn't dead.

There's no life to the creature in front of me despite the illusion it's wearing like the elegant black cloak it has wrapped around its neck. It wears the visage of a man, the body of one. But it's not alive. I can detect no *talent* there as such. Quite the opposite. There's an absence, a blankness, a sinkhole where all the vibrancy should be when I *look*. It makes me feel unwell. Though that may be the opium withdrawal.

The being tilts its head. It reminds me of a vulture I saw in the northern stretches of the Sahara, assessing me as threat or treat. Except now I'm the one trying to make that assessment. And this thing is the one that seems to be a corpse.

Undead creatures are not unknown, and some even maintain at least the semblance of rationality upon their changing. Ones who are welcomed in Talented society are more of a rarity. I've never heard of such a thing in Leandre's service.

The tall dead once-man bows deeply, sweeping his hat off his head. 'De Moriéve at your service.'

His voice is peculiar. There's a silkiness to it that speaks of cultivation and manners, of high birth and higher status. But underneath, there's a gravelly tone, a parched cracking like a pinned butterfly's wing crumbling to dust. And, of course, he's given me a name. So, no matter how much his unnatural state may raise my hackles, I can no longer think of him as an *it*.

'You're not Leandre.' I am clearly not on my finest form. Repeating the obvious seems about as much as I can manage at the moment.

De Moriéve treats me once more to that prey-bird squint. 'Did you believe the ruler of Paris at your beck and call, Good Man?' There's a genuine puzzlement to his tone, a wonder at the audacity. 'He has more pressing matters than to attend your summons. No, I am here to ask the questions on his behalf.'

'Don't you mean answer them?' I can feel some part of my sluggish brain shouting for my attention, but I'm not able to get what it wants me to notice.

The creature draws up, towering over me, and spreads hands with nails longer than a knitting needle and sharper than a butcher's cleaver out in front of him. 'I said exactly what I meant, fellow. My questions are asked on pain of death. Now, what are you doing here in my liege's territory with neither permission nor penitent excuses? Only aggravating demands for parleying when my sources tell me you've been here for *years* and never once approached the Prince or paid him his due.'

That was the message my hind-brain was screaming at me that I failed to hear. Predator. Threat. Run away. Looks like I've well and truly drawn the Prince's attention. Once I sent the message, mind, I expected little else.

'Death is exactly why I'm here.' There's no point in beating round the bush. I suspect I'm only a few turns of conversation away from torture, and I need to get to the point before he tears me apart with his own.

The dead man looks at me with large empty eyes and scratches at his chalk-pale temple. I'm amazed he doesn't shave a peel of skin away in doing so. It must not be quite as papery as it looks. A part of me starts categorising that he may not be easily perforated if I pull my blade, that a magical attack might be more effective, musings about the effectiveness of bale-fire and burning. I shush it down. I'm not here to fight.

I'm here to die.

'What do you mean?' The confusion in De Moriéve's voice is strong. I'm not surprised. He probably came here expecting me to challenge his liege, to seek either to seize a piece of Paris or the Prince's seat itself. The very thought makes me want to laugh, if the thought of making such a noise in a world without my wife in it didn't fill my throat with salty bile.

I try to resist the urge to jig up and down, to scratch the back of my hand until I draw blood. The need, the restless hunger is starting up properly now. Insistent messages are travelling between my various extremities, all suggesting that the absence of opium is entirely unacceptable. I know from experience those demands are only going to get more strident.

Something unexpected happens. The muscles around those cold lifeless eyes relax, and —though this takes me a moment to recognise— soften, along with his expression. He moves closer, and I flinch back, expecting the conversation to be already at an end, for this body to follow close behind. Instead, he spreads his hands placatingly, though the razors at the end of each fingertip undermine that slightly.

'So the rumours I've heard are true,' he murmurs, a sad rattle to that gravel undertone like a funeral carriage's wheels down a gentry's driveway. He reaches into his inside pocket and pulls out a thin metal pipe and a glass vial. In the bottom I can see the tar-like brown-black that I value more than gold, more than anything. He tips a tiny amount out and hands it to me, producing a tinder box from another pocket. As I place it to trembling lips, he strikes enough sparks as to light up the opium, and the first numbing smoke tendrils dance down my throat and wrap their calming, constricting barrel hoops around my heart again.

De Moriéve smiles. At least, I assume that's what that particular spread of his thin bloodless lips means. The expression he wears makes me deeply uncomfortable and inexplicably ashamed. It's a sorry state of affairs to be pitied by a dead man.

'I, too, know that feeling. The inescapable urge. The cloying, endless demand.' I suspect the once-man's not talking about drug addiction. Discussing his burning needs, the thing he's driven to seek over and over doesn't exactly set me at ease. I'm here to ask for help, not to be his lunch.

I take a moment to let the pipe calm me, but I don't draw too greedily despite every element of my being crying out for me to do so. The Good God knows I want oblivion, crave it constantly. Again, though, that's why I need to say what I've come to say.

'I seek Leandre's help.' To the point. Make it clear, keep it concise.

De Moriéve strokes his chin, somehow avoiding giving himself a fatal shave again. 'Such a thing is possible, I suppose. We have access to many physicians and alchemists. Your detoxification could be aided if what you offer the Prince is sufficiently interesting.'

Oh. He thinks I want help to shed my addiction. I hurry to clear up his misunderstanding. 'No, sir. I don't seek help to live. I seek help to die.'

The dead man looks baffled but, to his credit, adjusts quickly. 'A sad waste, but I can accommodate that if final oblivion is your preference.' He steps towards me, his razor-tipped arms spread to give a finishing embrace, and I have to move equally quickly backwards.

'No, you misunderstand!' I don't want to die now. It'd mean starting all over again. And having the memories back. I can't. I won't. Not till I know for sure.

The arms falter and drop back to his sides. 'What is it that you mean then, Good Man?'

I sigh and let the comforting numbness loosen my tongue, to spill the truth out. 'I want it all to end. Not this life. All my lives. Every time I die, I come back. Reborn over and over again. The only way I know to finish it is…impossible.' The idea of reaching Perfection again, of becoming a holy person once more, is anathema to me. Not only will I never seek that, I'll never deserve it either. The gutter's where I belong. The gutter or the grave.

Understanding lights up in De Moriéve's face. 'Ah. I see. Of course. I've heard of your...' He pauses, searching for the right word. 'Condition. You must excuse my absence of mind.'

He didn't say no. I'm trying not to get too excited, but he *didn't say no*. 'Is it something you can help me with? That Leandre could undo? Is my death possible?'

The dead thing that might have been a living human once looks at me with a compassion that would break my heart if it weren't already nought but a broken shell.

'No.'

Ah. Apparently it can still break further.

I look up at him with an intensity bordering on rage. 'Why? Why won't you help me?'

And still this former human doesn't change expression, his sympathetic pity so clearly readable, I want to erase it from his face almost as much as I want to erase myself from existence. 'What benefit is there for my liege in that? The gratitude of a dead man? The magic inherent in you that allows you to come back time and again, to take dead forms and wear them anew? That's powerful *talent*, not to be lightly messed with.' He smiles sadly. 'Take it from one who knows.'

'I'll stand service for him. Tell me what he needs. An enemy slain, a territory conquered. A... a...' I search desperately for anything of worth I can offer him that won't keep me here in this life for overly long. 'A lover for the night. Whatever he needs.'

So grief will make a whore out of me. It feels like I'm bringing a stain of shame to the honour of the oldest profession. I'm desperate though. Anything for this all to cease.

But he shakes his head. 'Even if it were possible, which I doubt, there's nothing you offer that Leandre cannot already have at much lesser risk. Unravelling your existence might unleash power to level half of Paris or more. There's nothing to be gained and much to be lost.'

'Please!' The begging tone's clear in my voice, obvious in my hunched-up posture. My legs don't feel able to support me anymore, and I'm down on my knees, down in the muck and mire where I belong, tears and mucus streaming down my face and staining my clothes and my soul. 'Please help me, please.'

De Moriéve pats me with an awkward gentleness. I'm not sure if it's because of the uncomfortable nature of having to comfort a stranger or because he's trying not to eviscerate me in the process. Either way, it has the desired effect. The effort of that forced humanity reminds me to be ashamed of my own pitiable display, and the tears dry enough for me to regain my last shreds of dignity and rise to my feet again.

Leandre's man nods. There's no way to tell if the approval is real or not, but I appreciate it nonetheless. 'Good. Go now. You may head where you will. If you return to the dens, then Leandre will not hunt you down. I'll speak to your harmlessness.'

Downgraded to harmless, of being unworthy of consideration by the great and good of the Talented world. I should be offended. Instead, I'm immensely grateful. The dens aren't closed to me. The doors haven't been slammed shut by my failed roll of the dice. A little oblivion, a tiny momentary cessation still lies open. An escape of sorts.

I wipe at my smeared eyes with the back of my sleeve, though it's so filthy, I do nothing but aggravate the situation. By the time I manage to clear my vision sufficiently to look, De Moriéve is gone. So too is the little comfort his pipe granted. Reality is about to come crashing back down on me.

As fast as my filth-hardened trousers and broken hope allow, I hurry back to the only comfort left in a world without Susane, back towards the lamp-light siren call of the opium dens and the nothingness it can offer.

CHAPTER SEVEN

TOULOUSE, 9 JUNE, PRESENT DAY

Eight hundred years later, and Almeric is still a religious nutjob. Luckily it's our job to crack nuts. Ideally, by cracking them in the nuts.

Turns out Isaac was taking a little bit of dramatic license. Frank Phillips/Almeric isn't actually on the flight yet, but he's probably at the airport waiting to board. It's an overnight flight due to land in the early hours of the following morning. All of which means we're looking at pulling an all-nighter. There's nothing for it but to pile into our own vehicles and chase the parting night westwards, the arriving dawn warming our backs.

The thing I'm seriously confused to the point of being worried about is where he's landing. 'You're sure it's Bordeaux?' I ask for the seventh time as we pull up to the airport.

Isaac rolls his eyes. Jakob answers for him, managing to keep a more gentle tone than his brother could probably muster. 'We've checked the flight logs, and, ahem, accessed his booking. It's definitely this flight, definitely landing here.'

It doesn't make any sense whatsoever. That makes me more edgy than a fourteen year old rattling off troll comments on the internet behind a proxy server. De Montfort's been following our progress. Hell, Susane was his spy in the Mother's camp. With Susane dead, I don't doubt for one moment the Mother would be happy to get her hands round his scrawny neck and extract a little vengeance for making her word look questionable.

While I won't go so far as to say we are best buddies —I don't think she's about to invite me round for family dinner, even if I did save her daughter— the Mother has named me an ally of the Sistren, and an enemy of mine landing in her territory? Is liable to find themselves in all sorts of hot water. Or cold, drowning in the freezing tides of the Atlantic, wearing the magical equivalent of concrete boots.

Mind you, De Montfort hasn't exactly been making friends at many of the bigger airports. Leandre might be going for the whole "neutral party" stance, but that's all politics. I don't doubt if Simon tried to saunter into Paris Charles De Gaulle, he'd find a whole host of Talented badasses waiting to snatch and bag him for the Lutin Prince. Lyon? Well, he might not have upset the Tarrasque personally, but it's still the fucking Tarrasque. Just because he's an arsehole doesn't mean he'd help De Montfort. He's an equal opportunities wanker. He hates everyone and fucks with anyone he can.

There's Marseilles. I don't know what the international schedule in from the USA is there, but I'd have thought it'd be better than Bordeaux. However, in Marseilles, there's no solid structure, no equivalent of Leandre. It's a constant battleground of rival factions built on shifting sands of alliances and betrayals. Choosing who to approach to secure passage would be tricky. And by the time you actually needed to transit through, the whole political layout might have changed all over again.

Still, better options remain. Either fly into another country's airport —Barcelona's only just over three hours away from Toulouse, hardly difficult for him to get to wherever his secret lair actually is— or pay a private jet and land at a smaller, less tightly guarded airport like Tarbes. I don't believe for a moment that a man as well-prepared and as cunning as De Montfort isn't sitting on a small fortune. I don't get why he wouldn't go for something more straightforward like that. This all reeks of poor planning. That doesn't fit with my profile of the man. I hate him with a fire that burns down to the very core of my being, but I respect him too. Underestimating De Montfort is a good way to make sure of getting caught out. I've no intention of letting that ever happen again if I can help it.

While we loaded up the cars, I put in a quick phone call to the Mother and filled her in on what's been happening. I didn't give her the whole story, obviously. We're not besties, just temporary allies, but I let her know what had happened to Susane and that De Montfort was behind the whole affair. I also told her that, seeing as how she couldn't get me those two, if she could deliver Phillips to me, then our debt would be squared. If I know the Mother, that'll be motivation enough. Talented don't like having debts hanging over them. They tend to crop back up at the most inopportune times and cost you more heavily than you ever intended. If anyone knows there's always a price to pay, it's the Mother of the Sistren of Bordeaux.

So Simon De Montfort, master trickster shithead and planner extraordinaire, is flying his star chess piece straight into enemy territory, and it's making my brain go fucking loopy. I know he's up to something; I know there's a plan in there somewhere, and I can't get anywhere near it.

Overhanging glass suspended at swooshing angles underline the aerodynamic connection of Bordeaux's airport. It's pretty enough but hardly hugely original. Considering how stressed I am, it'd need to have been designed by Salvador Dali for me to pay it even a flicker of attention. Even if the control tower *was* melting over the terminal building, I doubt I'd properly notice.

We instinctively form a huddle around Jakob. He's wearing a disguise spell they integrated into the design so he doesn't even have to really use any *talent* to hide. If someone bumps into him though, they might realise he's a seven-foot tall robotic killing machine — even if he *is* significantly better at making tea than wielding death. As this is an airport, people bumping into each other is a constant hazard. As much as I love the idea of Jakob forcing his way through security and grabbing Almeric, dishing out the whole "dead or alive, you're coming with me" schtick, one pitched gun battle in twenty-four hours is more than enough.

There's a major shock waiting for me in the airport lobby — the Mother herself is here. More surprising, she hugs me and kisses me on both cheeks. Maybe I'm paranoid — scrub that, I'm definitely paranoid, albeit justifiably — but I flick my eyes left and right, looking for witch ninja assassins to drop from the ceiling, her having marked me like Judas. But, no, apparently that's how Moms and I roll now. I'm not, however, suicidal enough to refer to her as "Moms" anywhere but inside my head.

'There is a little time before the plane is due to arrive. There has been access arranged.' She quirks an eyebrow at me, looking me up and down. 'There have been some improvements made to your looks since last you were seen, Cathar.'

I swish myself back and forth at the knees, miming swirling the dress I'm not wearing because nope, just nope. That blasted ballgown I inherited along with the body was more than enough for the next few lifetimes. 'Oh, this little thing? Just something I borrowed from Maeve.

The Mother's right eyebrow climbs so high, I think it's about to go bungee jumping off one of her locs. 'There is quite a story to be told there, I think, Good Man. Should time allow, then there will be feasting to fete the telling were you to accept.'

Well, blow me down with a feather and call me Billy-Bob. Apparently, we *are* close enough that I'm getting invited round for family dinner. Quite the honour, all things considered, and I'm feeling pretty chuffed with myself. It even distracts me from the constant worry about what De Montfort has planned. As soon as I think that, of course, the worries come hammering back down on me like fist-sized hailstones.

'Have you any idea what the hell he might be up to?' The Mother is very damn smart, with that kind of predatory intelligence that means there's every chance she'll have spotted something I haven't.

The creases that form on her face suggest otherwise. 'There is something afoot. What, though...' She shrugs helplessly. We aren't the only ones feeling frustrated by the whole shitshow.

She whisks us off through a private security channel, where the security guards stare determinedly straight ahead while a *creature built of metal* walks through their detector, which starts screaming like it's just been goosed by a horny baggage belt. Nobody moves, and the noise eventually dies down. I have no idea how they're going to explain that one to the airport authorities in case of an audit, but I don't doubt the Mother has a plan in mind. Even if said plan is just "throw the two patsies on duty under the bus".

It also, of course, goes nuts when Aicha goes through. She does a miniature half-pirouette in the middle of the scanner screaming blue murder, so she can glare at me. A glare that says "why didn't we do this when we flew to England?" and also "don't you dare make me give up my weapons ever again". I try to wiggle my eyebrows to say "we don't throw people under the bus, Aich". Unless it's De Montfort of course. Then not only will I throw him under, I'll switch places with the driver afterwards and drive back and forth over him till he's a smear of sticky paste across the floor, just to make sure.

We're taken through to an area airside, underneath a fabric awning off the side of the building. It gives us a clear view of the whole airport. Two cars screech up next to us, and a group of witches dressed in a mixture of airport security and customs agent uniforms bail out. No one is about to sneak up on us. We can see clearly in all directions, including up. I guess the plan is that when the plane's landed and parked, these guys are going to rush onboard and grab Almeric before he can disembark and head through security. It's a good plan. Stop him from getting into the building itself, where De Montfort might have agents ready to spirit him away. Everything is as carefully prepared as it can be. So why do I feel like I'm about to have a heart attack from the stress?

Because it's too easy. It's all going our way, and it rubs me up entirely wrong. Something's got to give. It has to. I can't work it out for the life of me, but De Montfort has a plan, and I know I'm going to kick myself when I finally find out what it is. Good God damn it, I don't want him to get another win, but I can't work out his angle, and I'm terribly afraid he's going to outplay us once more.

One of the agent witches is monitoring Flight Tracker on his phone and tells us the aircraft's about fifteen minutes from landing, currently tracking downwind, and we should be able to see them. I peer in the direction he's pointing. At first, I assume he means we should be able to see them if we're fucking Superman or equipped with binoculars, but eventually, I do spot a black dot that might be moving and might be an aircraft.

Sweat cascades down my neck. My heart's going so hard, I feel like someone slipped amphetamines into my coffee this morning. Something's going to happen. Soon.

Still, the seconds tick by, and the only thing stopping me from pacing like a caged lion is looking out of control in front of my new BFF, the constantly cool and under control Mother.

The agent monitoring the app informs us the aircraft's turning onto finals and about five minutes out from landing. I gear myself up for go-time. Looking over at the Mother, I nod my head towards one of the cars so we can go meet the plane. She graciously assents, and I head over, swinging myself in...just in time for shouting to start outside.

I leap upwards, smashing my head before stumbling back out to find absolute panic.

Seems De Montfort is making his move.

CHAPTER EIGHT

BORDEAUX, 10 JUNE, PRESENT DAY

Waiting till I got in the car? Just plane rude. And part of me feels sure De Montfort did it on purpose and is sitting somewhere laughing at me.

Several witches are pointing and shouting towards the aircraft, but I can't see anything. The Mother remedies that. She puts her finger and thumb on each hand together, then stretches them out. The motion forms a panel of compressed air that acts like a zoom lens. We can see what's happening at the aircraft. I almost wish we couldn't.

It's wobbling fairly strongly, its wings dipping, and it's not that windy out. The Mother moves the screen around expertly, and — there.

On one of the passenger windows, towards the front of the aircraft, are tiny shapes, like a dispersed cloud of bees. She angles it round and zooms in further, and I can't quite believe my eyes.

Fucking pillywiggins.

There is an insane number of hidden species still living alongside us today. How the Talented world hasn't ended up getting blown wide open is beyond me. Mind you, there are vast swathes of the population who believe the Earth is flat and that YouTube videos hold better information than scientists, so maybe it's not that surprising. If you'd asked me, 'What is the species least likely to turn up to fuck up your plans?', pillywiggins might well have been the guess I'd have gone for.

Pillywiggins are fae but about the most harmless of them in existence. They're what most kinds of literature since the nineteenth century present when showing faeries. Tiny little flower huggers that flit around in clouds of pretty dust, drinking nectar. Admittedly, also fucking like rabbits, which isn't something children's comics and cartoons tend to highlight, but otherwise, they're the sort of creatures that are bottom of the food chain. I know a lot of fae kill them on sight, just biting their heads off. Probably because they feel they undermine the rest of Faerie's street cred.

So I expect to occasionally come across them frolicking in a meadow, supping from a hanging buttercup, or going at it hammer and tongs on a lily pad, making me want to bleach my eyeballs and just generally ruining a summer's day for me. What I don't expect to see them doing is sawing out an aircraft window.

First, let's just take a moment to dispel a myth. That whole thing of people popping open an emergency exit in flight? That ain't happening. They're made to stay shut while pressurised; the difference in pressure between inside and outside the plane keeps them lodged firmly in place.

But if you cut your way in from the outside? It's not going to work quite the same way.

As there's what looks to be about a hundred of them, they've already managed to slice through the airframe. The window pops out, wiping out about twenty of the little fae fucks as it gets ejected into the atmosphere, narrowly missing smashing onto the wing. One agent has pulled out a handheld CB radio, apparently tuned to the tower as I can hear the pilot shouting about a decompression. At this altitude, it's not life threatening, but it can't be comfortable, and I can only imagine what the panic must be like inside, with the air rushing out probably sounding like a compressed hurricane erupting around the passengers.

Now Isaac acts. People are in danger, and he steps up. Nith's energy erupts out towards the plane and cocoons it, blocking the window and steadying the aircraft. The pilots regain their approach trajectory, and I hear them telling the tower they'll be making an emergency landing, stopping on the tarmac for an inspection.

I'm ready to jump back in the car, to race there to meet them so we can grab Almeric's Modern Life, and get gone. The Mother's not stopped watching though.

I look back over to see a crack team of pillywiggin commandos —which is the most ridiculous fucking idea I've ever heard of— fly back out, carrying a limp form between them, straight through the angelic field surrounding the plane. Apparently, they slipped inside when the window went. But all this should be entirely and utterly impossible. Pillywiggins only form of exercise is coital, and they weigh about as much as a feather each. There's no way even ten of them should be able to carry a person. And that's before the whole "flying through an angelic barrier" aspect.

I glance over at Isaac, who's gritting his teeth, a single sweat drop beading on his forehead. 'What the fuck, man?' I can't keep the incredulity out of my voice. What he's doing is unbelievable, protecting the aircraft and everyone on board but letting what is presumably Almeric get away? We still don't know his plan, but all things considered, it might potentially be putting the whole world at risk.

'Demon energy,' he manages to grind out, and I swear profusely.

Apparently, demon energy really is like fucking angelic kryptonite. This would have been useful to be more aware of at an earlier date. Looks like the little constantly-losing-Sunday-league team is actually able to kick the shit out of those local winning rivals after all. That was never my understanding of it previously.

I'm looking around for anyone who can help. Up in the air, they're away from anything I can affect. It's clear, cloudless, so I can't even try to smite them with lightning. Hell, there's not even a breeze I can augment and hurl at them to scatter them away, not enough trees to borrow their memories of the gales that can blow in off the ocean. They're way too far away for Aicha to fuck them up. I look over desperately at the Mother. She looks pissed, absolutely furious, but she shakes her head. There's nothing she can do.

'Get us out of here, back to landside — now.'

She nods, and two of the agents rush us through a nearby door and into the baggage collection area. We're as close as it's possible to be to security. We can get through the airport and to the carpark in a few minutes. I suspect it'll still be too long.

'Can you track them, Jak?' Isaac has stayed behind, keeping the aircraft safe until it touches down. We'll swing back and pick him up after. I'm hoping that Jakob might be able to tell us where they're going by tracing their demonic energy signature, but he's shaking his head. Whether it's some sort of object they're carrying or another form of possession like what happened to poor Otto, I guess they've simply used the countering effect it seems to have on angelic *talent* to bust through the forcefield and then either dropped it or masked it somehow.

A few more steps, and we're outside. I'm swinging my head around wildly, trying to spot them so we can give chase, but it's just clear blue sky as far as I can see. Aicha calls Isaac, who pops us on speaker phone, and I scream at him, her, Jakob, the Mother, anyone. 'Where are they? Where?'

No one can tell me. The sky's clear in every direction.

De Montfort has Almeric. He got one over on us yet again.

Chapter Nine

BORDEAUX, 10 JUNE, PRESENT DAY

So sick and tired of losing. Sick of being so damn tired. Running on absolute fumes.

The yelling turns to screaming, ululations of strung together swearing syllables, all of the worst bad words I can think of in a myriad of languages until my throat gets hoarse, cracking and dying as I stomp up and down the rows of parked cars. I may even have broken my toe by kicking a concrete bollard. This only causes me to scream even louder, cussing out every single thing in existence, particularly because the bastard bollard is entirely unbothered by the whole performance. It could at least have the decency to act hurt. Rude.

The Mother is waiting for me, once I calm down enough not to break our new bestie status by swearing profusely at the scary witch queen ruler of the coven controlling a large swathe of the west coast. Her arched eyebrow makes it clear that she, too, wants answers.

So I give them to her. All our adventures thus far, since everything went spectacularly to pot —hell, passed through pot as a gateway drug and headed straight to a crack pipe and injecting heroin directly into its eyeballs— with me getting my magic eaten by Melusine. Maybe it's too trusting on my part. Those *talent*-imbued skeletons are no minor artefacts. They're the sort of MacGuffins you could build a whole eighties action-adventure franchise around and make a fortune. Any Talented who got their hands on those bad boys could pull off some serious world domination if that was their dirty little megalomaniacal kink. They could certainly wipe out annoying rivals who happened to live a short distance down from your town in the blink of a Sauron-like giant glowing eye.

But if there's one thing the Mother has shown herself to be since our misadventure in Lourdes, it's honourable. I'm not suggesting for one moment she isn't a political animal nor that she'd turn down the possibility of getting her hands on anything that might further cement her power and provide future protection for her progeny when she passes over the reins. But she only has a progeny —only has that possibility of a future— thanks to the sacrifices I've made. The prices I've paid. And I just don't believe she'd screw me over after all that.

Yeah. I know. I'm a fucking idiot. But right now my only concern is stopping De Montfort. I'll worry about how I'm going to get stabbed in the back once I've stabbed him in his front. Repeatedly. Perforating every single major organ in alphabetical order.

The Mother is moving even before I've finished the story. Lackeys and lieutenants come rushing over. At first I assume she's summoned them through psychic connections, ties that bind them to the whole coven structure. But as I continue deeper into my tale, detailing Scarbo's betrayal and our fugitive run through the mean streets of Paris, I notice tiny expression changes. Eyebrows quirk; lips purse. Subtle combinations that seem to act as summons. Then as they close in, her fingers flash, lightning gestures that pause in positions that aren't any form of sign language I've ever seen. Looks like the Sistren have their own secret code. And that they don't rely on their mistress' magic to get everything done. Wise witches. My own story stands as tribute to that. The body I'm wearing — and how the former occupant got evicted by Aicha shows how even god-like *talent* can get outclassed by forward planning and animal cunning. Not that I'm calling Aicha an animal. I'm not in any hurry to get evicted, thank you very much. Nor eviscerated.

'So what is there to do next, Good Man?' I don't feel like much of a good man right now. A useless man. A wrong-footed, off-balance, failure-yet-again man, perhaps. Every time I think we're taking a step in the right direction, it turns out instead to be a step straight onto a bear trap or a pit filled with sharp stakes that De Montfort's put straight in our path. It means I'm second-guessing every possibility all over again.

Which, of course, catches me a slap round the back of the head. Through the stinging tears that the blow causes to spring to my eyes, I can still make out the expression on Aicha's face. She doesn't look very impressed by me falling into an existential crisis yet again.

'Stop over-complicating it, you twat. Keep it simple, dickhead.'

'I'm pretty sure the anacronym is KISS, Aich.'

'Okay. Keep it simple, stupid dickhead. KISSD. As in "the very thought of you being KISSD makes me throw up in my mouth a little". Better?'

'Let's go with "yes" just so that we stop this conversation, shall we?'

The Mother sighs impatiently, but I see her mouth quirk. We're hilarious, and she knows it. 'There is truth in what her highness says.' Her highness? Fucking hell. Two things pop to mind. One, that I've never heard of the Mother showing anyone such respect. Two, that I'm never going to hear the end of it from Aicha.

The Mother continues, 'There is a tendance, a temptation to complicate such scenarios. What options are there on the table? What must be achieved, prices be damned?'

Cold passes through me, a shivering chill that travels to my core and is gone. For the Mother to talk of ignoring the costs in order to get what needs to be done *done* is terrifying. Because it shows me just how terrified she is. That the Mother recognises the seriousness of this situation, precisely what sort of threat De Montfort poses with almost all of the skeleton parts in hand. With what he already had, he could probably have ruled the world. And he's just gained a major top-up thanks to snatching the latest Almeric incarnation from under our noses.

Okay. Stupid levels of simple. Aicha's right. I can manage that. 'Right, let's break it down. One, he needs the original Almeric's skull, currently located' —I wave my hand at the golem housing Jakob and Nanael— 'in the T1000 over there. Which should be, thanks to the in-built angelic defence system, safer than Fort Knox.'

Except the thought comes to me of another time I believed a holy relic was safe. When I thought the Grail was locked up in Foix, which was the equivalent of Fort Knox in medieval Occitanie. Sure, there wasn't an angel that time. But our overconfidence still led to the evil fuckers getting their hands on that holiest of items. And there's another problem.

I turn towards Isaac as he finally rejoins us. 'Except he's not safe, is he? What the hell was all that with demon essence? I thought demonic magic was like gnat bites to angels? How did it break through your warding?'

My oldest living friend shakes his head, pale-faced and drawn. 'I've no idea, lad. *We've* no idea. Nithael's telling me it should be impossible, which, honestly, is putting him in a right old tizzy. He's practically sulking over it, which is even more annoying from an angel than it is from you. Pretty good going.'

I get the feeling that the words aren't only for us, but a very unsubtle dig at his other-dimensional lodger. Looks like this is the source of some disagreement between Isaac and his angel. Trouble in paradise, if you will.

While I hate not having answers to that particular conundrum — and if it's annoying me, it must be driving Isaac absolutely loopy — it doesn't change much other than not relying on the angels. We still have to keep Jakob safe. No question he's going to be De Montfort's next target.

'Okay, so one, get them somewhere protected. Two, find De Montfort and...' I break off, look over at Aicha. 'Rescue this Frank Phillips?' She shrugs. 'His bones at least.' This gets me a nod. I guess having read about his particular beliefs and having seen how much of a murderously prejudiced arsehole Almeric's been across every single lifetime, she's not bothered if we get him back dead or alive as long as we get him back. Can't say as I disagree.

'So two, find De Montfort. Get all of the bones, including Phillips', back.' There's an important conversation to be had about how that particular treasure trove of calcium and terrifyingly powerful *talent* gets divided up afterwards. We'll worry about that once we get our hands on them or more precisely get De Montfort's off them. 'Then three, find a way to kill or imprison Demon Fart permanently, so he doesn't just start up all over again with whatever the fuck he's up to.'

'Shouldn't there be...' The Mother breaks off as she shakes her head slightly, like she's trying to dislodge water from her inner ear after a trip to the swimming pool. 'There is a *pet name* for the villain?'

'Of course.' I shrug. 'It takes away a little of his power, a touch of his mystique and menace. Reduces him in our collective imaginations instead of building him into some unbeatable evil genius Big Bad. And his name is De Montfort. *De Montfort.* It was absolutely begging for ridicule.'

'Plus he's an utter prick.'

'Plus —yes, top marks for that one, Aich— he's an utter and total, unbearable, insufferable prick, and I will take great pleasure in telling him the ridiculous childish nickname we've created for him as I flay the flesh from his bones and play a Santana guitar solo on his ligaments.'

The Mother thinks about this for a moment, then tips her head. 'There is reason within.'

I think she actually said she approves of my train of thought. Go me!

You can see the Mother backtracking, searching through the conversation's thread like Theseus in the labyrinth of the ADHD minotaur. It seems to happen a lot when people end up talking to us. 'Shouldn't there be a fourth point? There is the question of the man's aims.'

'Nope.' I shake my head. 'I don't give a flying monkey's winged fuck for what he wants to achieve. As long as I can stomp all over his plans, crush them into the mud under the heel of my size ten boots along with his rotten skull, listening to them both splinter underfoot, that's all I care about.'

I can see from her face that she doesn't agree with me, that she wants to argue. And she's probably right. Maybe if we could work out what he wants, what he's up to, then it'd help us unravel his plans and put a stop once and for all to the utter shitgryphon.

But the problem is I've been trying to work that out ever since he trapped me in that cave in Faerie. Hell, longer really, from the moment he sauntered into Melusine's chamber, all nonchalant arrogance, and robbed me blind.

And really, the answer is simple. Some evil shit with the bones. Trying to work out anything more than that isn't going to get us any closer to me burying my boot up his backside.

'There is a threat here.' The Mother's expression is serious, taut, and worried. 'There is a threat that carries in the air and earth and through the waves themselves. That whispers in the fire's tongue.'

Well that explains why the Mother herself came here to meet us, apart from how much she loves hanging out with me, of course. Looks like she's been picking up on some bad juju vibes either through augers or just the same gut instinct we all have, fine-tuned like a Stradivarius violin by her position in the Talented world.

She carries on. 'There are forces that move now which contain within them doom most terrible. There have been visions and seeings that cannot be questioned. There are calls to be made. Alliances to be demanded.'

It takes me a moment to decipher her going all 'I was there three thousand years ago', Elrond in her pronunciations, but I get it. She's definitely had some sort of prophetic vision, and it's enough to put the willies up the Mother herself. That on its own should be enough to scare the shit out of anyone sane.

Clearly, this has grown beyond the standard remit of "sort out your own shit in your own backyard". It's bigger than just the south of France. Beyond our capacity to sweep it under the rug and wipe our hands off, job done. No, for the threat posed by an utter arsegrape like De Montfort possessing as much magical power as he now does? We're going to need to call in every favour we've ever earned. Reach out to every single Talented who'll talk to us and might answer the call. For this one? We'll need everyone on board.

I see Aicha realise this at the same moment as I do. She turns to me and can hardly keep her voice level. 'It's a fucking *Infinity War* moment, isn't it?'

She's right. Looks like it's time to call in all of the big guns we can. Full on Avengers team up mode.

CHAPTER TEN

BORDEAUX, 10 JUNE, PRESENT DAY

Briefly considering making another crack at Aicha about her being Black Widow. Except I'm afraid she might live up to that and bite my head off. Literally.

There's not much more to say right here, right now. The Mother's already on board, but neither of us can do much from Bordeaux airport. She needs to head back to her seat of power, and we need to do the same. Recharge, ready ourselves, reach out to everyone we can. Every single person we've ever allied ourselves with, willingly or otherwise. Persuade them of the level of threat we're facing here, make them understand this isn't your normal "evil mage dickhead threatening to undo reality itself".

Make them understand that this time, the evil mage dickhead in question might just have the power to do precisely that thanks to those bones.

We jump back in the cars, and while Aicha drives, I start making calls. First one is to Leandre.

Well, first one is actually to Al-Ruhban to get Leandre's phone number. He *hems* and *haws* for about thirty seconds before I remind him what *hemming* and *hawing* cost us last time, then coughs up the required digits. I take a second to fill him in sufficiently, which consists of, 'Shit's about to go down. Make sure you're ready. You owe us on this one,' then I hang up and hammer the Lutin Prince's number into the car's touchscreen.

He picks up on the fourth tone. 'Talk to me but make it snappy. I'm in heads down mode, here.'

'Leandre, it's Paul. Paul Bonhomme.' Two things keep me from making a joke, answering him like a 1980's business bro. Perhaps something about ringing the bell or Wall Street calling and asking for its lingo back. One is the seriousness of the situation. The other is that I don't want to piss off the uber-powerful ruler of Paris and have him paint the car's windscreen with my grey matter.

'Ah, Paul, el mano himself!' The warmth in his voice sounds genuine. Mind you, with Leandre, I can never tell how much is real and how much is this persona he projects to keep everyone from freezing in terror each time he speaks to them. Make sure they're relaxed and off-guard. Much better to catch them talking shit to your face than plotting your downfall behind your back. Far easier to work out whose heads to explode to 'maximise synergistic energies' or however the hell he'd put it.

'Listen, Leandre, this is serious. We need you on the team.' I wince at that appalling bit of boardroom slang, but I get into the details with him. Of De Montfort sending innocents to the slaughter against the angelic power of the Bene Brothers. Of him finding a way to nullify their other-dimensional *talent*, although I don't tell him how, of course. The less people who know about that the better.

I do tell him of De Montfort's assault on the landing aircraft and how he grabbed Frank Phillips, latest incarnation of Arnaud Almeric and owner of the last set of bones. Of how much raw *talent* he now has at his fingertips, owning two almost-complete sets of bones. But it's when I tell him that the Mother is on board, of her apparent vision that he interrupts.

'And you're sure she said it was a vision?' There's an intensity there, a demand that I qualify it, clarify the details. 'Zoom out, give me the big picture. What are the optics looking like?'

'Like a row of bottles full of alcohol stacked up behind a bar.' Brilliant. That's Aicha's addition to the conversation. I can't keep myself from wincing. When Leandre did his equivalent of the *Bewitched* nose twitch and insta-teleported Scarbo into Al-Ruhban's kitchen, he said he was able to pull it off due to the contract Scarbo had signed. That, of course, doesn't mean he was telling the truth. Were I in his place, I'd be telling all of the porkies about my powers. And considering the lengths he already goes to in order to make people underestimate him? I don't doubt he does too. I'm steeling my nerves, anticipating blinking out of existence any second only to find myself in his torture chambers under the heart of Paris. Probably themed like the Wall Street trading floor, but voicing that would only add insult to the undoubtedly numerous and agonising injuries he'd presumably then inflict upon us.

That doesn't happen, though, thankfully. Leandre barks out a laugh that sounds half-forced. 'Yes, bish bosh, top marks.' The words are there, but he's clearly distracted, aware a joke has been made, not truly focused on what said joke really is. Which is probably a good thing considering it was at his expense.

'It was definitely a vision,' I throw in hurriedly to keep his attention there so he doesn't rewind mentally and realise Aicha was taking the piss out of him. 'She talked about a threat carried towards us.'

'On all four elements.' Aicha doesn't sound like she's joking around anymore. She's deadly serious.

'Right!' I wait for Leandre's thoughts on all this. Silence reigns from the other end of the line. I cast about desperately for something to persuade him further. 'Didn't you say yourself that you'd known something was coming? That's why you locked down Paris after all.' A lockdown that single-handedly failed either to stop us from getting around or Scarbo from stealing the rib cage for De Montfort. I decide not to vocalise that part though.

And still the Prince says nothing. I'm starting to sweat by this point. 'Look, you saw how much power there was in that one set of bones. I don't doubt Al-Ruhban told you about our little adventure underneath the Grande Nef. How close those Nazi fuckstickles came to bringing something unnameably horrific through from some other dimension. Melusine spent over a hundred years as the bogeywoman of the Talented world thanks to just a sprinkling of the lesser bones bound together. A collection which *allowed her to grant wishes* and allowed De Montfort to travel back and forth between Faerie and here *without Oberon or Maeve knowing.*' I'm really stressing those points now, leaning in on them, trying to drive them home into Leandre's brain. Trying to force him into realising just how unbelievably dangerous the threat facing us is. When you deal with magical politics, it's easy to get blasé about such things, to assume it'll all just fall into place, that someone will shut the latest version of a Talented equivalent of Doctor Evil down. Why? Because someone always has. Which is, of course, the story of humanity's continued survival. That someone always has persuaded that madman to step down, rallied the troops at the precise moment to change the course of the battle, convinced that president not to press the very shiny big red button just to see what happens.

Our not ceasing to exist has been as much due to bumbling chance, though, as to the right person with the right words or the right equivalent of a righteously big heavy hammer being there at the right moment. It could so very easily be that *this* — this moment right here — is the one where words fail, and the hammer just isn't large or weighty enough to crush the verminous bastard's head in. However much I want to watch Demon Fart's brains go splat. We need to stand together, to unite, or I have a terrible feeling crawling up and down my spinal column that we won't have anything left to stand on. Whether that means our own legs or the world itself? I can't say. Neither sound like particularly good options to lose in my opinion.

Finally, the Prince speaks. 'And what happens with these bones, assuming we win?'

Inwardly, I want to groan even as my brain notes he's not using the jargon-filled speech patterns he's always chosen up until now. He's a businessman — or a businesslutin these days, I guess, him having given up his humanity — first and foremost.

'I want them gone.' Honesty is the best policy here. Part of me wants to promise him the moon on a stick and the sun in an ice-cream cone for dessert. Anything to get him on board. But my gut tells me it'll backfire either now or later. 'If I can destroy them, I will. If not?' Fuck, I don't want to do this, but I can't see any other option. 'We'll divide them amongst us. Spread them out between those who stand together, to keep safe.'

It's the equivalent of arming all your political rivals with ten-tonne warheads, but there's no choice. It's still the best plan even if I can't help having visions of some other evil wankshaft going on his own version of a main story mission to gather them back up at a later date. Or else one of my current allies deciding to do the same.

That's a problem for after ensuring reality doesn't get shredded by whatever the fuck De Montfort is up to first. Silence falls again, but I can tell the Prince is considering it.

'What do you need me to do?' he says at last, and I could cry with relief, possibly even do, a few tears escaping as I blink them away down my cheeks. Paris is with us. An ironic thing for me to be cheering about, considering what the northern Francs did during my first lifetime, when I cursed Paris and all its occupants on a regular basis. This time though, it might just turn the tide the right way.

'De Montfort's family were established at Montfort-L'Aumery.' I can't believe he doesn't know this, can't believe he hasn't had some element of his staff researching the fuck out of the man believed to have stolen from him. But then, the Prince is too canny to do something until he's sure of winning, and he knew how much magic De Montfort had on his side with the stolen ribs. 'That needs to be hit like a crack den SWAT raid, okay?'

'Roger, roger.' I can almost hear the relief in Leandre's voice. He thinks that's all he'll have to do. Makes me suspect that he has the place under observation after all, that he's sure De Montfort isn't there. I'm pretty much certain too. Demon Fart would have to be a fucking idiot to be hanging out in such an obvious locale after we almost caught him with his pants down in Kenilworth Castle. And sadly, he isn't, much as it'd make our lives easier.

I disillusion him rapidly. 'Then gather up every single individual you can muster. Call up the reserves like you're marching to fucking war.' My thoughts flick back to the magically possessed Grail hunters De Montfort sent against us at Isaac's. I wonder how many more like that he has stashed away, ready to be thrown against any foes. Hell, we might be doing just that. 'We're going to get back behind the wards at ours. That'll be the rallying point.' It'll also probably be the warzone. De Montfort needs that skull Jakob and Nanael have taken up residence in again. My hope is we can gather enough allies at Isaac's without Simon knowing and thus catch him off guard when he launches his full offensive. Enough to turn the tide and overcome the advantage he has in terms of *talent* and planning.

'Okay, copy that, sterling work.' The false bonhomie returns to his voice. Guess he's not surprised by my demands. He's back in character. Whatever. As long as he's onside, that's all that matters. 'I'll crunch the numbers, scout out the opposition HQ for a hostile takeover, then report back post-reccy to put our heads together for a brain-storming pow-wow, okay?'

I take all of that to mean he's going to go kick the fuck out of whoever he can find at Montfort-L'Aumery, then rendezvous with us at Isaac's. 'Got it.' I hesitate, but then add, 'Thanks, Leandre.' Thanking the fae is a bad bloody idea as a rule of thumb, and he's definitely still fae. Isaac's words in testament to his character ring in my ears though, and I honestly don't expect to make it through whatever comes next. Let him come calling in the favour from my dead and buried bones. See how far it gets him.

'You're welcome?' I can hear the confusion there, and I wonder if anyone has ever dared to thank him before. It's quickly gone. 'I'll go get the gears spinning, pivot the thinking round, get the synergy aligned and widen out the bandwidth for the whole team. Ciao for now!'

The line goes dead, but it's all I can do not to pump my fist in triumph, which would be a bad idea as I'm driving and likely to crash the car, which would be a good way to cut my celebrations short.

Leandre is on board. We might just have a chance after all.

Chapter Eleven

BORDEAUX, 10 JUNE, PRESENT DAY

We've just swung the odds
dramatically in our favour.
Which is good because they were
previously so small, you'd have
had better chance persuading
the fucking Tarrasque as to the
importance of dental hygiene.

We spend the rest of the drive brainstorming other candidates for our burgeoning alliance and reaching out to them where we can reach agreement. Faust and Mephy are an obvious choice. A sudden, terrified thought strikes me, as the burring tone of the call kicks in on my mobile. What if De Montfort got his hands on Mephistopheles? The moment I think it, I realise it's the most plausible option. He's the only demon ever to take up residence on Earth that we know of. I'd have said capturing him would be impossible, but considering Ben's recent successes with caging angels, all guided by De Montfort pulling the strings, anything seems possible.

So I'm greatly relieved when Faust answers the phone and I can hear Mephy shouting questions to him in the background. Of course, I only have to ask them to come for them to agree approximately a second later. I don't mention the demon energy thing. There'll be time enough to get into that when they get here, and I'd rather they concentrate on booking flights over from Salzburg, but I'm hoping Mephy might help us understand and nullify this weird impossible essence De Montfort has somehow got his hands on. Magic even the angels don't understand. Perhaps a demon will have better luck.

It takes some arguing with Aicha, but she eventually agrees to me reaching out to the Caliburc, the Golden Goat who rules the Cote D'Azur. She has a real bee in her bonnet about him that I've never understood. He's always been delightful and helpful whenever our paths have crossed. There're rumours he's the original owner of the Golden Fleece — as in, the one who grew the fleece itself, brought to France by a voyaging Jason after his main adventures. Other stories say he's a powerful magical being summoned from another plane by Abdelraman to protect the fabulous riches he left behind when he returned to the Maghreb until his never-achieved return. Either way, he's a major Power, possibly tens of thousands of years old and one even Leandre would think twice about tangling with, I suspect. To my delight and Aicha's susurrant bitching, he agrees to come meet us the following day. I'm not a fool. I think the promise of a share of the magical bones is the persuading factor, but it's worth it to have him on Team Bonhomme.

As revenge, Aicha suggests calling the fucking Tarrasque. This nearly causes me to swerve into oncoming traffic, as well as to dry heave at the very thought. Luckily, nobody has any way of contacting him —because who in their right mind would want to— and anyway, there's no way he'd help us out. Not least after Nithael humiliated him so very effectively. He'd sign up for Team Demon Fart in a heartbeat. Plus, it'd involve me *talking to the fucking Tarrasque.* I already did enough of that recently to last for a lifetime, thank you very much indeed.

By the time we get back to Isaac's, we're running low on ideas. It's not that most Talented are fundamentally evil — that's just not the case, or the world would have boiled away into the vastness of space in the ensuing magical wars many times over — but they are generally pretty self-centred and not really interested in what happens outside the boundaries of their own petty principalities. Plus, I don't have that many of their numbers. They don't seem to want to be friends with me for some reason. Not even when I make popcorn.

I give Craig, the Magus of Blackburnshire, a call. A call that mostly involves me explaining the situation repeatedly while he gets distracted on tangents. He manages to get the gist of it — that I'd like him to jump on a flight and head over — but he doesn't really have his head around the rest of it.

'So we're gunna hit the town, reet? Get fucking mashed up and do our funky thing, innit?' Because despite me trying to make him understand, he's still convinced I'm calling him up for a date.

'Sure, whatever.' I can't keep the frustration out of my voice, which makes me feel a little bit like I'm kicking a puppy. A very, very stoned puppy, but that only makes it even worse. 'I'll be delighted to do that once we take care of the *menacing evil threatening all of existence.*'

'Reet, I hear you, like, but I ain't quite got me head round it.' That much is obvious. '*How* is existence under threat, exactly, love?'

'*I don't know!*' I can't help shouting at him, and it's totally unfair. Because he's right. I have no idea. Not a fucking clue what De Montfort is up to. What he's planning to do with his very metal bone collection he's gathered. But I don't need the Mother's visions to know it's nothing good.

And that's the real source of my frustration. Where is De Montfort? What is he up to? Why isn't he attacking? Because he has to know that we saw him take Frank Phillips. He must have been monitoring what his pillywiggins were up to.

So why is he giving us the time and space to gather up our allies? It's scaring the bejeezus out of me. I'm constantly on edge, waiting for the other foot to fall because everything is going far too bloody well.

Still, maybe it's just because we've disturbed his plans enough to keep him off-balance. He didn't expect me to get free and start running around opposing him. Perhaps we're still ahead despite his win in Bordeaux. If we can gather all these various Talented together, then either find his hideout over at Lavaur maybe or Montsegur itself or else let him break himself against us, attacking our arrayed strengths on our home turf...

We can still win this.

'Are you still there, like, or what?' Craig sounds puzzled rather than pissed off.

Guess I got lost in my own thoughts for a moment. 'Sorry, I am. So can you come?'

'Aye, I'll be the-'

I wait for a moment, assuming he's just forgotten what he was saying mid-syllable. But after a few seconds, I pull my phone from my ear to see I've lost signal. I'm about to head back inside when I feel it happen. The wards springing up.

And not our wards. Not the wards I walked into the soul of the streets of Toulouse, ingraining my essence into those slabs of concrete, claiming them as mine. Nor the angelic ones that Nith and Nan wove from them, light years beyond my understanding and capabilities magically.

No. They aren't ours, but I know whose they are. These are his wards. De Montfort's. As soon as that horrible sticky feeling of his magic surrounds us, I can *see* them in the distance as they pop into being. It's a wall of shimmering sickly, putrescent green, like the very air is rotting, turned rancid and corrupted. Streaks of black run through it, and I know it's the demonic energy, built from an essence that shouldn't even exist in our reality.

And I realise it isn't a wall. No. It's a dome, a curving arc that extends high into the soaring blue sky above us, turning it that same diseased colour, infecting it too. That it extends all the way over our heads till the few clouds are shaded too, like pustulent scabs on the sickened heavens. As I crane my neck back, my body turns, and I'm following the path of that ascending parabola, looking for the source. My body swivels around southwards, and I can't contain my gasp when I spot it.

Because it looks like one of the mountains in the Pyrenees has been turned into the magical equivalent of a volcano.

A spewing plume of rotten *talent* explodes up from a single point in the mountain range, hitting the sky and then pouring outwards in a bubbling, roiling storm of rotted energy, surrounding the Pyrenees in an arcing circle for hundreds of miles.

I spare a glance across at my companions, see the same shock reflected in their features. Even Aicha can't keep herself from biting her lip. The question is clear on my own face, the head shakes and blank horror obvious answers on theirs. None of us have ever seen a working like this, never even heard of the like.

Looking down, I see the signal's back on my phone. I hammer in the numbers, hoping beyond hope that this barrier dome has extended as far as Bordeaux.

'Are you inside?' I can't quite keep the desperation out of my voice, the need to hear the answer I want.

'There is some distance from the wall to Bordeaux,' is the answer the Mother gives me, and I feel like weeping. And not in relief like when I called Leandre. Because it means we're in here.

And every single one of our carefully won allies are out there.

There's the feel of a hand gripping my shoulder with force but only a fraction of what it possesses. I know that because my shoulder blade doesn't get pulverised into dust. Looking round, I see Aicha's there, her eyes locked on mine, and she gives me that smallest, most minute of nods. It's a nod that doesn't just affirm her presence but that somehow lends with it a smidgen of her essence, the tiniest part of her strength to fortify mine.

So I don't break down. Instead, I marshal my emotions, pulling myself together by force of will. Both my own and that I've borrowed.

Let's get to the important question. 'Can you get through it?'

'There are... possibilities. Tests that must be made. Efforts and energies invested.' Delays at the very best then. 'Stay where you are. There is safety inside your own barriers.'

Basically, she's telling us to sit tight and wait for the cavalry. Except that's not going to work. I shake my head, and maybe it's in answer to what she's saying, maybe also at the further incomprehensibility of what's happened.

'We can't do that, Mother, because there is no safety here.'

She sucks in a breath. 'Why is that?'

'Because there are no wards anymore.'

And that is the part we're all struggling with. Why disbelief has pasted itself across the expressions of all of my companions. Even Jakob shows it, his head twisting back and forth, looking for something no longer there, as if were he just to look a little more, they'll maybe reappear. Because somehow, piling impossibility on top of impossibility, when this new uber-powerful ward went up, blocking us in and our allies out...

It destroyed our own wards. Broke them or pulled them down. I'm not sure which. It doesn't matter. What does matter is it leaves us totally exposed, sitting ducks.

Toulouse —my home, my own — holds no safe haven for us anymore.

CHAPTER TWELVE

BORDEAUX, 10 JUNE, PRESENT DAY

And he's one step ahead of us once again. What will it take for us to get in front, to trip him up? Ideally to face-plant straight onto a bed of the pointiest spikes known to man.

T he ensuing discussion after the phone call ends is terse but short. Isaac is all for heading towards Bordeaux. His thinking is that we meet up with the Mother and her team on the other side, combine our strengths to focus on a single portion of this malicious working and try to force a way through.

It's a good plan in many ways. Most of the time I'd be on board.

But I look over at Aicha and read the same idea in her eyes as is running riot in my mind. The single thought running rampant, screaming blue murder and ringing every single alarm bell it can get its hands on. A very simple thought. That it means going on the defensive again.

And if I were De Montfort? That'd be exactly what I'd expect me to do.

Which means it's exactly what he wants us to do. So that means we need to do the opposite of that.

Unless of course he's expecting us to realise and do precisely that...

I feel like I'm somehow in the Battle of Wits from the *Princess Bride* and I have the terrifying sensation that I'm Vizzini in this setup, trying to out-bluff a deservedly confident Man in Black. Every time we think we've come up with a way to out-think him, to change the board in our favour, he pulls off some impossible save that makes it seem like we've done exactly what he wants thanks to his immunity to iocane powder.

But I'm sick of going on the defensive. So I put forward my counter-proposition, and Aicha nods her silent assent. It's very simple.

We go find the heart of this horrendously fucking toxic ward that's just sprung up to cover half of Occitanie (and presumably a chunk of Spain to the south as well). And kick the shit out of whoever or whatever we find there.

Isaac is not entirely convinced by our way of thinking.

'That's not a plan. It's a bloody suicide note, lad!' His outrage is palpable, present, a pressure that sits heavily on my heart because, of course, I know there's a good chance he's right.

I sigh, trying to push air into my chest, trying to make it rise against that burden of paternal fear. 'It might be, 'Zac. It's also the only thing he won't expect.'

'Of course he'll expect it! It's what you do every bloody time! Go charging headlong off into danger without a bloody care in the world...' His voice falters, cracks, and the words are lost to the weight of emotion. I don't miss his eyes darting sideways, to the reflective metal carapace that houses the other family member he stands to lose. The one he only just got back. The one residing in the thing that De Montfort now desires most in the world and that I'm suggesting taking straight to him.

'But he won't expect it this time.' It's hard to bite back my own impatience, my desire to act, to do anything rather than sit here and wait for doom to swoop down on me from above, a vicious half-starved eagle's shadow descending from the mountain eyries. 'Look, when did the ward go up?'

'I don't know, half an hour ago?' He's being deliberately obtuse, and he knows it. I shoot him a hard look I learned from him. Defeated, he sighs and nods. 'Once we got back home.'

'Right. And we know from speaking to the Mother that Bordeaux isn't included. He let us back in, 'Zac. He gave us the time and space to stick everyone on high alert, to get everyone on board, "woohoo, go Team Bonhomme", and then what?'

'Sprang the trap.' The words are dragged unwillingly from his tongue. That's the curse of the true academic of course. If you can present a carefully constructed argument, they'll respond to it with due consideration however much they don't want to.

'Which tells us two things. One, De Montfort doesn't care about the whole of the rest of the Talented society ganging up on him, so time is short. I don't care how powerful that boundary is. Between the combined magics of the Mother and her connection to the Garonne, Leandre and his powers of bypassing all locks, and the Hob King and his nullifying effects on wards, he can't hope it'll hold them out for long. Obviously, he still expects it to be long enough.'

'And secondly?' Good God, he sounds miserable. I hate doing this to him, but I need him on board. We all need to be in accord before we walk off into Mordor.

'Secondly, it means he wants us to rely on them. He wants us to either wait for them or go try to help them to get in. The evidence is clear. We're outclassed, outgunned, outmatched. The sensible thing to do is to find a way to pull down these barriers and bring in the backup. He'll expect you three to make me do the sensible thing.'

'He might know you, Paul Bonhomme.' Aicha's grin is wild, fierce, and packed with a ferocity that shakes its fist at society's expectations, fully ready to see it crumble and fall before the raw force contained within. Aicha Kandicha is a force of nature, a force to be reckoned with. 'He might know you, but he doesn't know me. Sensible? Let's go kick him in the sensi-balls.'

'Fucking A.' I look over at Jakob first, deliberately forcing myself not to look at the man I love more than I did my own real father. It's Isaac who's marched through the years next to me, wiping my tears and sticking a plaster on my metaphorical bloodied knee. And still I make myself not look at him, to not see the pain and fear on his face. Because I know it's there. And I know it's not for him.

'What do you say, Jak?' It's hard to read the metallic face. There are features, sure, and the metal moves. But skin speaks a language we learn from our first time touched to our mother's breast, and there're none of those linguistics there. I just have to wait for his answer, studying the impassive visage.

It comes eventually. 'I think we go, my dear boy, though I am...' His lips, sun-glinting, twist for a moment, and it humanises the golem so much it hurts. 'Though I am afraid.'

When an angel-bearing master Kabbalist wearing an impenetrable metallic golem speaks of their fear, only a fool would ignore it. Luckily I am such a fool. He's given me the answer I want. That only leaves one more.

'What do you reckon then, 'Zac? At least I'm not suggesting leaving you on the benches this time.' The joke falls flat, of course. There're no benches to sit on. We're all going to win or die. Or both. Or possibly neither and only wish we did die instead of whatever De Montfort has cooked up for us, waiting in the mountains I once called home.

He looks at me, and I can feel his studying gaze. I know he's looking inside me, seeing my own terrified inner child bawling and mewling, who wants to go and curl up in a dark corner until all of this horror and misery and unbearable weight of responsibility just fucks off and leaves me alone. And for a moment he looks old. Ancient even. If there have been moments where I've felt every day of my long life during recent events, well... In that moment he wears his, carries them in every line and patch of weathered skin. Then he sighs and nods.

'I trust you, lad.' Four simple words. Four simple words I've always known and never understood how I could possibly have achieved such a hefty honour. Four simple words that, in truth, I've never felt I've merited. Never felt worthy of that complete, whole-hearted, unconditional trust. 'Let's saddle up, shall we?'

He pats the side of the car fondly, like the noble loyal steed he's conjuring up in the image, and just like that the argument is settled.

I trust you, lad.

Guess I'd better finally prove, once and for all, that I'm worthy of that trust.

Chapter Thirteen

TOULOUSE, 10 JUNE, PRESENT DAY

The only thing worse than walking into a trap? Knowing you're walking into a trap but not having any idea exactly how those steel jaws, full of torso-dismembering teeth, are going to close around you. Only knowing that they will.

Everyone's in for this trip. Part of me still desperately wants to leave Isaac behind, to somehow persuade him to wait this out at the house, but he's never going to buy it. I'd say Jakob too, but a super-tough metallic angel is a useful team member even if he's only playing defence. I'm less than happy about turning up to De Montfort's front door with the last piece he's missing — the skull Jak and Nan are currently using as their cockpit for the mecha-body — but it's all constant second guessing anyhow. Maybe he wants us to leave them here while we charge in, and he'll swoop in behind us and grab up the pair of them. After these impossible wards combined with the whole pillywiggins escapade, anything seems possible. There's no safety anywhere now, not inside the territory he's claimed with this rotten, rotting magic. None except what we find by standing together.

Otherwise, there's not much we can do. Given time, given a bit more recon info, maybe we could come up with some nifty *talented* gadgets or pick up some more military-grade hardware. As is, I've kept one of the machine guns the Nazi fucks were packing and so has Aicha. Shoot-outs aren't really my area of expertise, but I'll take anything that might help right now.

I pop the Veil of Veronica in my pocket. It takes me back to where this whole absolute farce started. The last thing I want to do is forgive De Montfort, but if it gets him gone? If it means he really never comes back ever again? I'll happily swaddle his face in it, basking him in whatever combination of innate *talent* and imbued belief allows it to pardon all sins instantaneously of the wearer, giving him a final send-off. While I choke the fucking life out of him with my bare hands.

We jump back in the cars and head for the motorway that goes south before bending east towards Narbonne. It's a couple of hours drive. Aicha and I are in the lead car, the body-sharing brothers following. There's no banter, no jokes. No attempts to lighten the mood. We don't even put any music on. Nothing's going to reduce the tension on this journey. Nothing except getting where we need to be and doing what needs to be done.

As we're driving, sudden inspiration strikes me. Of an ally we still have. Someone who can still come help us kick that grin off De Montfort's face. Or ram a shotgun barrel into his bollocks.

Someone who'll take great delights in doing just that.

I hurriedly redial the number Isaac gave me last time. 'Gwen, it's Paul.'

'Is he dead yet, Good Man?' The demand is clear. Mainly because she probably can't imagine why on earth I'd be calling her otherwise.

'No, and not only that, he's fucking winning. Again.' I can't keep the frustration out of my voice. Good God damn it, I am sick of saying that. 'How would you like to come help us stop that and, as an added bonus, help us kill him as agonisingly, painfully as possible in the process?'

'Did you never hear the story of the grieving mother and the torture kit she built out of some household accoutrements and some careful Black Friday purchases?' Fuck me. Gwendolyne is utterly terrifying at times.

'Brilliant. He's in the Pyrenees, practically on your doorstep. I reckon he's probably at Montsegur. You've seen the barrier that's gone up? That's him. Start heading that way, and we'll meet you there.'

Silence. Silence that drags my momentarily lifted spirits rapidly back into the depths of hell, like Orpheus threw them a cheeky back glance just as he reached the exit. Then Gwen speaks. 'I'm outside the barrier.'

Oh fuck. Fuck fuckedy fuckaroo. 'Of course you are. How come?'

'I got a call. Supposedly from a Cagot community by Bilbao that needed my help for a difficult birthing involving a pairing with a Talented. A story that was sure to get me moving. One I'm no longer convinced will turn out to be true when I arrive.'

Of course. What a perfect tale to motivate Gwendolyne, considering what she's already been through with Susane. The whole thing reeks of yet another master stroke by De Montfort. 'Any chance you can turn around, get back through it?'

'I'll be trying, boy; you can bank on that.' The line goes dead. I guess she wants to concentrate on pulling some sort of screeching one-eighty and heading back in our direction.

Sadly, I doubt it'll make much difference. Another ally efficiently and effectively pruned away from us in our hour of need. Fuck my life.

We turn off just before Carcassonne, the site of many turns of ill-fortune during the Albigensian Crusade, and I'm glad not to have to pass it. That'd feel like a bad omen, and I can do without any of those.

The mountains rise up to meet us. The June sky should be bright blue with careless happy-go-lucky cloud puffs bobbling about in it. Instead, it's like the stratosphere is flayed flesh that's been stretched out and left for days in the early summer sun. It festers, and the odd waft of cloud is like a scabbed sore ready to weep. Perhaps for us. Perhaps for the earth itself. Suitably dramatic, perhaps, but not a comfortable vista under which to drive towards your doom.

It's a shame in many ways that the mood is so weighted. It's a breathtaking drive normally, once we break off from the motorway. We scoot along the side of the Aude River, the overhangs of the mountain crowding in on us. Normally it's vertiginous, but today it feels oppressive. The shadow of countless millennia is almost too much to bear.

In the distance, I catch a glimpse of Rennes-Les-Chateau. A place laden with power and full of mysteries. Not least of which is, "How did it enable Dan Brown's books to become so wildly popular?" but there's plenty more besides. One thing that isn't there, though, no matter how many people believe it, is the Holy Grail. Sadly, much like Otto Rahn, I doubt they'll believe me if I tell them.

And then finally I track the storm funnel of putrid *talent* we're driving towards and clock the place we're going to.

Not Montsegur after all.

But Bugarach. Oh. Well, I wasn't expecting that.

I should have been really, now I think about it. Thing is, I was so convinced of the other logic — that it'd all tie back into our past that once I saw it was in the mountains — I was convinced it'd be Montsegur, that site of the Cathar's last stand, where the faith had fallen once and for all.

Instead, it's Bugarach. And it makes perfect sense.

There are points in the world where the walls are thinner. Not just between other realms and dimensions, like Faerie or the higher and lower realms.

No. Where the walls are thinner between worlds. Between realities. Between possibilities and impossibilities and all the options that rest in between them.

The Pyrenees are just such a place. Wrapped around a heart of iron that can throw a compass and make it lead a person through paths that never used to exist a second previously, through ravines that close up behind them and swallow them whole, never to open again. Lucifer's heart, some say, or his crown. A fallen star perhaps. Or a star that fell through a million existences and carried with it the memories of its passage before lying dormant underneath the craggy heights of this strangest of mountain ranges.

And Bugarach is perhaps the strangest of them all.

It's a place shrouded in tales and steeped in mythos, not all of which are true and some of which have cost many unTalented dear. It's even named after two fae, Bug and Arach, who supposedly created it. For one brief moment, it became the most expensive land on Earth per square metre, when it was predicted to be the only place to survive the oncoming Mayan apocalypse in 2012. When 2013 turned up to smear egg on the face of the owners of said land, they got the double kick in the groin of watching their land prices slide off into the obscurity of worthlessness. Although who they thought they were going to sell them to had they been right in the first place, I have no idea.

It's also the location of the highest concentration of UFO sightings in Europe. And not in the "buzzers" sense of bored little green men scaring yokels who nobody will ever believe. This is more flying orbs and inexplicable sightings. Haunting phenomena that have a simple explanation. Even the unTalented only need to have the tiniest sensitivity towards *talent* here to catch glimpses from beyond a certain veil. Not one that separates life from death. No. One that separates reality from the other.

Because Bugarach is supposedly home to a portal, a weak point in the world where you might wander through to somewhere *else*. Maybe just a tiny bit different, where everyone calls you by a different name and laughs when you insist that you've always been Carl with a C, not with a K, and your wife doesn't remember your first date and weren't her eyes blue not the brightest of greens? Or perhaps somewhere entirely different, where all your dreams will come true. Including the ones that wake you up screaming in the night.

A place where the walls of the worlds are thinnest. Where you could tumble them all down if you had something powerful enough to do so.

When I see Bugarach itself, something catches in my throat. The way the plateau at the top sticks up prominently from the mountain range makes me think of the images I've seen of Ayers Rock. It seems like something out of the Dreamtime too. And though it's not red, these are the Iron Mountains. Here, too, is ancient landscape we can never hope to tame.

Time is not on our side; sure, Time's pretending to be neutral, hanging out on the sidelines, but I can see him giving the opposition instructions with subtle hand gestures. The only gestures he's making at us is to call us wankers. I'm genuinely terrified about just rolling up to Bugarach, especially considering what happened the last time I caught up with De Montfort in the mountains of Faerie, but I'm even more worried by the idea of leaving Almeric in his grubby little paws while the zombie version of the Northern Lights crackles overhead. Whatever is going down is going down *now*. The time for caution is at an end.

We spend a while on the last part of the drive, thrashing it out, trying to look for the main risks now we know where we're going. There're so many of them, it's hard to know where to start. We don't know where on the Mount he is. We don't know who's there with him, what other soldiers or creatures he might have by his side. There's no telling what he's actually up to. And that's before we get into all the unknowns revolving around this fucking demon essence he shouldn't have access to but somehow does. All we know is that whatever he wants, it's going to be bad news for us and probably the planet as a whole. So we need to get in there and put a stop to it before he completes whatever it is he's doing.

I feel locked in a loop as we approach, like I got touched by Punxsutawney Phil's shadow ever since I fell into the shizzard's clutches. It's the same things repeating time after time. Ben wanted to use the skulls to break through reality. Melusine used her ossuary sceptre to reshape it. De Montfort forced us to follow him through to the fae realm, using it to create his own way in and out. Hell, even the rib cage that he nicked in Paris was being used by Thule Society idiots to weaken the barriers between our world and the next when we took it off them back in the seventies. Bones and forced doors and broken walls. And now it all leads to Bugarach.

My nerves are shot as we get out of the car, slamming the doors shut behind us. I feel rabbity right at the moment. And not in the verbal diarrhoea sense. More in the "trapped in the headlights, about to be made into bright red rabbit jam" meaning. Nervy doesn't even cover it.

It takes a couple of minutes for the Chuckle Brothers squared to catch up in the other car, and I spend it scuffing at the gravel of the parking lot with my shoe, trying not to think the same things over and over and failing miserably. We have to assume De Montfort has this place under observation. Sneaking up isn't going to happen. There are too many known unknowns, as well as too many unknown unknowns for even Donald

Rumsfeld to get his head around. There's no option but to go in and improvise. Which, to be fair, is my normal course of action — run in headlong and see what happens — but this time I really don't want to for a whole host of reasons. Because I don't want to lose this body. Because I don't want to get outsmarted by fucking De Montfort again.

Because I can't stop thinking about that cave under the hill in the Wilds.

I'm afraid of what's coming, of what De Montfort has in store for us, of ending up back underground and never getting out again. And everyone's looking at me to lead the charge, to be full of vim and vigour, to drop snarky jokes and light-hearted banter, and to look like nothing in the world can ever bother me. All I want to do is hide in a dark corner, to dive under the covers until the bogeyman goes away. Till my mother comes and tells me it's all just a bad dream and kisses away my tears. Good God, I miss her. Now I can remember her face. I'll not let that go again, however much it's a double-edged sword.

So I do the only thing I can do. I bluff it out.

'Right, Aicha, guard the rear. Isaac and Jak, in the middle. I'll take point. Can Nith and Nan give us any idea where to head?' It might not be my funniest call-to-action for the team ever, but, hey, I'm talking and suggesting we move forward instead of running away. That counts as a win, right?

Isaac and Jakob pause and then both point in unison to the top of the mountain. Because of course they do. Where else would we need to go?

Just before we start off, a thought occurs to me, and I pull Aicha to the side. 'The White Lady, is she here? Can she help us? Will she?'

Bugarach is a portal, after all. And the White Lady is the Guardian of the Portals. Having her on our side might just tip the odds back in our favour.

There's a moment. It's strange, and I can't quite place why I find it so unsettling, but something passes across Aicha's face that I've never seen before. It's lightning fast, so quick I can't identify it properly. Regret? Shame? Sorrow? Then it's gone, and her impassive, stoic beauty is locked back down tight.

'She's near. There's not much she can do. What she can, she will.'

Oof. That's a host of extra questions raised, but I can see from Aicha's expression I'm not going to get answers to any of them. Still, it suggests the White Lady is on our side, at least. Even if "not much" wasn't quite the contribution I was hoping for from her. Anything is better than nothing, I guess.

We start off up the path, through the forested undergrowth, towards the peak. It's a pleasant three-hour hike on a normal day, but I get the feeling we aren't going to be allowed to just merrily traipse our way up there, picking daisies as we go. For about an hour, it'd be a pleasant enough romp, if it weren't for the sky being tinged like gangrenous meat and whatever world-ending fuckery De Montfort has waiting for us at the top.

I'm just about to turn and comment to Aicha about how comparatively stress-free the climb has been so far. And right then, on cue, there's a rustling in the nearby vegetation that definitely isn't friendly.

Looks like the fun starts now. Hooray.

Chapter Fourteen

BUGARACH, 10 JUNE, PRESENT DAY

Anyone want to take odds on the bush-rustler being a harmless badger? Note — badgers can only ever be described harmless in Europe, as opposed to their American cousins who look like they smoke meth from pipes made out of squirrel skulls.

Whatever it is, it's nice of them to announce their presence. It gives us a chance to pull swords (in mine and Aicha's cases) and ready our *talent* (for everyone).

Sadly, it makes little difference.

There's a blur just beside me, almost out of my peripheral vision. It's enough to draw my attention, and I turn towards it, raising my sword as I do.

The turn probably saves me from dying.

It moves damnably fast. I don't even see it, only a dark shape, green-tinged and about a metre high, hurtling past my shoulder. I'm about to sigh in relief that it missed me until I realise it didn't.

Not entirely anyway. It's gouged a chunk the size of a tennis ball out of my right shoulder, which starts to scream blue murder at me. Luckily, we're out in the middle of real wild nature, and I've already spooled my *talent* up. I stop it bleeding and switch my sword to a left-handed grip while it heals. My right arm isn't useless, but it's a bloody mess, and it's not as responsive as I'm going to need it to be considering the speed of that thing.

I catch peripheral movement as it blurs towards me again, but this time, it doesn't manage to sink its teeth into me. There's a loud *clang* as Jakob slides smoothly into its path. A weird howl, more of a rumble than an ululation, echoes out, but the tone of pain is still clear. The mystery thing's obviously not capable of tearing a chunk out of a titanium body.

'A bit of "be thou not afeared" angelic help would be awesome right about now!' I hiss, which is perhaps a bit ungrateful considering the save Jak just provided, but honestly, Nith and Nan aren't really pulling their weight at the minute.

Jakob shakes his shiny head, which makes him look a bit like he's glitching. Natural movements still aren't quite there with the new body. 'Demonic energy, my boy.'

This is fucked up. Demonic energy again? Like, where is De Montfort getting it all from? Despite all the press given by horror films and pop culture, demons don't come over to our dimension very often. You can't summon them easily. They just don't want to come. They're very happy where they are, doing their own thing, in their own world, with their own kind. I only know of one successful summoning. I know of a whole host that ended in the summoner being turned into mincemeat and the creature fucking off back home for the demonic equivalent of Netflix and chill.

De Montfort doesn't strike me as the sort to be taking that kind of risk. I'd love to know how he even worked out demons could nullify angelic magic. It's not like he could have just worked it out via a process of trial and error. Finding angels to test it on is as impossible as... well, getting hold of demonic energy. Once again, he's streets ahead of us, and it's driving me up the metaphorical wall so hard I'm getting whiplash from colliding with the ceiling. Vaulted ceilings at that.

I don't have time to think anymore on that additional mystery, though, because the greased lightning critter he has guarding the path launches itself at me again. It's clocked on to Jakob being a non-starter and so has moved round to the opposite side. Clearly, it's decided I'm the weak one, the runt of the herd — the prime target. To be fair, with my right arm slowed down, it's not far wrong.

That, and the fact that I have some seriously badass amigos. The thing's moving at freaking warp speed, but Aicha's still there to intercept it.

The clash between them is so fast, it's difficult to pick out what's going on, especially with the shady foliage overhead and evening coming in. It's like one of those shaky cam big budget fight scenes that were all the rage for a while in Hollywood movies. Every time I try to focus, the two of them shift, and all I can see is that whatever it is, it's long and tubelike, tapering down to the bottom. It looks like it has both of its feet together and is bouncing in to attack, like one of those Chinese jiang-shi vampires.

The battle only lasts a few seconds before the thing leaps into the foliage. A blade flash, an accompanying snick, and that rumbling howl comes back, loud enough I momentarily think it's the precursor of an earthquake. Something thumps to earth with a thud, lying on display in the parched brown grass. It's left behind a souvenir. On the path is what Aicha trimmed off it as it hurtled away. A big toe. A very big toe.

The Druze warrior is sweating, which tells you just how hard she was fighting. Aicha doesn't break a sweat for just anybody, I can tell you. She looks up at me, her eyes sharp beneath the aquiline shading as they roam the surroundings, hunting her foe. 'Came-cruse,' she hisses, never breaking from her search.

Ah, shit. That makes sense. It wasn't on two feet bouncing around; it was on one. One foot and a dismembered leg. Maybe.

No one knows what the fuck the came-cruse is or even if it should be 'the' or 'a'. For all anyone knows, there's a whole tribe of them kicking around the Pyrenees. Most people hope not, though, as one is bad enough.

You know Thing from *Addams Family*? The disembodied hand that scuttles about and basically fucks anyone up who messes with it? The came-cruse is like the lower limb equivalent. But it's not just a foot. It's a whole leg, right up to the top of the thigh. There's even a bit of bone sticking out.

I've heard all sorts of theories about where it came from. One theory is that the ogre, Papu, tore it off himself when it kept doing its own thing instead of what he wanted it to do. Then it stomped him to death in revenge and fucked off. Others say it's the result of some seriously fucked up necromancy even by necromancer standards, going even more awry than raising the dead normally does. No one can say. What is sure is that it's a disjointed leg on its own that manoeuvres at speeds just shy of a Harrier Jump Jet and can devour a human in a few moments *despite apparently not having an actual mouth*. Which, when that's the least weird thing about a monster, shows you just how totally fucking strange it actually is.

So to kick off our adventure up arguably the world's weirdest mountain, we're going to have to battle arguably the world's weirdest monster — a super-speed, ass-kicking disembodied leg.

Because, apparently, the day just wasn't going badly enough already.

We bunch in back to back, and I can't help but notice that despite the angels being pretty much useless and the brothers not being much better, everyone seems to cluster me inwards, only adding to my sense of being the lame herd member. In both senses of the word.

So I, of course, feel duty-bound to prove the opposite. When a rustle in the bushes gives me the exclusive heads up, I leap forward, my sword raised, ready to deal death to the fiendish limb and once more prove myself a useful, productive member of the team.

Which is when it leaps from the other side of the path and kicks me clean in the back with about the same speed and impact force as a Dodge Charger with a battering ram strapped to the front.

I get treated to an unexpected crash course in flying, with the emphasis on crash. Bracken and branches tear at my face, then my arms as I throw them up to protect myself from losing an eye. I don't know whether it's instinctive *talent* use or just nature being sympathetic to my fae makeup or sheer chance, but I don't smash into anything hard enough to break any limbs. Not even my thick head. This is good news in terms of physical operability. It's bad news in that it puts me hundreds of metres away from the group, sailing downwards through the greenery. Going over the edge of a path on a mountain is pretty much always a guaranteed drop. This is no exception.

Now I'm almost wishing I hit a few more things because I'm picking up velocity as gravity decides to join forces with the kick up the backside, meaning I'm accelerating. I feel a bit like Gandalf falling in Moria, only diagonally. And through a forest rather than the inside of a mine. And instead of being hurled down by a flaming Balrog, it was a sucker punch (or rather a sucker kick) from a disjointed appendage. So not really that much like Gandalf in Moria.

Until the darkness takes me.

Chapter Fifteen

BUGARACH, 10 JUNE, PRESENT DAY

I've said it before, and I'll say it again. Dark for dark business. Sadly the business in question seems to be Fuck Paul Bonhomme PLC.

I don't mean I lose consciousness, although I wonder for a moment. The darkness actually takes me, like I'm a Pokémon it captures and stuffs down into a Pokéball until such time as it wants to release me to battle savagely against other poor, enslaved magical creatures. Pokémon trainers are the worst. Except, perhaps, for whatever this darkness is.

It wraps itself around me, and I can feel its movements despite the fact it only seems to be an absence of light. It's incorporeal but very much still a physical presence, which is odd. I'm more worried about the fact I can't see where I'm going at all now. I've not received any more body blows, so I don't think the came-cruse is with me. This isn't natural though. Either I've stumbled into the lair of some strange being that lives on the mountain or this is another layer of De Montfort's defences. Lair or layer. Neither sound particularly good.

I smash at accelerated speed into what seems to be an immense pile of leaves, like someone's raked them all together to make an autumn bonfire. In June. As much as it's mitigated my injuries from major breakages to me just being heavily winded and having some bruises that are gonna shine like oil slicks when they pop to fruition, the whole resemblance to a pyre makes me nervous. The fact I can make out that they're leaves means I can see again. Sadly, as I can't move for the moment, it doesn't really help me much.

For the time being, though, I lie here. I have to. Getting up isn't really an option until I get my breath back. I can't help wondering if I've cracked a rib after all, whether it might be pressing on a lung because I'm really struggling to get any air in. It's not getting any easier the longer I lie here. In fact, it seems to be getting progressively harder.

I'm gasping for every miniscule air particle, grabbing at it greedily, trying to force it into my lungs. Lungs that seem flat and lifeless, incapable of inflating. Surely, I can't have punctured both of them without realising? I can't feel any dampness to my skin or pooling around my back, as I'd expect if I collided with something that punched through me hard enough to pierce both lungs without instantly killing me. I wonder if I'm paralysed, if I've lost sensation, but I can feel the leaves crinkling, the light scrapes against my back. That's not helping me though. It only adds to the sense of disconnect, of not understanding why my body's reacting the way it is.

Panic's setting in now. I'm helpless, and the dark takes me again. Some part of my animal brain is howling, like a paw-trapped hyena, and if I could bite my own lungs out to get away right now, I probably would. I knew it. I knew it. I knew the dark would come and claim me back, that I'd never really escape from its clutches. That eternal blackness and suffering were my fate, and the escape back to the light, to life was just a temporary illusion, a mirage before the desert of my mind burned them all away.

I try to roll over, but I can't move. Deep-seated dread fills me now, and my back might not be broken —though I no longer believe any of my sensory inputs apart from the nothingness my eyes tell me I'm surrounded by— but I'm just as effectively paralysed. Shallow, rapid gulps of miniscule amounts of air aren't enough, not even close, and my constant high-pitched breathless gasping is the soundtrack to my reality narrowing into all-consuming panic. Death is close, so damn close, and if you could promise me I'd be gone, away from this endless night's smothering embrace, I'd seize it with both hands. I don't believe this feeling is ever going to end though. The eternal shadows have claimed me back, and I'll not escape a second time. My chest's compressed state won't let me howl my primal terror out, and it's unbearable, a torment all of its own. It's like that old Harlan Ellison story. I have no lungs, and I must scream.

My salvation feels like my death arriving for a split second. The weight on my chest triples, quadruples momentarily, and I'm sure it's going to cave in. Then, miraculously, it lightens and, with it, my vision does too. The endless dark fades to grey and then the evening's low-angled light once more streams through the wavering canopy overhead, just like the air does into my starved, endlessly grateful lungs.

I still can't move for a moment. The last vestiges of that inescapable dread linger, and I have to wait for them to leave, to evaporate under the light of day once more. The night and I used to be friends. That's no longer the case.

Noise to my left pulls me back to the realities of what is happening. There's a reason we're on this mountain. What's more, I'm not alone.

Jakob gleams in the setting light like he's made of molten gold, each shifting movement making the light dance textures into his smooth cold carapace. He looks like Achilles in the armour of the gods, like Hephaestus himself crafted him as a gift to humanity. Or to me, at the very least.

He's wrestling with what looks like a decrepit old woman — if said woman had arms like withered oak branches and claws like shark's teeth. She's wrapped around him, her bark-like legs crossed behind his back, and she's squeezing him in a lover's embrace. There's no care in her coupling though. I can hear the squealing chalkboard nails of metal under stress. Bending titanium should be impossible with raw strength, but it sounds like she's doing it.

Jakob's grappling her, rolling over, trying to get her underneath him. But she's like a greased pig, like they're in water, and she's overly buoyant, constantly rolling back over to pop out on top. He has his grip on her, though, too. He's trying to pull her off, trying to get his hands under her arms and force them apart, and my heart sinks. I know what he's trying to do. He's trying to subdue her. Non-lethal force while she crushes him with her incomprehensible strength. I need to get up, to move, to help him, but I'm drained, sapped of any sort of capability.

It's not good enough. Jakob saved me from that sarramauca — a night hag. Normally, they're content to drink just the fear of those they pin beneath them, locking them down in the dark's terror. Not always though. Sometimes, people disappear from their beds, from their tents, from their lives. The night-time swallows them whole. Or rather, a sarramauca does, just like it almost did me. I need to return the favour. I need to save my friend.

Forcing down the last vestiges of primeval dread, I open myself up to the land beneath me, to the ebb and flow of cyclic life and death, to heal me and fill me with existence's destructive glory.

I'm too late.

Not to save Jakob's life. Not to keep the creature from victory over him, to stop her from stealing away his essence with her uncanny embrace. No,

I'm too late to save him from staining his soul in a way I know will mark him deeply.

I see the moment. The denting is visible now, and I can't be a hundred percent sure, but I reckon if Jakob's as fully integrated into that body as I think he is, it has to hurt. His hands, constantly flailing to corral the wriggling, greased-hog-like hag, suddenly seize on her neck. I think it's by chance, and for a moment they just cup her throat, like a lover making promises of futures bound together. Then determination arrives, and his fingers interlace and his palms apply pressure and he squeezes, pushing his thumbs downwards harder and harder till they tear through her throat, crushing together like a kid squeezing a juice box, desperate to get that last drop.

Her head comes off and bounces away through the undergrowth, tumble-weed through an Old West ghost town.

The remainder of the creature goes slack, and a torrent of black ooze erupts, coating Jakob from head to toe. It adheres to him, so that though he tries to scrape at it, it won't come off. It's just being smeared around, tarnishing more and more of him.

He's panicking. I can tell. I recognise myself from just a few moments previous.

Now it's my turn to help him. I reach out to the roots surrounding us and persuade the trees to lean closer, to bring their branches around him. They enwrap him in a loving embrace, then rub him up and down, like a parent fluffy-towelling a kid fresh out of the shower or maybe nature's version of one of those automatic car washes. Whichever image you prefer, within a few moments, he's buffed up bright and clean.

Sadly, I suspect it might take longer than that to get him feeling similarly spotless on the inside.

I can't be sure, of course; I've not walked with Jakob on his life's journey, on the wild and wonderful turns it's taken him along, on the tragedies it's led to, like Ben's machinations and amorous manipulations. That being said, I'd lay money this is the first time Jakob has killed, well…if not a person, then a properly sentient being. The man I'd say couldn't hurt a fly just popped a head off like a champagne cork. That has to be causing him some concern.

I push myself up onto my elbows, levering myself to try to get a better look both at the decapitated corpse and where we came from. 'What happened to the came-cruse?' I expected it to follow on behind me to smash my face into the metaphorical curb like Romper Stomper.

There's a peculiar vibratory movement to Jakob, and it takes me a moment to realise what it is. This is his body's version of trembling. Shit, he may be going into shock. I need to keep him focused. I click my fingers at him, snapping his attention back to me, away from the headless form at his feet. 'Hey, Jak. The came-cruse. Where is it? Is it coming?'

He looks at me, though I can tell he's fighting not to let what's in front of him drag his eyes back down. His head twitches left, right, a jerked no. 'Aicha engaged it, my boy, as soon as it caught you. She looked to have it firmly under control. Sent me to come rescue you.'

His cranium keeps twitching, and to my astonishment, I see what looks like liquid, like molten mercury, roll down his alloyed cheeks. I suddenly realise it's not physically there. It's his *talent* manifest, a mix of his own power and Nanael's angelic essence. He's crying angel tears for the life he had to take.

I'm up on my feet in a second and over to him. Cold metal or not, I wrap him in my warmth, enfolding him in my arms. For a moment, he tenses, and I think I've made a mistake, remembering that's how the hag-thing wrapped herself around him, crushing him. Then he's holding me, his steel-like visage buried into my shoulder, and he's sobbing like a newborn babe. Perhaps, in a way, that's exactly what he is. Reborn and reforged in both form and choice.

'You did save me, Jak.' I murmur the words into where his ear would be. I've no idea if he actually uses this form's physical attributes or if it's just a conduit for the *talent*, but I'll not treat him as different, not as either more or less than human. 'I was dying. She was killing me. Without this body, I'm useless for the upcoming fight. You saved me and did what needed to be done.'

For a moment, I don't think he heard me. Then I hear his quiet, muffled buzz of an answer. 'Doesn't make it any easier though, does it, my dear boy?'

I don't need to answer that. He knows. *I'm sorry, Jak. It doesn't.*

It never does.

CHAPTER SIXTEEN

BUGARACH, 10 JUNE, PRESENT DAY

Trauma stains and streaks a normal soul. When you've lived for centuries, sometimes it's all that's left to see. A rainbow miasma of pain marks.

Once we both get over as much of our trauma as is possible —or at least bottle it up and bury it deep inside for our therapists to go hunting for like Long John Silver searching out Captain Flint's treasure— Jakob helps me back to the path. We have to battle through some dense foliage to get there, but between my power to persuade flora and his inhuman, angelically overcharged metallic strength, we're back on the ascent and catching up to the others in record time.

I'm hurting. I definitely did break some ribs. And my shoulder's a mess, ripped up and shredded. Luckily we're out in nature, and I'm able to draw on that to heal up, but I'm having to do it slowly for two reasons. One, because I'm also trying to spool *talent* into myself, to fill up my beaten-up, aching body for when we get into the big showdown. And two, because we're inside the fucker's wards now. Everything feels tainted, harder to pull on, to persuade to my aid. He's perverted Bugarach itself, and it's a huge bind on my abilities.

Just what we need.

When we catch up to the others, Aicha's breathing hard, leaning up against a sturdy trunk twice her width. She's also still missing three fingers on her left hand, and the thumb and little finger are nothing but nubs. They're regrowing, but not quickly. I don't know how much of that hand or arm she lost, but the blast she took from De Montfort is clearly still affecting her. She looks a long way from fully fighting fit. Mind you, so does every single one of us.

Fuck my life. We are in a mess. Only Isaac looks even close to normal, but I can see just how worried he is about all of us, about what's still to come. He wraps his brother up in an embrace, and Jak doesn't try to keep him at arm's length. When we're put through a crucible, when we start to doubt our own worth or, worse still, our own humanity, a loved one's touch is an unwavering anchor to hold us steady through the roughest seas.

'What happened?' Isaac looks at me, but it's his brother who answers.

'A sarramauca.' His voice is muffled but clear, steadying. Looks like Isaac's comforting clinch is helping Jakob regain his equilibrium.

I don't get that, the whole thing with the sarramauca. Because they're not team players. They're creatures of nightmares. Not something you can normally command or control. Same thing with the came-cruse. These aren't faeries, cruel but with social structures that resemble human ones. Their existence defies our logic. You can't bargain with these sorts of bogeys. So how did De Montfort get them working for him? It doesn't make any sense.

It also, honestly, doesn't matter. Whether it's a side-effect of the Grail magic or the bones it infuses. Whether Bugarach calls them, and he's simply turned them more rabid, less cautious, froth-mouthed watchdogs to guard his six. Whether it's a working of the impossible demonic essence he's laid his hands on. None of that is the real point.

Whatever the reason, we still need to push on. We just have to be aware that anything, anything at all might attack us at any possible moment. It's going to make our escape run through Paris look like a walk in the park.

And we've lost a lot of time already. The sun's angled itself behind the thrusting grasp of the Pyrenees, and the shadows are lengthening at a rate of knots.

Night is falling. The dark comes, and bad dreams walk abroad.

It's a nerve-wracking walk by were-light up the path towards the mountain top. Every twig-crack, every leaf-whisper seems laden with the promise of miserable death, of untold suffering, and I'd be ready to scream that scream I've been holding in from earlier if I wasn't sure it'd damn well kill us all. I'm used to being the scariest motherfucker in the room — or at least having her on my side. This is how quarry feel. I don't like it in the slightest.

The only thing stopping me from shrieking like I've caught my balls in my trouser zip every time there's the most minute noise is that my heart's in my throat, blocking it up. I can feel my pulse where my Adam's apple would be normally, and my heart's going at about a thousand beats a second. My body's awash with stress hormones, and I'd be worried about the long-term effect on my physical well-being if I honestly expected to survive the night.

And I'm scared to die. Scared of what De Montfort might make happen after I die. Scared of what terrible sacrifices still wait at the top of that mountain, things I'm not ready to offer, prices I really don't want to pay. And those are just words because really, the terror is more primordial, more simple than that. I'm still terrified down to the very atoms of the marrow of my bones of waking back in the dark. Waking again and again endlessly to die in agony over and over, forever and ever. Amen.

Death is terrifying.

But I won't let him see that. Won't give him the satisfaction of letting him taste one iota of my terror. It's game face on, best foot forward, and I'll walk to my downfall. Hell, I'll do the fucking Can-Can all the way there if it'll please the gods that I get chewed up and spat back into the never-ending night to go mad for all eternity.

Just let me stop De Montfort first. Please.

It's been so long since I believed in any higher forces. That's not changed, but it seems some instincts are deeply ingrained, like the drive to beg a favour, a trade from an uncaring, indifferent universe when the odds seem insurmountable. *Please. Please, just let me stop that mad, murderous bastard first. Do what you want with me after, but please. Please.*

Empty, unfinished pleas and open-ended promises. It's all I have to offer for the moment as the night swallows our footsteps, and the weaving, bobbing light guides us up, half-walking, half-scrambling. The path becomes semi-carved steps, more worn by passage than by design, and the ascent steepens. I'm glad none of us are clumsy. A fall in the dark would make my brief test-flight earlier look like a breeze.

Please.

I don't for one moment believe it's because of my asking, but we make it the rest of the way without any more unpleasant surprises. Either De Montfort's exhausted his unnatural allies —and, let's be honest, probably enslaved allies, who would willingly team up with him?— or he's keeping them back to engage us when we reach the top.

Which is a cheery thought to have as we crest the plateau.

Chapter Seventeen
TOULOUSE, 15 MAY 1917

S pring shouldn't be like this.

The symbology has a basis, roots if you like. Rebirth is a real phenomenon. Calves and chicks, the sprouting bulbs. The lengthening of days and the sounds of new lives.

Not right now. Not for the people in Europe.

While in Toulouse, I was far enough away from the action as to remain untouched by it on a personal level. I keep my interactions with the unTalented as limited as possible, so the countless deaths from the surrounding towns and villages, the bright-eyed boys who walked away to get mown down by machine gun fire? They've not tugged my heart-strings in the same way as they do for their loved ones, the neighbours, the friends who watched them grow, only for the reaper's scythe to call for an early harvest. Just names murmured in the morning queue for the bakery. Eyes glistened wet all around me when I walked through the overly quiet streets, but they were just things happening to other people. No business of mine.

But then I had to go and look, didn't I? Had to give in to that innate curiosity that always wants to know what's going on. Not to go and fight obviously, by the Good God, not at all. But to observe. To see what we've decided to do to our nearest neighbours in the name of country and flag, of blood and sport once more.

I wish I could say it was inhuman, all the countless deaths suffered in the surrounding towns and villages I pass as I travel back from Arras, riding trains where services still run, hitching lifts where not. Sometimes simply wandering my way back down the country roads, the idyllic blossoms of the fields and forests unable to lift the horrors from my eyes. Sadly, though, I suspect the carnage is entirely too human.

Perhaps a little of my naivety, that final trace of faith and hope in our species, just got lost in the blood-made-mud of Vimy Ridge as I walked among the dead and dying and wondered who had it worse — them or those left behind.

I saw the staring, terrified eyes, the traces of madness that had taken aching bites out of the remaining souls. Smelled flesh rotting in sodden boots as trenchfoot seized hold. Trembling hands rolling cigarette after cigarette to calm nerves too shot to ever be soothed again. The moments when the ever-present horrors of this terrible new mud-born world were forgotten for one tiny instant, a smile would break out, a laugh, a song. And a head would raise too high, then explode in a shower of brains and trauma, painted across their friends' faces and minds. The endless tears and boys — just children, signed up under false pretenses and faked ages, calling out to an uncaring sky, lost in the shriek of falling shells, like the stars themselves were being shaken from the heavens by the endless noise. They cried for a mother who'd never hear their voice again.

And for them, I wasn't even there. Didn't fight their pointless fight. No, I only observed, wrapped up in a *don't look here*. Watching. Weeping at the senselessness of it all.

And now here I am. Home again in Toulouse. The wards welcome me back in as I half-stumble towards the nearest ale-house. Good God, I need a drink. Something to wash the bitter taste of humanity's failings from my mouth. What dregs we are, worse than any left at the bottom of the barrel. A scraping of a species. It makes me spit.

I know I should head back to Isaac's, see if he's there. Last I knew, he was about to go chasing yet another rumour of Jakob, this time over towards the Black Sea. He didn't tell me much. I think he saw my itchy feet, was afraid I might insist on going with him. The love he holds for me hasn't diminished in the slightest in the centuries we've been together. Sadly, I fear he has. The lessening of the greatest soul I've ever known is a tragedy I'd called unmatched if I didn't just see what I did.

I find myself standing on the Pont Jumeaux, staring down into the racing waters underneath. The spring run-offs and rains have sped up the river's pace till it practically tears down the channel, refusing to be limited, corralled, contained. So full of life while I feel dead inside.

Maybe it's ridiculous to let it affect me so deeply. It's hardly as if the darkness present in humanity's collective soul is new to me. My whole ridiculous saga of an existence kicked off with me trying to be the best human being possible, to promote love and patience and kindness. Which resulted in the assembled forces of the establishment deciding to wipe us off the face of the planet. As a species, tolerant we are not.

But there is something about this one...

I've seen our ability to slaughter accelerate endlessly, as we turn our ever inventive characters to discovering new ways to kill and maim. But this...

Seeing the youth walk, their eyes wide with knowing terror, their backs stiff, holding themselves from blindly fleeing by will alone, knowing a bullet in the back'll come almost as quick as the machine gunfire from the front. Watching them get chewed apart by incomprehensible artillery fire. The pounding, thumping rhythm of explosion after explosion. The smell of mustard gas and the sound of the broken sobs of broken boys.

It's as if our destructive capacity has finally caught up with our inner darkness. And what world will be made from such a power as that? It's more terrifying than any magical working I've ever witnessed.

A shadow casts over the lip of the bridge, lengthened by the lowering sun till it touches the water and darkens the speeding current. A hand as large as my face, the pale green of a three-months drowned corpse caught up in seaweed, grips the parapet. It looks capable of tearing the stones straight from the mortar and crushing them to dust with a squeeze. Sounds plausible. I reckon the hand's owner's entirely capable of just that.

'Hello, Franc.' I study the whipping froth foam browned by the sluicing deposits of farms and factories springing up along the Garonne's banks further upstream. 'I guess it was too much to hope you'd have fucked off and died in my absence.'

A gurgling chuckle like the last air bubbles popping out of a waterlogged mouth answers that one. 'Why, my little lordling. What greeteries and gallantings is that for poor Franc? I bided and bidded my brigandings and bright boys to keep a-watchful listeneries upon our shared aboding. All as promisings, all as pledgeried, is it not? And that's the well comings of comrades and all lying allyings, upon my oath.'

Apparently, Franc's upset I've not thrown my arms around him and kissed him on both cheeks like a long-lost brother. I don't know about that, but I might be about to lose my lunch at the very idea. 'Franc. We're not friends. We've never been friends. Never will be. So why are you here?'

'Why am I here, does my ears a-hear and turn like hares a-coursering? Why, 'tis you your nobling self-sort who does stand a trip-trapping 'pon the passagings above mine own twistery silvering splashes. A poor sort of sorry neighbourings would it be if I did not come slice a slivering of breezery with your fine self, would it not?'

'Know what, Franc?' I worry a lump of the masonry mortar loose and let it drop. The water pulls it in, swallows it whole, leaving not a trace that it ever existed. Gone. Down to the depths.

'Possibilings, Undyer, that I mayhaps and mightery. Dependeries upon what the "what" what you is wotting was.'

That whole sentence makes my brain hurt, so it takes me a moment to decipher it. I think Franc's telling me to get to the point. After a bit of internal tussling, I carry on rather than drive my sword-point through his shit-eating grin to shatter his ruined dentistry even more than they already are. Just.

'What the "what" is, Franc, is that I absolve you here and now from all neighbourly duties of care. You don't need to check up on me or pop over for a cup of tea. Just keep your end of our deal, and I'll keep mine. Okay?'

'Fine as trilleried trimmeries 'pon silkened gowns all a-twirl at the gal-lanting's balleries.'

A simple yes would have sufficed. Despite the torturous acknowledge-ment, Franc makes no show of shoving off. Instead, he continues to lean on the brickwork, putting enough of his weight on it, I'm amazed it doesn't just collapse and send him plummeting into the waters below. One can only hope. The Good God knows I could do with a laugh round about now.

'Times and tidings most interesting, all hop-skippering up the currents comes currently.' Oh, good. He's not done. Just when I thought my day couldn't get any worse.

'What are you talking about, Franc?' I don't have the mental energy to deal with his horse-shit today. I want to get mind-obliteratingly drunk. For the next month, at least, until the grief and fury in my mind at my own species —and myself for my own inactions— dissipates. Hell, at worst, it'll probably be over by Christmas. Funny how that never seems to turn out to be true.

'What carries is the fall and carrion with all the carrying-on 'pon the northern fields a-fallowing.' I have to run that one back through my mind. Twice. Not because I didn't understand it but because I did. I'm not used to that ever happening with Franc.

I nod. I've nothing else to say to that. Sadly, Franc does. 'Have you been there, all look-see and curiouser of thinkery? That's where you've gone, gallivanterings in your absentry, is it not?'

There's a strange tone to his voice. Curiosity, yes. But something else too. A strange, mournful tone, like when we remember long lost loves or prices paid but never recovered from, in lives that are no longer our own. I look over at his monstrous face, a ruinous flesh-mass, bulging and bloated, knotted hair waving in a breeze no one else can feel, eyes curdled milk-tops, bleached blankness. But there's something else in there today, weaved into his expression. A certain understanding.

'Are you feeling sorry for me?' It seems inconceivable. I didn't think Franc was capable of feeling sorry for anyone but himself.

'Of sorts, little lordling, of sorts and sore sortings, when all does fall quick-step one-two into categorisings and calamiteries. I've seen those painful priceries, oh yes, have I not? The twisterings and turnerings that cost so much, bitter in their biteries, though claret pours drip-drop out all the same, upon my oath.'

The river rushes by beneath us, implacable, unending. I wonder if it ever wishes for a finish, a moment when it crosses the line and is done with its unstoppable racing. Whether the tides and current ever dream of being done.

'There was blood, all right, Franc.' My voice surprises me. I didn't mean to speak, but apparently my words are bursting their banks, breaking their dam. 'Blood and body parts as never I saw. Not on the most vicious field of combat. Kids forced to walk to their deaths, torn apart by barbed wire and bullets. Rot and despair with hearts and minds breaking every single second. And for what?'

For a moment, I'm back there. Amongst the churned-up, turned-mass-cemetery soil. I wonder if the blood spilled will stain it red. Surely there's never been so liberal a watering of it.

'For a few metres of land no one really wants. For a war fought because it's been too long since sabres were rattled, and isn't it jolly good fun to go have a game of battles, to remind the other bastards that we're the best? To send out lads dressed in patriotic bonhomie to die together? Whole villages. Whole towns. All their futures dead in a futile, gallant charge to achieve nothing.'

My voice rose till I was shouting to the wind before it dies down, the anger stolen by the breeze. Only the grief and guilt is left behind.

'And I was as bad as any of them. As bad as those bastard generals sat miles behind those nightmare trenches drinking tea and plotting death like picking a team for a game of rugby. I went and watched and did nothing. Just watched them die.'

Deep down, I know it's not my fault. What could I have done? Reveal myself on the battlefield in a maelstrom of magic? My resources aren't unlimited. I'd be chewed to pieces by machine gunfire in a matter of minutes. Then I'd have the entire Talented ranks hunting me down for revealing our existence, and I'd have achieved precisely nothing.

But maybe that's the real problem. I'm not convinced I've ever really achieved anything. Sure, I've saved a life here. Thwarted a villain there. Loved and lost and grieved. But mainly, I've just watched. Watched a species I'm no longer sure I'm part of expand and learn and grow. And die. So much death. And now, to see this? It is like witnessing all of the endings I've seen over the centuries compressed into a few short minutes. The distillation of death. The perfection of slaughter.

'I can help, my little lordling.' Franc's voice is calm, unusually level. There's none of the usual ostentatious flamboyancy to the words, none of that sneaky obsequiousness that normally permeates them. It's unnerving.

'Help in what way?' I hardly believe Franc's offering to curb the blood-thirsty tendencies of humanity. If he's that powerful, he'd have taken over the world long ago.

'With an ending. Finishings and forgetteries.'

For a moment, it feels as if I forget how to breathe. 'Are you telling me you can help me die? Once and for all?'

The monster next to me wraps his fingers along the wall, tapping out the 'Shave and a Haircut' rhythm. 'If you comes a-seeking that last little eye-closeries and off and gone into the dark, where never a please or by your leave might let the light come traipsering in again...' The knocking pauses. 'I may be able to bring assistings and serviceries to bear, Undyer.'

It's a strange thought. My mind goes back to all the times when I hit rock bottom. When the world was too much, and all I wanted was a way to snuff out the lamplight and call it a day. To go to my rest once and for all instead of starting over again endlessly. I've never been able to find a way out. None except that of becoming Perfect again, but sadly, wishing to die tends to mar perfection.

And now, right here in my home city, on my own turf, I'm being offered what I sought so many times. A real escape. An easing. An ending. Thinking about where I've just been, it's tempting. The misery. The suffering. The limitless capacity we carry to impart pain, to spread terror and anger and hatred like a plague. Why should I stay? What reason do I have?

Except.

Except, despite it all, there are other thoughts, other memories. Even there, even amongst all that horror, where Death walked proud-backed and men fell left and right, I saw the best, down there among the worst. I saw boys throw themselves on grenades to save men they didn't know, saw them sharing smokes and stories of home to calm the terror rattling every single nerve, saw them talk down those walking that fine line of the mind breaking, shattering under the unbearable pressure, lessened just enough, just enough to survive by that bond established — a word, a nod, a passing feather-light touch.

And on top of that, I've my moments of joy. My own times where I was saved. By love, by friendship. By a selfless gesture from someone who owed me nothing and knew me less than that. Those thoughts are the glowing embers that breathe fire into my soul, and when I look, I can see that even the misery I've just witnessed hasn't snuffed them out completely. Not yet.

'Thanks for the offer, Franc. I'm not ready to call it a day yet.' Saying the words makes them true, makes me realise I'm not ready. Not now. Perhaps not ever.

'As you wish, my little lordling. I remains ever your servant, all honourings and tideries upon you, on my oath. The best of the brightenings to your returnings and patheries, Undyer.'

'And a good day to you too, Franc.' I drop another piece of mortar into the water, watch it tumble down towards the rushing current, expecting it to be pulled under, smothered by the movement and mass. Except it isn't. It lands and somehow rides the crest of the tiny spurned up waves, bobbling along, still on the surface despite the forces seeking to drag it down.

I want to track its progress, so I turn to cross to the other side of the bridge. As I do so, I realise I'm alone. Franc has disappeared, gone back to wherever he is when not annoying me or communing with his lovely lads and lasses. The strangeness of the conversation — a pinnacle of weird in a forced partnership that has never been anything but undoubtedly odd haunts me. I can't help but wonder what magic it is Franc has or thinks he has that can unpick my reincarnating magic. A shudder runs down my spine. The day when conflict comes, it'll be one to watch out for.

By the time I reach the other side of the bridge, there's no sign of the piece of cement. Whether it's already floated away, ripped downstream by the water's demands or else sunk, traceless after a valiant effort, I cannot say. Only that it's gone. Only that I remain.

The sky's darkening. Clouds draw across to curtain the sun, proliferating shade and shadow, and the wind picks up, its teeth a reminder that the cold is still lurking, that its time is not entirely done. Drawing my trench coat closer, I turn once more towards the lights of Toulouse, towards the lure of the drinking house. Somewhere out there is a beer calling to me.

It might not be the best reason to live for. But right now, it'll do.

Chapter Eighteen

BUGARACH, 10 JUNE, PRESENT DAY

There's no one else I'd choose to stand with me than these three. Here, at the end of all things.

I wondered whether De Montfort might be at the highest peak as we climbed, but he's been sensible enough to stop where the land flattens rather than going for the dramatic satisfaction of the highest crest. Of course, that's how he is. Annoyingly practical. Not leaving vulnerabilities with stagey theatrics. There's nothing more annoying —or deadly— than a practical villain.

The plateau's not as flat as it looked from down below. It really gave this image of a shaved crew cut of a mountain top. The reality's far more vertiginous — a sloping angular slab of green creeping up the granite protrusions. The wind's stronger up here, moving with that single-minded purpose that the lack of breaks and shelter allows. It's not a full-blown gale or anything —it's still night-time in June— but it brings a brisk freshness, and it only adds to that sense of precariousness, of being on the edge in so many ways. Not just spatially. Perhaps tangentially too. Perhaps if we fall from here we won't just go down. Maybe we'll go across. Tumbling over and across through unseen walls, unknown ways. I'm just not sure to where.

The lower ground stretches out until it vanishes, merging into the pitch-black extremities. The sky though — the sky's on fire. Stars burn, flickering scintillations making them like the candles of the gods held up in silent vigil. The moon waxes full and engorged. Perhaps it's her pull that keeps us on the mountainside, that stops the Earth from pulling us back down from these hallowed peaks. I've climbed higher mountains, but I've never felt closer to the celestial bodies, like one step might take me to their surfaces, like I'm a hair's breadth from escaping orbit. There's a holiness to this place. Albeit one now tinged with that same sickened, sickening green tint from the terrible barrier that's drawn us here.

I expected it to be thicker here, where the barrier explodes upwards, but somehow it's not. The layer is thinner, like even it can't hold back the strength of the heavenly orbs, like no simple earthly power can ever hope to restrain them, here on this place that stretches a finger to touch with the forces above us, Sistine-chapel like. The purity of this place remains despite the sordid magic spewing from the top of it. I've precisely zero doubt that De Montfort's going to do something that'll defile even that though, just like Nicetas did with the Holy Grail itself. That seems to be all they're capable of doing. Tainting and besmirching. Pouring down ruination on anything sacred. It started eight hundred years ago, but by the Good God, it has to end here tonight. I just wish I felt more confident it'd end well.

De Montfort sees us, of course. I don't think anyone expected we'd be able to sneak up on him, but he dispels the very idea. 'Made it at last then! And the whole crew's here. Splendid!' He gives us a cheery wave, then turns his back on us, fiddling with the two skeleton-strapped tables he somehow lugged up a mountain. Although I suppose having a sceptre that allows you to teleport probably makes that an easier task.

Or 'did' because he's broken it down into its component parts.

During the climb, visions of some semi-portable Dr Frankenstein-esque laboratory kept me company. The skeletons aglow like algae-possessed coral strapped to operating tables; Simon prancing about, demanding lightning and screaming about them being alive.

However, there's a part of me that can't help thinking he's already accomplished that before today. That I'm the Monster, and De Montfort is the mad scientist Victor who's made me what I am today by playing God. If I am his creation, though, I'll not mourn his passage. I'll wring his neck for what he's done to me.

I want to reply to his greeting, to hit him with my hardest sardonic comment ever, a single one-liner that'll destroy him forever. But all my snark and sass have deserted me. I can't feel frivolous, can't fake the funk and act all nonchalant. Not right now. I look left, right — at my friends. Let's be honest, my family. These people here matter more than those who I left in the dust to be dust so many hundreds of years ago. I look at the gleam of Aicha's blades, which match the glitter of her deep-set dark eyes — readied albeit running on empty. I see the glint of them reflected in the dented and darkened sheen of Jakob's metallic form, brand new but already marked by our travails, though less than his soul is. And I see Isaac. The man who saved me from the start, who's saved me over and over. He's pulled me up and kept me sane and made me be the person I'm supposed to be. I can see the tightness around his eyes even in the half-gloom of the moonlit mountaintop. I don't know what I'd be without him as a tether. I don't ever want to find out.

So we stand. Four of us. Six if you count the angels. And Good God, I hope we can count on the angels. De Montfort's nullified them most effectively so far, and I fear he's going to pull the same trick again. So... four. Four immortals, heretics to many of our faiths — a Druze warrior princess, a Bene Elohim and human golem, an angel-wrapped rabbi, and a once-Perfect, wholly fallible man wearing the body of the fairy queen. Exhaustion hangs over us like a weighted net, but already I can feel the adrenaline starting to pump all over again.

This is what it's all been heading towards. This is why we've scaled the heights. To see if we can save the world from being dragged down into whatever murky depths De Montfort has planned. If tomorrow comes, there'll be prices to pay for all the hormones that've coursed through our bodies and kept us going. Part of me knows how unlikely that is, for our quartet anyhow. If I can make the sun come up, make the day dawn for the rest of the world... if they can never know about this moment but carry on along in blissful ignorance...

Then it'll all be worth it.

We gather up our last morsels of strength and step forward, advancing on whatever horrors De Montfort has in store for us at the summit of Bugarach.

Aicha pauses mid-trudge. 'So a Cathar, a Druze, and two Kabbalists walk up a fucking mountain in the middle of the night.'

I snort. I can't help it. 'Go on. Tell me how this one's the Cathar's fault.'

She looks at me, blinking owlishly. 'Sorry, is it my fucking nemesis dripping magic I spilt over a bunch of utter lunatics eight hundred years ago standing over there? No, dickhead, didn't think so.'

'Okay, it probably is my fault.'

'See, that didn't hurt so bad, did it? Now take the next step in embracing the truth. Repeat after me: I am a twat.'

Oh, it's too easy, and Good God bless her, she knows it too. 'Aicha is a twat.'

She gives me a playful smack in the arm that'll still leave a bruise if I still own said arm in the morning. 'So close, yet so far. Dickhead.'

I think that's as close as she'll ever come to saying how much I mean to her. I'm going to take it that way anyhow.

We carry onwards, and as one, we draw our swords. The sweeping *cling* as they come free synchronously is deeply pleasing.

'Oi, Count Rugen,' I yell, hoisting mine aloft. Then I let my voice drop, let the wind carry my words to him, instil them with the right level of menace. 'Prepare to die.'

Aicha gives me a nudge. 'You've done that bit already, *saabi*. Not bad though still. Never has been.'

'No, it's not, *laguna*. Ever a pleasure, never a chore.'

'You're a twat, Paul.'

'You too, Aich.'

Then without another word, by unspoken, silent agreement, we break into a run, eating up the distance between us and the utter bastard waiting with a calm, serene smile. I dream about beating his smug face into a bloody pulp — a delightful daydream as I pound across the potholed, scraggy grass.

Of course, I know it's not going to be that easy. But a man can dream.

De Montfort sighs and walks to meet us, unhurried, unbothered, the long grass whipping around his ankles in the gathering breeze. I have to change my angle though because he's not walking exactly to us. More crossing the plane, drawing us with him. He swings his own sword, that pirate-style cutlass he favours, in lazy figures of eight, its whirling cut through the air creating an almost hum. It's hypnotic, drawing my attention in until all I can see is my tunnel vision, leading straight to me plunging my sword tip through the bastard's heart.

Which is, of course, exactly what he wants.

The eruption of aching in my temple is quite astonishing, especially considering he hasn't moved. There's a millisecond of dullness that grows exponentially to a roaring throb threatening to render me senseless. Darkness gathers at the edges of my vision, trying to smother my sight; my knees half-buckle, my feet turning in their struggle to hold balance as I stagger sideways, my direction altered by the momentum of the blow I've taken to the head. My attempt to stay upright falters, then fails. One knee goes down, and I'm face-down in the loam, earth flicking up into my mouth, the taste of grass and soil filling my senses.

I draw on that, using my connection to the ground to steady myself as I flop over. Now I can see who sucker-punched me.

The skeleton. The one that was on the right table, the one De Montfort was fiddling with. And it's not just ambulatory, free from the operating restraints. It's screaming what sounds like promises of hellfire. And it's wearing skin. On its face, at least.

That's when I realise what's weird about them, what De Montfort kept me from realising by making sure our attention stayed focused on him as he walked away from the two tables. A fact that seemed trivial until one of the skeletons got up and punched me in the back of the head when I wasn't looking. Both skeletons look complete. That shouldn't be possible. We still hold the original Almeric skull.

The bag of bones that cold-cocked me isn't wearing just a skull. It's wearing a whole human head severed at the neck and then somehow reconnected to the top vertebrae. What's more, it's a man, and he seems to still be alive, to both his horror and intense outrage.

He wasn't a spring chicken even before he got his head lopped off and kept alive like a reverse rooster. The grey hair covering his ear tops and nape only highlights the bald patch consuming most of his head, like a circle to point out the liver spots peppering it. The wrinkles speak of a man in his later days, certainly past sixty, though with the way he's screaming blue murder, it's difficult to tell exactly how far past. He's screwing his face up so much, it's driving the creases into his face like origami folds. And despite how animated he is, especially for a head stuck on the top of a fleshless corpse, there's a deadness to his cold-steel grey-blue eyes. That's not just because of his decapitation. I suspect they've looked like that for decades. Probably since the moment he was born.

In fact, I reckon they're more alive right now than they've ever been, with emotions like panic and confusion sparking across them before being subsumed in vehement rage. Spit flecks form at the corners of his mouth, which, considering he's missing most of his respiratory system, is bizarre. There's no point trying to understand impossibilities like that once you get too deep into the insanities that *talent* can breed. 'Because magic' becomes your go-to answer.

'Villainous hellspawn! Sodomites and philanderers! The god of Moses will strike you down for your whoring and dark magics!' His skin purples, mottled white spots only accentuating his rage.

It doesn't take a genius to work out this is Frank Phillips, religious extremist and all-round shithead — even though now he's just a shit head. What surprises me more is how entirely obvious it is that he's Arnaud Almeric come back to life. Physically, he doesn't resemble the mad monk, but that same high whining tone of entitled outrage, the way he structures his promises of religious retribution on all those below him? I could be back in the halls of Lavaur all those centuries ago.

What's particularly odd is how he's moving. His eyes are mainly on De Montfort, and it seems to me that all his venomous wrath is aimed at the man who was once his ally even if he doesn't remember it. The skeleton, however...

It may only be the bare bones of a body (heh), but it's responding like it got dipped in adamantium. Which, considering how radiant it is with *talent*, might not be too far off. The skeleton is engaging Aicha now it's knocked me down, pressing her, wielding its own forearm bones like maces, blocking and striking, looking to break her defence. It's really odd though. It'll lead with graceful sweeping gestures, then suddenly halt, its movements becoming like the air's turned to tar and only effort of will is making it move through the treacle. The skeleton goes from moving like a ninja warrior to looking like an early Harryhausen animation, all stop-motion jerking. Then it slips back into a flow and moves like a bushido master again. A bone-shido master, maybe.

Aicha's holding her own, more than holding, but the problem is she has no path to a victory. Her blades bounce off the bone like they're diamond. She times a strike perfectly, sliding it between luminous ribs into where a heart would be, triggering a burst of *talent* inside like a miniature sun, setting up a firestorm inside the cage. It's a brilliant idea; perhaps there're invisible or *talent*-made organs pushing it onwards, and her blast of power might disrupt the creature. Instead, it crunches in on itself, trying to close up and trap the blade while bringing down a hammer fist to crush her hand holding the grip. She twists and rolls, coming back up with a block from the wakizashi to meet the other arm looking to bludgeon her skull so hard she'll swallow it in tiny shards.

The head on top is still screaming bloody murder at De Montfort, and I notice that De Montfort isn't looking well. He doesn't look quite right either. I'm close enough now to get a better look. There's a waxiness to his skin, a greyness that wasn't there the last time I saw him. His face is still carrying that nonchalant smarmy confidence, but I can see now it's been pinned on.

He sweeps his gaze across the plain, and lying on my back, still winded, I follow it. Isaac and Jakob are crouched about thirty metres back, each with one knee down, their hands flat against a barrier I can see when I *look*; it is a deep red bordering on purple that I assume is demonic. I'm not *looking* at it too hard though because both Nith and Nan are out to play, no doubt majorly pissed off at being blocked once more. These impossible other-dimensional entities push through into our plane of existence, all neon-white highlights against the sky as they batter against the barrier, their translucent electric fists hammering down again and again, their galvanic wings making swooping beats, propelling them with unimaginable force. And still the barrier holds. How De Montfort worked out this trick with demon essence I have no clue, and I've zero idea how he got hold of so much of it, but it's pissing me off a whole ton. I can only imagine how vexed the Bene Elohim themselves must be.

And even without *looking,* I should be bleeding from the eyeballs and singing hallelujahs right now. That barrier must be even stronger than I'd have ever imagined possible.

I'm about healed enough to get back in the fight, and I struggle to my feet, my eyes locked on De Montfort. He's definitely not right, less in control than he was. His eyes keep flicking to the head/skeleton monster mash-up he made. That's not surprising considering said head is cursing him out constantly with a stream of religious insults I'm pretty sure would put him on God's naughty list. What is surprising is he's not looking at the skull.

He's looking above it.

So I open up my own *sight* just a touch. And now it's my turn to gasp, to feel the colour drain away from my skin.

Arnaud Almeric isn't the only one tied to that skeleton.

He's not alone. I really fucking wish he was.

Chapter Nineteen

BUGARACH, 10 JUNE, PRESENT DAY

I didn't ask for this. I deliberately didn't say, 'At least things can't get any worse.' Murphy fucking with me anyway seems damnably unfair.

A spirit clings to the creation, tendrils of essence wrapped around the bones. It pulls on them like puppet strings to dance with Aicha's swords as if it's doing the Ghillie Callum. It's fighting to grip on, like the skeleton's covered in Teflon, and perhaps in a spiritual sense it is. There's a pale-green *talent*, the colour of scum-tinged sea foam, flowing down from the outraged head. The spirit's coils of power grab hold again and again, but Almeric's own force, consciously or not, wrestles it for control of the assembled bones.

The spirit's magic appears to be stronger, but it seems cautious, wary about Almeric's power, almost like it gets hurt every time it grips it. Its own *talent* is shot through with putrid tinges of the same colour, its edges yellowed and looking gangrenous, like infections are rotting away the very soul. Problem is, from the colour of the rest of its power, I know who it is, and their body decayed centuries ago. I'd hoped they'd disintegrated along with it. Apparently not, or at least not entirely.

The remainder of the being's power is red as a garnet filled with firelight, red as a burnished dragon scale. It's as red as the essence of fire distilled, and it's the same red I walked through when I thought I went to my death on the pyre at Lavaur so very long ago.

It's the red of a *talent* I thought I'd destroyed, that I was willing to give my own immortal soul in order to defeat.

It's Papa Nicetas. The mage who tricked all of the Cathars, who aimed to twist the Grail to bring something terrifying and unholy through to our world, infinitely worse than any demon you could ever imagine. The bastard who killed Ben, who made Almeric kill me.

The one comfort I carried through the long years alive, all these centuries when I should have been nothing but long-forgotten dust, was that Nicetas was done. Gone. Wiped from the face of the earth just as his actions had eradicated the peaceful dream of the Cathar faith.

Looks like even that turned out to be too much to fucking hope for.

There are times when languages fail, when no matter how much mastery you have over words and meaning, they just fall flat in the face of the task set before them. To try to tell you how I feel, seeing Nicetas' essence floating above that skeleton, to know that the one truly good thing I believe I did, the one action that gave my existence *worthiness* didn't actually happen? There's so much inside me, it's indescribable.

There's a Russian word, *toska*, that can mean being mournful, but it's more than that. It has many different levels, but at its most intense, it refers to the idea of a soul in anguish, pining for something else. Perhaps that's closest to how I feel right now. My whole being yearns for the moment previous, when I didn't know Nicetas had survived, to exist once more in a world where he doesn't, even for a moment. His presence bruises my soul; it paints it in purples and greens that ache unbearably. I think for a moment of the Man in Black telling Princess Buttercup that life is pain and she should get used to it. Nearly a thousand years of living later, I'm still not.

I stumble back up, searching my mind for something to dispel his noxious presence as well as I can without dipping into my mind palace. But as I regain my feet properly, wondering if gnostic harmonies might disrupt his malicious energy and if they'll still work when I have a singing voice so out of tune, I'm worried it might add to his discordant powers rather than dispel them, instinct makes me sway backwards. Doing so means my fringe catches a trim, as does the tip of my nose, which stings like fuck. It also means my face doesn't get cleaved off my skull, so I'll take the stinging, thanks very much.

Wheeling round, I see De Montfort has closed on me while I was distracted. He's not looking great. Hardly something I'm liable to shed tears about. The only way I want to see him looking well is well-done when roasting on a spit, but it's unnerving. This is his moment of triumph. So why does he look like he's moments away from losing both his lunch and his ever-loving mind?

His flesh is a sallow yellow-grey, which isn't a healthy skin tone for anyone but certainly not for a fae. The muscle under his eye twitches uncontrollably. He's a far cry from the confident fiend who sealed me away in my own private nether world, condemning me to perdition.

Somehow, despite getting hit for six by fucking Skeletor, I've kept hold of my sword, and I bring it round to catch the back-sweep De Montfort transforms his movement into. He blurs away, and I only just have time to block another downstroke that twists sideways at the last moment, almost sliding inside my guard and disembowelling me. A desperate wrist flick is all that allows me to deflect it and keep my organs on the inside.

He may not be in the most tiptop shape of his lives, but De Montfort is still no slouch with a blade. I think I'm pretty handy in a sword fight. That may be true, but I didn't spend every single life ever drilling as a warrior. I've never worked as a sellsword or soldier of fortune. De Montfort has dedicated his existence to two things — military excellence and revenge on me. Three things, assuming the resurrection of Nicetas was always his endgame.

Add that to his fae form, and he's a whirling dervish of swashbuckling blade mastery. I'm keeping up. Just. It's damnably hard though. His sword acts as an extension of his will, changing direction mid-swing without seemingly a care in the world. By contrast, what I'm doing is requiring every last drop of my concentration, and I'm spilling sweat by the bucket-load to make sure I'm not shedding blood in equal amounts.

Out of the corner of my eye, I see Aicha's doing better than I am, but it's making no difference. I feel the moment when the pressure changes, and she clouts Jack Skellington's less charming cousin with a column of compressed air, wrapping it round and squeezing, trying to grind the bones into meal or break the bonds keeping them animated anyhow. The bones compress together, so the head dips down a few more inches, then springs back when she releases it. Aicha must be burning through her *talent* like a booze-hound through a six-pack, and we're a long way from our home turf. It's a major worry. All Johnny Blaze-ing shithead over there has to do is ride it out till exhaustion, physical and magical, kicks in, and he'll be able to pound her into the dirt.

I can't concentrate on that because if I do, I'm going to end up getting a belly button extension up to my throat. De Montfort is far too deadly to allow any sort of drop to go unpunished. Even that momentary check on Aicha costs me. I turn back in time to move but not enough, and the right side of my head lights up like someone's just pressed a burning brand into it. I speak from experience. Amazingly similar sensation. Sensory overload of the nerves in action. I look down to see my point-tipped ear lying on the floor next to me. If I were a real fae I'd probably be horrified by the disfigurement. As it is, I'm just glad it was my ear rather than something useful, like an arm or an eye.

I need to come up with a better option, though, than us just throwing down with these two until Aicha and I keel over. I desperately want to know what Isaac and Jakob are up to, but I daren't let my attention waver again.

I need to change the script. A clash of arms is only playing to De Montfort's strengths. That's what we've been doing all the way through these miserable past few months. Playing to his strengths. Dancing to his tune. A tune that is probably fucking 'Crazy Frog' as well, the irritating sodding shitstain. So time to change it up to something with a decent beat and enough groove that I can dance to it.

Talent. If swordplay's not enough, time to bring magic into the equation. Which is always handy when you do maths, as you can just cast a spell to make the other side equal x rather than having to do algebraic calculations.

I send my power rippling out through my feet, searching, asking. The seeds of the scrubland heed my call. They drink up what I send and spring outwards.

Vermillion blades shoot from the ground, wrapping and warping together. They take form, shaping into a pretty decent replica of Finn the Human's grass sword, though it's the ground itself that's wielding the weapon. Stretched strands tie it back into the soil, long enough it can dance effectively, bobbing like a stem in a spring breeze. I may not have the mental capacity to be original, having borrowed the design idea from *Adventure Time*, but it's effective. The grass sword is totally independent of me. Animated by my fae *talent* but given autonomy. Sweet. Time to give De Montfort a right royal grass-kicking.

It's now effectively two-on-one, which changes the dynamics totally. Now I'm pressing the attack. Fast as he is, he's not wind-whispered-sward fast. The grass isn't as sharp as steel, but it's like getting struck by a thousand paper cuts, and Imperial China knows what's up with that as a form of execution. De Montfort's blocking is top-notch; I've not landed a hit, but there's that iron-rich tang in the air that says he's bleeding. Call me a shark because it's making me press all the harder.

Of course, he's not done. He shapes his mouth in a peculiar way, pushing his lower lip to the side like Popeye without his pipe, and gives a warble like an amphetamine-jacked wren. The sword wavers for a moment, twists like it's looking for the danger even though it doesn't have eyes. Then it strikes out again. De Montfort snakes right, pushing sideways in the rotation, trying to pivot on his heel around the stems and bring his sword spinning round in his off-hand towards my left bicep. It forces me backwards, creating space for me to bring up my own blade and parry, and it's a close-run thing. I make it though, and I'm half-rejoicing because he's left himself open for a strike from behind, and the grass sword is swinging round into position to punch through his lower back.

My luck doesn't run that way though. The breeze snickers, and I've just enough time to realise that isn't a normal noise for any sort of wind to make before my body instinctively decides to fling itself out of the path of stamping hooves that hardly make a whisper. An impossibly bright, impossibly quiet white stallion dashes past me so close that the heat of its breath sends fresh stinging pain through the wound where my ear got lopped off.

It shouldn't be so damn quiet. I don't know if you've ever been near a horse at full gallop, but that's a whole world of noise. Pounding hooves are loud on any surface, even when unshod. This thing moves like it has silencers strapped to its incredibly powerful legs. It takes me a second before I realise why. It's not touching the ground.

The creature is running on air, and now that I look closely, I can make out that the air is running through it. Behind that luminous brilliance, I can see through the creature's body, can see the grass sword as it closes in on it. De Montfort has summoned or created some form of Cheval Mallet from the wind and sky, filling it with starlight. Which sounds beautiful, and it is, but this is De Montfort in action too. The creature opens its muzzle, and in its mouth is a row of teeth that'd give a piranha razor-envy. It wraps a whipping black tongue, like it's the horse version of Venom or something, around the grass sword once, twice, binding it tight, and it should be tearing itself to shreds on the razor edges, but it's not. It's engulfing it in this impossibly long appendage, and still it's not slowing down. The horse powers on as though it has all the leverage it could desire even though it's not touching the ground. The sword gets ripped out by the roots and goes limp. The white air-horse gallops away, retracting its impossibly long tongue, drawing in the blade-of-blades to chomp it back to chaff.

Now we lock back sword-to-sword, and of course the advantage has swung back to my bastard of an opponent. He has the edge on me physically, and he presses, putting his weight behind the strike. I can feel the twist to his wrist as he re-angles the blade, forcing mine slightly under, so that his pushing is forcing me back towards the soil. I've not taken a knee yet, but it's only a matter of time.

So I do what anyone with any sense would do in such a situation. I push back as hard as I can; his blade wavers an inch towards him. Then I relax and fall backwards.

The sudden dissipation of pressure catches him entirely off guard, just as I hoped. I keep my blade to his, guiding it and keeping it away from my body. Right foot planted firmly into the earth, I kick out hard with my left foot, connecting right with the De Montfort family jewels.

I don't hear them pop, which is a shame, but I might just have broken his reincarnation magic because I seriously doubt he'll be having kids anytime soon. The combination of the unexpected drop and the force of the kick to his bollocks sends him flying over my head and into a crumpled heap, landing face-first a good ten metres away. He's not impaled himself on his sword, which is a damn shame; he rolls over, his blade ready.

I risk a quick glance around. Aicha's still dancing with the weird human-headed skeleton. She's not running on empty yet, but it's only a matter of time. I glance over at Isaac and Jakob. Isaac catches my eye. He gestures wildly like he's trying to lay a really complicated bet at the horse races. I take a moment to decipher it, but then I get it. They're nearly through. We're about to get some serious angelic back-up.

Ooh rah.

CHAPTER TWENTY
BUGARACH, 10 JUNE, PRESENT DAY
For once, the momentum seems to be swinging in our favour. Fuck. Just pretend I didn't say that, okay?

I'm not slacking off the pressure on De Montfort during all this. If we can get him polished off, perhaps the bones will all just disintegrate into dust while Nicetas goes screaming off into the void of oblivion. And unicorns will fart nitrous oxide, and it'll rain whisky for a week.

It has to be worth a try though. De Montfort's recovering fast; he's fae and out in a place about as wild as it still gets in western Europe, so he can draw on nature's integral power to heal, but he's still on the floor, giving me the high ground. I rain down blows on him that he successfully parries. When he turns my blade aside, forcing me to shuffle my feet to keep my body angled towards him, he tries my own trick on me, lashing out with his calf-high leather boot at my kneecap, aiming to pop it out and bring me down to his level.

Last moment, I see it coming and twist, taking the blow to the thigh as his foot scrapes upwards, missing its original target. Damn, that hurts. I use the energy to turn my twist into a full-body swing though, pivoting my sword round to take his arm off at the elbow. He only avoids it by throwing himself flat at the last moment. Sadly, I'm carried too far round by the motion to capitalise on it, and by the time I reverse my grip, ready to bring the blade hammering down into his chest, he's scrambled far enough backwards as to regain one knee.

It's too damn even. On the one hand, Aicha and I are keeping them busy while the Bene Elohim equivalent of a SWAT team smashes the metaphysical door in with a battering ram and then will, hopefully, proceed to kick the shit out of all the villains. On the other, it's also allowing Nicetas to strengthen his grip here on the mortal plane, which I reckon ranks firmly in the "bad idea" category.

The Aicha vs The Evil Dead battle drifts over towards us. She's still trying for the fiery inferno inside the ribcage. It's not working, per se, but I wonder if I can see the starting of a blackening char to some of the bones. Maybe it's not pointless after all. As I advance on De Montfort, my eyes meet Aicha's for a moment, and I flick my glance towards Isaac and Jakob. I don't need any response. I know she gets what I mean. The pleasure of working with a consummate professional.

Simon's almost up, but a two-handed strike he only just blocks drives him back to his knee. I'm not ready to let him regain his feet.

'Why the fuck are you doing this, you utter prick?' I can feel my lip curl, the distaste at even talking to this spunkbubble threatening to make me gag. 'Hating me — fine, I get it. I ruined your plans, cost you your son, elaborate revenge schemes, yada yada. Got it. But bringing back that arsehole Papa Nicetas? Do you really hate the world that much?'

He's scrabbling, trying to get to his feet in between blocking my blows. Or so I think. As I bend closer, he hurls a handful of dirt at my head. The injection of *talent* means it feels like I've just caught a face full of gravel from the wheel spin of a rally car. Cheap trick, but it's enough to stagger me back for a moment, enough space for him to regain his feet. He presses his momentary advantage, his blade slicing death through the air.

'Yes.' His eyes are aglow with the depths of his own distaste — for me, for the world, for the whole of humanity. 'I hate everything about this wretched existence. Gone? He was never gone. I've heard him whispering to me, demanding, cursing me out, remonstrating my every weakness. Every second of every day. Life after life. A constant misery, never letting me sleep, waking me with his demands when exhaustion bore me away. And you ask me if I hate the world?' His blade is a rhythmic drumstick, beating down a percussive accompaniment as he hammers at my defences again and again. 'Yes, I hate it. I hate you. I hate life. I want it to end. All of it.'

I've had to give ground, stepping back under his furious assault. Without my realising, we've drawn closer to the other pitched battle. There's a moment when Aicha spins into my field of vision on the right, her own strikes producing a hollow high sound like a cowbell.

As the Nicetas/Almeric skeleton/head mishmash passes a metre or so to my right, De Montfort *pulls* with his *talent*. Not on the creature itself; he's not about to do our dirty work for us. No, he pulls on the miniature firestorm Aicha has going in the empty chest cavity.

The flames leap outwards. Let's be honest, there's not a lot keeping them there apart from Aicha's will, and she's too busy, the interception too unexpected for her to counter De Montfort stealing her fire like the world's shittest Prometheus impersonator. It roars out from between the ribs like a molten phoenix and shoots towards me, whipping around to engulf me in an inferno hot enough to make a crematorium furnace envious.

I have seconds. Even as it rips over the grass, blackening it as it goes, I can feel the incredible temperatures. I throw up a shield, enough to hold for a moment, but it won't last long. Between the surface-of-the-sun-level heat and De Montfort's methodical hacking, it'll burst in seconds, and it has already taken a good bit of my internal power reserves. I need something and fast.

The smouldering grass gives me an idea. It may be June, but we're high up in the mountains, and the temperature's dropped hard and still descending. The greenery surrounding me is covered in dew.

I pull it all towards me, drawing all the moisture drops inwards. They flick up like reverse rain, splattering around the firestorm. The grass itself pulls up from its roots. The sparse trees reach down into the ground, and they all fling the liquids they can find, more even than they can spare, their leaves curling inwards to allow them to send more water to my aid.

It cocoons us, me and the fire. The water turns oranges and yellows, so that I must look like I've been preserved in amber, a dug-up relic from an epoch long past. Mind you, there's no one on this mountaintop alive or dead that doesn't apply to. De Montfort's fallen back, wisely fearing the water might turn on him. The flames hiss, fizzle, and fight back, trying to break through the aquatic barrier, but it's no use. For every drop evaporated, another two takes its place, and while the heat may be stifling, it's the fire itself that's being suffocated.

Now De Montfort presses forward, advancing closer, forcing his own *talent* in again, trying to feed the fire, to restore it to a full-blown blaze from the damp squib it's rapidly becoming, emphasis on the damp. It's not a bad idea. I'm running low on *talent* and oxygen in my little protective bubble. If he can keep it going a tiny bit longer, he might just have me beat.

He can't. The fire goes out completely. De Montfort howls in frustration and pulls back his sword to strike at me, to vent his spleen on my shield.

I pull back the wall of water in one tiny, very precise spot.

High pressured steam shoots out like someone shot up a Wild West locomotive engine. I'm no physicist. Science is a consummate, incomprehensible wonder and should be treated with baffled awe at all times, but I do understand that tiny gaps and compressed gases result in concentrated expulsions.

The cloud of scalding gas pours out straight into De Montfort's face, and he staggers back, screaming. I drop the water, sending it back to its myriad sources with my gratitude, and drop my shield too, drawing on nature to replenish my depleted *talent*.

De Montfort's dropped his sword, and he's clawing at his face. I can smell that sweet crackling pork smell that made me glad to be a vegetarian from the first human burning I had to witness. He's stumbling towards the demonic barrier, towards where the brothers are close to breaking through. Perfect.

He's healing, of course, but slower now, and I can see the steam's stripped his skin back several layers. His face is red-raw, crisped, and crinkled; it must hurt like hell, every nerve feeding back raw agony. He obviously managed to angle his head away at the last moment because his left eye is still relatively normal, while the right is cloudy, bulging, obviously affected by direct contact. Either that or he's concentrating his healing on one eye, then the other, making sure he can still see me. Sensible, but it's not going to save him.

He throws up a shield of his own as I slam my blade down at his head hard enough to strike sparks from the hardened air. I feel his magic worm out through the earth, asking it to swallow my foot, to form a mound of earth to trap it as I step on it. It forms but dissipates as I march across it, and down comes my sword again, slamming so hard into his barrier that he flinches uncontrollably.

'Problem is, *old boy*,' I say as he wriggles backwards, his eyes wide now, his breathing hitched, his weapon lost as he looks to escape. 'You've fucked with the wrong type of magic for a fae body.' His shield is weakening with every strike, and I'm relentless. Each time the blade comes down, it gets closer and closer to his accursed neck, and Good God help me, I'm ready to bathe in his fucking blood. 'Magic bones? No problem.' *Clang*. 'Evil spirits? Sure.' *Clang*. 'But resurrecting the dead? Necromancy?' *Clang*. *Clang*. 'Fae magic is life magic. And just like life, it can be properly fucked up and hella dark.' *Clang*. So damn close now. 'Death magic like this? It goes totally against what life is all about. Your magic is deserting you. Life itself' —*clang*— 'is on my side.'

He's scrabbling with his hands now, trying to claw his way across the ground to get away from me quicker. He's mere metres from where Isaac and Jakob stand, and I hear Jakob give a tiny delighted cry that tells me he's cracked the puzzle. Aicha's forcing the Nicetas/Almeric creation closer and closer to the brothers.

Now it's pressed against the barrier itself, its arms a blur as it tries to parry the flurry of blows from Aicha's two swords, desperate to regain its balance but failing miserably. De Montfort's mad scrambling quickens, so he has his back to me now, only throwing wild glances at me as he tries to escape, and I'm laughing without even realising it. A half-mad, half-exultant cackle that we have them on the run. Against all the Good God damned odds, we're turning the tide, and we're actually winning.

Which is, of course, the moment when it all goes to shit.

CHAPTER TWENTY-ONE

BUGARACH, 10 JUNE, PRESENT DAY

Fuck you, Murphy. Fuck you right in the ass. Fuck you very much, very hard, over and over, you smug, self-contented prick. And fuck your law even harder still. Arsehole.

I know what you're thinking, and you're right. It's entirely my own fault for celebrating way too early, for getting carried away when there's still the hard yards needing to be put in. In my defence, have you seen how many losses we've taken recently? It seems only karmically fair that once, just once, everything goes our way. We win spectacularly, tidy up all the loose ends in a wondrous display of deductive genius, and then go get rip-roaringly drunk to celebrate.

Sadly, Karma is already out on a bender, getting absolutely out of her skull on Writer's Tears and Guinness with Murphy, and they're both finding it absolutely hilarious to piss on me from a great height. As per usual.

So as De Montfort's shield drops and the skeleton/preacher combo is pressed hard and Jakob starts to open the barrier...

Simon looks over his shoulder at me, and I don't see terror or fury or even resigned acceptance.

I see glee. Pure, malicious glee. Not the look of someone who's lost, but the delighted expression of someone who's watched everything come together exactly how they wanted it to. The look of someone who's sure they've won.

A momentary glow, a split-second only, is all the warning we get. Then the screaming head of the confused fundamentalist preacher suddenly silences. His eyes roll backwards into the skull, and his mouth gapes open, like he's died from sheer terror. I daren't *look* at him, not with the Bene Elohim warming up to storm the castle just behind, but I can guess what's happened. Nicetas has wound his tendrils into Almeric's brain. What comes next confirms it.

I don't know if you've seen *The Exorcist*, that scene where the possessed Linda Blair spews forth literal bile to accompany her verbal form. It's a bit like that but without the head spinning, and the bile is red, that dark, rich, troubling red of Nicetas' *talent*. The substance pours out of the distended mouth, slamming into Aicha before she can throw up any form of protection. It's not thin liquid though. This is a rich gunk, a scarlet sludge that adheres to her even as it throws her backwards, slamming her to the ground some way off and sticking her there.

At the same time, De Montfort launches himself forward — but not at me even though I've braced myself, expecting him. No, instead he springs like a pouncing tiger straight at the animated skeleton.

To the surprise of absolutely no one, though, De Montfort is not turning on his master of centuries. This is, yet again, all part of his cunning, scheming plan.

Did I mention at any point exactly how much I fucking hate Simon De Montfort? I hate him more than the fucking Tarrasque. By a considerable margin. I think no more needs to be said.

De Montfort barrels into the skeleton, connecting at the sternum and shoulder, barging him backwards.

Straight at the barrier. Straight for the metal golem hosting Jakob.

The demonic energy barrier travels with them. It's pushed back into Jakob, then clings to him, literally stopping with him half way through it. The energy surrounding him glows the red of a forest fire on the horizon, closing implacably, and I can't work it out for a moment. Then I get it, the importance of the barrier stopping half-way; it's keeping Nanael from striking at them. It's giving Nicetas and De Montfort access to the skull at the same time.

The skeleton stretches its arms out wide, and the titanium metal, this impossibly durable substance, just melts as the spine collides into it, the rear leg and arm bones cutting through it like a hot knife through butter. Almeric's head whips backwards like he's trying to headbutt Jakob with the back of his head to break his metallic nose. There's no crunch, though, from either of them. Instead, the two skulls merge.

There have been moments of terrible horror in the last period of time. Images that will stain and scar my psyche. Suffering that I'll carry with me until the end of my endless days.

This should be one of those moments. It should be horrific, tormenting, terrible. It's not. There's no bubbling, melting flesh, no screams of agony as souls are rent asunder. The two —flesh and metal— become almost transparent. Both skulls, so similar you'd think they came from twins, are all the eye sees. Everything else is irrelevant. The one on top of the skeleton just keeps travelling back into the one Jakob's occupying until they're overlaid, a double image as the metal golem gives way under the impact.

Then that sense of a double exposure, a failed photograph disappears, collapses in. The last hint of the metal skeleton dissolves as efficiently as if it got dropped in a vat of acid. And Jakob and Nanael...

Are evicted.

It should be impossible. I'd have laid money on Nanael being the most powerful being, alongside his brother, on this plane. That skull held Jak and Nan for hundreds of years. It might not have been by choice first time round, but still. Their connection with that particular bone prison runs *deep*.

Kicking them out like a pair of sleepy drunks at closing time should not have been doable.

Yet, I can see it. Feel it even. Displacing something that freaking powerful from where it wants to be carries outwards like ripples in a pond. Except, considering the size of what's just been thrown, it's more like tidal waves in the ocean. It batters against my senses for a moment; the unbelieving outrage of the dislodged Bene Elohim carries like a psychic trumpet blast being blown directly into my ear. It makes me wince.

I'm torn about what to do. Whatever Nicetas and De Montfort are up to is clearly where the action's at. But I can see Aicha's still coated in that claret goo and writhing. Jak and Nan might be incorporeal now, but I bet they can still kick ass. Two angels plus two magicians versus Nicetas and De Montfort has to be sufficient odds, right? Plus, being honest, compared to the heavy firepower already there, adding my pea shooter isn't going to dramatically change the outcome.

I dash over to my downed friend, knee-sliding to arrive by her side, one of my eyes still on what's going on with the others. Looking at her thrashing, I want to just start scraping the crap off her as quickly as humanly possible.

However, even I have enough sense to recognise that plunging my hands into something causing so much agony to someone who can regenerate almost instantly isn't the best of plans.

Instead, I draw on my depleted *talent* and send it back out once more into the earth. The fucking local flora must be about sick to the back-teeth or back-petal or whatever with having to bail me out by now. Still, they do me yet another solid.

The earth opens slightly underneath Aicha, forming a shape painfully similar to a shallow grave. I have to remind myself I'm doing this to save her so I don't end up having to bury her. Roots stretch up from the floor and bind themselves in whorled loops around her body. I'm worried they'll just dissolve or something on contact with the substance, but they seem to be able to lie across it without problem. I guess it only targets human flesh.

I flick my attention back to the fight going on at the barrier and nearly have a brain hernia here and now at the utter impossibility of what I'm seeing. That and what the overload of seeing two full-blown angels in battle mode causes to my central processing unit.

Nithael and Nanael. The Bene Brothers. Beings from a higher dimension. My goodness, don't they just look like it? It's like someone gave Michelangelo the ability to paint with forked lightning. Their wings seem to encompass the starlit sky themselves, pinions stretching to touch the horizon, each individual feather carved in electric blue. I couldn't tell you if they're twenty feet tall or two hundred or both at the same time. The purity of their essence broils out of them like the cleansing heart of a furnace, and I feel every single one of my failures and foibles, each petty or selfish action or failure to act from my parade of existences simultaneously while knowing they understand and forgive me for each and every one. Shooting stars of blue neon ripple across their diaphanous forms to show musculature that would make Hercules weep with envy, that would make

Atlas do more than just shrug. They are impossibly perfect, too wonderful for our frail world to encompass, and it's only my love for my friend who may well be dying at my feet that keeps me on my knees in awe.

And they are impossibly both held in place, immobilised. By Nicetas. His presence has swelled to match their stature, the bordeaux-stained clouds making up his spirit having distended with a crackling green that no longer looks putrid. The grandeur of his intensified essence brings to mind Jafar at the end of *Aladdin* when granted the power of a genie. I don't think there'll be any restraining cuffs appearing, though, to bring him conveniently under control. His engorged energy blots out the night behind, obscuring it in a smoky-claret haze, like the sky is burning and the world is ending. Perhaps it is. Arms and hands have extended off him from various points to seize the angels, pinioning their limbs, wings, and heads in place. He's not hurting them, and it looks like it's taking all of his concentration, but they're not able to strike back against him either. It's a Mexican stand-off on a celestial level, written mind-bogglingly large.

At the centre of the red roiling emulsion, the skeleton head is screaming again. The two-become-one skull is coated in the same gunk covering Aicha, and the glimmer of Almeric's scum-green energy is only there now in one socket, flickering. Despite its fleshless state, despite lacking the muscles and tendons and *skin* that one would normally associate as necessary to show emotion, I can see the realised terror. Perhaps it's the ear-splitting howls, the mixture of words and syllables. I hear bits of it and hear a litany of prayer and curses, names and fears. The mouth screams out entreaties to a cruel Almighty. One he's served through multiple lifetimes, and I hear him scream out each of the names he's used between the pleas. I guess the memories of all those previous existences have all just come crashing in. I doubt Almeric ever recognised his own reincarnations, ever knew the source of that puritanical fire engraved on his soul. I almost envy him those chances he had to live fresh, anew even if he squandered it by making the same mistakes over and over. I don't envy him that forced realisation now nor what he's going through. I envy him what comes next even less.

A rolling noise rumbles at my feet. It's like the distant roar of a train far down a one-lane track, and I look down to see the roots have finished enveloping Aicha. Now they're spinning her like a fairground tombola, faster and faster, applying centrifugal force. They loosen their grasp as they spin, expanding outwards, and the Good God knows I owe them beyond measure because they take that poison onto themselves. The colouration changes the rough bark-like material, staining it like the trees have drunk deep from a battlefield, and I suspect they'll follow a similar path down into the darkness of eternal slumber after doing this for me. They split apart, crumbling away, and in the middle lies Aicha.

For a moment, she looks more angelic than either of the Bene Elohim behind me, all cares smoothed away from her features, at rest, her defences down. Then her eyes snap open, and I could weep because my best friend is back in the game. Nicetas might be able to hold an angel in each hand without breaking a sweat, but with Aicha Kandicha by my side, we still stand a chance.

I'm not sure how, but we do.

We have to.

Chapter Twenty-Two

BUGARACH, 10 JUNE, PRESENT DAY

Time to go battle...what? I have no idea what Papa Nicetas is, what he's become. I'm still going to try and kick him square in the nuts, the fuckweasel.

I hoist Aicha to her feet. Her face is drained of colour in a way that, were she anyone else, I'd say she was going into shock. It's that strange effect, like when someone reports bad news, as if our blood flow somehow gets diverted to our brain to help us deny the reality we're now faced with. As a species, we're so easily overloaded, it's amazing we've not been replaced as the apex critter long ago. Probably only because our vulnerabilities are masked by our imagination on one hand and our cruelty on the other.

Aicha's not in denial though. Just a whole fuckload of pain if I'm any judge. I can't tell if it's physical or psychic nor can I say which is the better option. I'd go with neither if really pushed.

We're both beat up badly. I try to wipe some of the grime off my hands, onto my trousers, and they come away wet, slick with blood. Apparently, I'm bleeding from multitudinous locations after my sword fight with De

Montfort. I didn't even realise, never even felt them. A quick internal check reassures me none of them are significantly weakening me, that I'm not at risk of bleeding out. I'm pulling in as much *talent* as the land can spare constantly, but I daren't divert it towards healing anything that isn't major. I get the feeling I'll need every last drop before the day is out.

If we're both limping slightly as we make our way across the smoking grass towards the celestial-scale battle going on, neither of us mentions it. We both still have our weapons and our *talent*, and we're both still breathing. I'll take the win for now.

De Montfort stands next to the now-complete skeleton. He's regained his cutlass, the flat balanced over his shoulder like he's striking a pose for one of the original pinhole portrait cameras. The absolute cuntbungle really believes he's some sort of swashbuckling pirate instead of an object lesson in why his father should have pulled out early on his very first life and saved us all the fucking misery of looking at him, ignoring his whole "destroy the world" spiel bullshit he's got going on. The one thing that makes me feel better is that he looks in an even worse state than we do. He's pouring sweat like he rocked up into a sauna wearing a mink coat, and despite his attempt to stand as bodyguard —or no-body-guard in the case of the skeleton, I suppose— his eyes are constantly roving all over the place. They flick towards his master, back to us, half-rolling back into his head. It's a long way from the cold sneering self-control I've seen up until now. If Nicetas' presence has been slowly driving him mad over the centuries, his reemergence into the world has pushed him totally over the edge. I have no idea if that makes him more or less dangerous. The former probably, knowing my luck.

He doesn't seem that bothered about what we're doing as long as we keep our distance. Isaac stands on the opposite side of the Kaiju-style grapple going on in the ether above. I wonder if the tears on his cheeks are from the pain being fed back through his bond with Nithael from the battle overhead. Perhaps not. There's enough other things to cry about. We drag ourselves over to him, keeping a beady eye on De Montfort and the skeleton of doom.

'Jakob?' I have to ask even though I'm terrified of the answer.

Isaac's face is streaked with grime from his fumbling about in the dirt, scraping sigils to disrupt the barrier, but there's a determined set to his jaw that reassures me. If he had lost his brother again after all this time, it would've marked him far more deeply. He raises a tired, trembling finger, pointing towards Nanael. 'Up there.'

I squint, that strange instinctive reaction we all exhibit as if it somehow activates a secret zoom feature built into our eyes but does nothing except obscure our vision with our eyelashes. Somehow it works though. I can see a shape whipping around Nanael's phosphorescent outline, like a comet spinning round the rim of a black hole. It's a bright white orb, reminiscent of a will-o'-the-wisp. I sag, relieved. Looks like Nan isn't any more prepared to let Jak go than we are.

That's one worry taken care of. Just leaves the possible end of the world. No biggie. I look at the team with me. I love Jakob. He's an amazing man, a saint in metallic flesh, not even counting the whole saving my life on the way up here. As for the other two? They're the people who matter most to me in all existence, the ones who make this fight deeply personal. Saving the planet is too abstract. Saving these three grounds it in reality, motivates me to go and kick the shit out of anyone in my way even if I'm finding just putting one foot in front of the other a Herculean task.

'Plan?' Apparently, one-word questions are all I'm capable of at the moment. At least I can manage that much.

Aicha inclines her chin towards De Montfort. 'Fuck him up.'

Now *that* is a plan I can get behind one hundred percent.

Isaac's preoccupied by the battle above, his forehead creased, doubtless trying to work out how to swing the odds in the Bene Elohims' favour. I'm more than happy to leave him to it. To be fair, that's where the real victory or loss'll occur. If he can influence the outcome, it'll be far more important than anything I can do. Compared to what's kicking off in the ether, the spiritual Brazilian jiu-jitsu match between the brothers and Nicetas, I feel about as significant as an ant at the battle of the Somme. I'm still going to go and bite the shit out of the arse I can reach though.

We advance together, Aicha and I, side-by-side, ready to make De Montfort tartare and then see what we can do about the screaming undead tethering Nicetas.

Unfortunately, Nicetas has other ideas entirely.

The skeleton's right hand lifts up and digs its finger into the eye socket where Almeric's spark lingers. It roots around, like searching for a pencil in a messy overfull drawer, then pulls back out, the dulled-jade spark held between its thumb and forefinger.

At the same time, it clamps its left hand onto De Montfort's shoulder, almost companionably, as though standing in solidarity. However, seeing Simon's face contort into an agonised rictus, I guess it doesn't feel like that to him.

The skull pops open its jawbone, and the swirling red miasma inside looks like a miniature vortex straight to the worst Hell imaginable. It pops Almeric's essence in like a delicious treat and sucks it straight down. I can hear a last ear-splitting, screeching wail from a spirit that has pursued an intransigent view of the path to Paradise through centuries as it gets torn to ethereal shreds, dissolving into nothingness, harvested by the same dark malevolent force Almeric once considered himself to be appointed by God to wipe out — or, at least, by the Pope, the next best thing to God in his opinion. It's taken a long time, but he finally pays the price for his conceit.

I really hope I'm not about to do the same for mine.

A noise grabs my attention, like a boiling kettle suffering from high-grade anxiety about its performance. It builds, escalating till it sounds like all the hounds of Hell whimpering in fear, their tails tucked between their legs. It's excruciating, making me want to clap my hands to my ears.

And it's coming from Simon De Montfort.

I almost don't recognise him. His hair, a cascade of sable curls previously, has turned the white of bleached bone with nicotine-stained blond highlights. He's still wearing the same ridiculous pirate outfit, but he's more Ben Gunn than Long John Silver now. It's like John Travolta plucked his face off and then crumpled it up like a paper ball as tight as he could before sticking it back in place. He's aged ridiculously, instantaneously. I've never seen an aged fae before; I didn't think it was possible, to be honest, and it's only the pointed tips of his ears that tells me he's not had his fae nature somehow stripped away from him by the malevolent presence gripping his shoulder.

Said presence is no longer wrapping its red energy tendrils like marionette-strings round the skeleton. Nicetas' spirit spreads itself from the skull, down across the shining *talent*-saturated bones. As it touches one limb after another, the same scarlet gunk that splattered across Aicha coats it, like dripping plastic onto a skeletal mould. It coats them entirely, passing from head to foot, and as it pours downwards, it bubbles and spits, boiling lava, cooling and thinning until it darkens to a blood red. It's hard not to gape as before my eyes, *talent* is making flesh. Parts change to tendons, the marbling of muscle clear and present, and I don't doubt organs are forming, hidden from our eyes by this outer layer. Above, the spirit-part never wavers, never lessens despite the investment into the physical. He still holds the two angels restrained, though I notice he's not struck out at any of the three of us here yet. I suspect it's taking a lot of his energy and concentration. Mind you, so it should. It should be fucking impossible.

The skeleton-corpse flexes a knee that's now shiny with new-formed skin, then rotates an ankle. And Papa Nicetas puts his foot down, walking abroad in our world once more.

Straight into Aicha's sword.

While I might have been suffering from my brain overheating due to the sheer implausibility and insanity of what I'm witnessing, Aicha hasn't been so easily overwhelmed. She has a plan, and it's a good one. It's simple, really. She waited till he, presumably, finished repairing his internal organs, then stabbed him straight through the heart.

It's a seriously smart move. Were he totally invested in the body, in the way one might normally imagine a centuries-old disembodied Talented doing —and it's fucked up that I say "normally" with that sentence— then you could imagine a moment of weakness as the spiritual ties fully to the flesh and is vulnerable for the slightest of times.

It doesn't work like that with Nicetas.

He glances down with a face that still looks like a kid took a matchstick to an Action Man in the name of science, shining goo and liquid eyes pulling into rough approximations of orbs at the sword sticking out of his chest. Fingers like sausages straight from the machine, the churning meat still visible through the opaque casing, run their way back and forth along the blade like the sweep of a bow on a concerto cello, dripping that same ochre mess all over the length of Aicha's katana. She's trying to pull it back with little success. It's as if it's wedged in stone, as if maybe were she able to pull it out, she'd get crowned Queen of England. But she's not Arthur. Not today, at least. It won't budge. She steps back and raises her wakizashi, thrusting it at Nicetas' fried egg of an eye taking shape. He whips up his other offal-packed carrier bag of a hand open-palmed so the point of her sword pierces the centre and wedges. The same grim gloop starts to cover the short sword too. Aicha wisely lets go and steps back, pulling two further knives from various concealed holsters, readying for combat. I guess she thinks he's going to take her weapons, turn them against her.

Instead, with the hand he's just liberally painted his viscous insides on, he flicks the sword-blade with his now almost-normal index finger. It makes the blade ring out, almost pure but with a discordant tone underneath, like a cracked church bell struck with force. The noise builds, joined by a second, similarly inharmonious higher note as he does the same to the katana. They crescendo, the jarring undertone rising higher and more dominant until there's a tinkling like cracked glass tumbling onto a cold tiled floor, and the blades shatter.

They don't just break into shards. It's like that tap snapped the molecular bonds or something. It looks as though the metal has turned to sand that then pours onto the ground before being whipped away by the breeze. They may have been Aicha's backup swords, but they were still masterpieces of craftsmanship, imbued with her *talent*. Turned to dust in a second by the creature before us.

His flesh has finished knitting itself back together, and his features have settled in place, solidifying. The hawk-like nose and beard bristles are those of a man who once blessed me and who cursed me at the same time. Perverter of the Grail, of the whole Cathar faith. Traitor to our cause and to humanity entire. Papa Nicetas.

But there's no human in this world and none that ever existed, in my opinion, who could grip two angels in the ether and hold them motionless. Papa Nicetas is no longer a man, if he ever was.

I pull a katana from storage and fling it over to Aicha as I charge up my own sword. The only good news in this whole setup is that restraining the Bene Elohim seems to be keeping a vast amount of Nicetas' power tied up, so he can't fling it at us. I don't know whether it'd kill us if he did, as in perma-dead, but I'm not in any hurry to find out. I am in a hurry to kill the fucker before he works out a way to get rid of either the angels or us, then probably destroys humanity as an afterthought.

There have been many times in my long life when I've wanted it to be over. Where the weight of loss or failure or weakness weighed so heavily on me that I'd have thrown down my load and walked away without a second thought.

Not now. Now I have people who matter to me, people who make this life worth living. Not just Isaac, who's always been there for me even when consumed by the grief of Jakob's loss. But Jak himself. And Aicha. Of course, Aicha. My soul sister, my best friend. Someone who'll save me just so they can tell me what a twat I am. I'm not ready to leave her, and I'm even less ready to lose a single one of them.

But this isn't about me. Not even slightly. It's about humanity — hell, perhaps life on this planet as a whole. I felt the depth of darkness of whatever lurked on the other side of that hole Nicetas tried to punch through reality with the Grail all those centuries ago. I might not know its precise intentions, but "nothing good" is definitely an apt summary.

I can see Isaac's taking it all hard. He's trying to keep calm, but flickers of pain keep coursing through his features, like he's getting jabbed in the side with a knife every few seconds. Nithael and he are integrally bound together; it's the only thing that's saved Jak —that total angelic bond— so I can only guess he's getting feedback from their struggle with Nicetas' spirit form. There are moments when 'Zac's skin tightens, as if he's tensing all his muscles simultaneously, that make me think it's physical, but there's a look in his eyes that tells me the metaphysical suffering is just as much, if not greater. He's constantly sketching in the dirt, scribbling Kabbalist lettering that hurts the eyes, loading them up with his *talent* as he does so. I can't tell what they do — whether he's investing that energy up to Nithael to strengthen him or trying to bind Nicetas' reformed body, but whatever it is, it doesn't seem to be having any noticeable effect. Though, as Nicetas isn't currently bathing in our collective blood while chewing on our gall bladders, perhaps it is.

Good God damn it. It wouldn't take much. If our allies turned up now. If the Mother broke through the barrier. If Mephy could turn up and counter this demon essence bullshit somehow. If Gwen smashed through from the other side and sauntered up with her shotgun over her shoulder. If Craig could roll up and clean up this mess, if the Caliburc could bring his strange ancient magic and Leandre could bring the whole of Paris, and just tag in so we could sit and grab a breather while they mopped up this shitshow for us, this could all be done and dusted, quick sharp, and we could all head off for celebratory pints at a job well done.

But it won't work like that. We're here and nobody else is. Doesn't matter how broken we feel, how close to burned out, how sapped to the very bottom of our souls. The three of us present, here and now, are the ones who are going to bring this to a close.

Isaac. Aicha. Me.

One way or the other.

CHAPTER TWENTY-THREE
BUGARACH, 10 JUNE, PRESENT DAY

Fighting dead evil wizards who can wrestle a pair of angels. That's another item on the anti-bucket list of things I never wanted to do before I died ticked off.

We advance slowly across the churned field, our eyes firmly on the reincarnated dead douchebag whose very presence pollutes the universe. A universe I'm quite fond of, thanks very much. He's like the worst of humanity writ large, and the worst of humanity writ small is hard enough to deal with. We don't need to be increasing the font size.

Still we close on him. Warily. We just saw him destroy two perfectly folded Japanese blades, tempered weapons made to kill monsters and invested with *talent*, like they were made of cardboard and sticky tape. I don't have a lot of idea of what to do next, and I'm pretty sure the sword I'm waving like an empty threat made solid in his general direction is liable to do fuck all. It makes me feel better though. I'll hold on to that for now.

He's looking at us now, at least with his actual eyes. His dual spirit self is still totally concentrated on the Nith and Nan tag team, and I'm exceptionally grateful. The intensity of his regard, still burning with red whorls where non-creepy, non-dead people have irises, is enough pressure as is. We split up, me tacking to his left, Aicha the right, trying to divide his attention.

I love that I think that sort of tactic is going to work with someone as run-away-screamingly powerful as the douchebag in front of us.

The beaky-faced prick, half-Julius Caesar, half-Sam Eagle from the *Muppets,* cocks one bushy eyebrow at our advances and sighs. 'Hello again, Paul.'

His voice still contains that musicality that was so hypnotic the first time I met him as a fresh-faced Perfect looking to make the world a better place. Now, though, I can hear that same discordant note layered underneath that speaks of his wrongness. This once-man shouldn't exist in our reality. He taints it, darkens it.

I don't believe in the simplistic views of right and wrong that religions profess and then promptly ignore when it doesn't suit them anymore. This thing makes Franc look like he was a saint. A placid smile and melodious voice doesn't hide the scrabbling corruption behind the eyes. Even without the malevolent force surrounding him, trying to make two actual angels tap out. Even if I didn't see him chew on Arnaud Almeric's soul like a penny sweet and drain the stupid shithead who spent centuries trying to bring him back of all his life force. Even then, the truth would be self-evident for all to see.

There is nothing good, not one iota of rightness in Papa Nicetas.

I don't reply. I've nothing to say to this thing in front of me that wears the shape of man woven from depravity. No pithy quotes or sardonic zingers to put a flea in his ear before I follow it up with a sword. I have no words to give him. I don't trust myself to speak. Don't trust him to hear. There's a part of me that's terrified he might steal my voice or build an inescapable labyrinth from the syllables.

He fills me with a primordial dread, such as a neanderthal might have felt on meeting Oberon or his predecessor when the gates came open. The realisation we're not the apex predator, not even the apex biped. Just apes in danger of becoming ex-apes rather than the apex. It's a long way to fall from the top. When man first saw magic, met the first of the gods, witnessed the first dragon take wing overhead or the first monster demand their firstborn, they must have felt something akin to how I feel now. A doom made flesh stands in front of me. An ending wrapped in tissue.

It's the shittiest gift anyone has ever given me, and believe me, over the centuries, I've had some doozies. Looking at you, Black-Plague-bearing, flea-infested jerkin. Straight from Genova, with love. Christmas 1347. I came with my own bubo-shaped baubles that year, all over a body I ditched quick-sharp.

I don't think this situation is going to be as easy for me to escape. And I think, if we don't stop Nicetas here and now, he'll put the Black Plague's death toll in the shade real fast.

The fact he's just standing there, one eyebrow arched, looking vaguely bored isn't doing wonders for my confidence. Still, I'll not be cowed by eyebrows. If Rasputin couldn't pull it off, no one can. I close in, my blade readied, pulling in *talent* till I must be glowing like a nuclear reactor overloading to anyone with *sight*. Aicha readies herself too. Her new katana is covered in fire so hot, the metal should be dripping. It holds solid though. I guess it's Nicetas' flesh she's looking to be melting off instead.

And he still seems entirely uninterested in the two immortal badasses advancing on him with what I think is considerable amounts of menace. He looks deep in contemplation of other, more significant things, like why he didn't manufacture a wristwatch when he reformed himself just so he could occasionally glance at it and sigh at the amount of his precious time we're wasting.

Nobody likes to feel like they're an irritating wastrel when they're attempting to be menacing. I realise, horrified, that this is how every unTalented idiot who ever tried to rob or intimidate me must have felt when I practically ignored them or belittled their try-hard efforts. Then I remember why I was like that — a supreme over-confidence in my abilities compared to theirs.

Shit. Nicetas doesn't even consider us a threat.

Well, best do something about that then. There's a particularly nasty spell I once learned while dancing naked in a freezing cold lake while my bollocks did their best to climb back inside me and up into my rib cage, in the Wicklow Mountains of Ireland. I'm not convinced any of that was necessary for learning the spell, but it amused the cailleach who was teaching it to me, and as that meant she wasn't trying to either seduce me or swallow my still-beating heart straight out of my chest, I was happy to play the source of amusement.

I've never used it. Not once. Which, considering the shitty situations I've found myself in should speak to how nasty it is. And, of course, the price there is to pay.

Death magic is frowned upon in most schools of esoteric learning and for good reason. First of all, because it's just weird and wrong. Most things aren't killed by *death;* they're killed by *life.* Either other living things and their innovative ways to use whatever they discover to murderise each other or by bacteria or just the in-built obsolescence that is an innate part of mortality. Using death itself, pure absolute absence of being, to snuff out life is against the natural order. And the natural order doesn't take kindly to that.

So to appease Nature and keep it from hitting you back with a triple dose of what you've just served up on someone else, the only option is to make a significant sacrifice. And not in a "here's a conveniently large and unimportant cow that we exchanged a bit of spare cash for down at the market". More in the sense of "here is my firstborn whom I love dearly, but still, please kill them instead of me".

Sadly, the only semi-child available is Simon De Montfort, and I don't think the universe is about to believe I'd be cut up by him dying. Plus, he's not really mine, except in the Immaculate Conception sense of blessing him (or cursing him, as you choose to see it) with his particular form of immortal life.

So I have to give up something of equal value if I want this spell to work. And there's only one thing I can think of. My own form of immortality.

I reach down, deep inside myself, following the fae *talent* traces like roots, to where they're planted in the soil of my soul. And there, buried inside it, is the seed that I've carried for eight hundred years, an emerald green kernel. The Good God knows I've wanted to be rid of it at times, but I've never been able to just dig it out and throw it away. Now when I don't want to give it up, when I want to hold it tight and never let it go, when I want to *live*...

Now I can burn it.

I let all the *talent* surrounding it turn against it. The power I carried before the Grail was activated now acts like antibodies suddenly recognising a foreign body in the bloodstream, and they attack it ferociously. I reckon I must be going full on Super Saiyan, but with my eyes pressed closed, it's hard to tell. And I doubt anyone has the spare capacity to break out the phone camera and record it, however cool it looks. My whole *talent* is ablaze, and that seed of eternal life...

Is turned to ash.

The power that rushes up and out of me makes the feeling when I took over this body, when I stood as ruler of the Court of Winter and did the whole "all shall love me and despair" shtick, pale into insignificance. This here is a force unparalleled, something that can finally even the score with this utter fuckstick who's come back from the dead to ruin my day.

I open my eyes and breathe out Death.

It pours out of me, that jaded green, no longer vibrant and alive. Now it's rot, toxins, spoiled flesh, and lifeless decay rolled up into a roiling cloud the colour of a water-swollen corpse. It streams from my nose and mouth, filling the air in front of me, and heads straight towards Nicetas to devour him.

Except he swallows it whole.

He opens his mouth and breathes it in like he's a Good Goddamned vacuum cleaner tidying up a little kitchen spillage. He pulls in every last drop of this, my last resort, my Hail Mary of a spell, and consumes it with the slightest of smiles on his face and not even a sign of indigestion as a result.

That was my best shot, and he didn't even flinch.

He gives me a faint nod as if acknowledging that, yes, that was as good as I could give, and, indeed, it was nowhere near good enough.

'Thanks for that, Good Man.' He inclines his chin graciously, and I can hardly keep myself from vomiting because I can still see the empty void inside his soul, the nameless, swirling horrors sitting just behind his regard. Then he sighs again, straightens up, brushes down his robe, and claps his hands together.

'Let's get down to business, shall we?' he says.

And everything goes to shit.

CHAPTER TWENTY-FOUR
BUGARACH, 10 JUNE, PRESENT DAY
That was it. My best shot. My reincarnation magic. My last chance. Hope itself. Gone.

He pulls his hands apart and expertly flicks his fingers just so at the same time, like a kid flicking boogers at a sibling. But nothing comes sailing in our direction. He's not thrown anything.

No. He's opening up the doors of Bugarach.

The air shimmers in front of him, a patch expanding outwards until it's the size of a pair of barn doors, boiling and freezing over and again as drops of congealed reality run down it like traces of a storm on a windowpane. Fractioned flashes of othernesses spring into my eyeballs without me consciously seeing them, filling me with numbing dread. I can't tell you what I'm seeing, but I know this much. It's horrific. More so than anything I've ever seen or dreamed of. A hell like the Catholics imagine to punish those who dare to disagree with their gold-cast reimagining of a Jewish carpenter.

More than I have ever been in my life, more than I felt at the thought of sixteen years of being stuck in that cave. More than when I gave up my life and my Perfection, expecting to become dust, to break the Grail, and foil Nicetas' scheme in my first life...

More than all of those times, I feel afraid because I know what Nicetas is doing.

He can't defeat Nithael and Nanael. Not yet, anyhow. So he's going to do the next best thing. He's going to banish them, fling them from this existential plane into some far-flung nightmare-scape. Doubtless, we'll be tossed in with them and have about as much chance of making it home again as Dr Sam Beckett. Less, even, as we won't have Ziggy and his nifty handheld computer interface to help us out.

Terror floods my every synapse, my every nerve, and drowns out my every thought. Whatever is waiting through there is misery unending, and I know that Nicetas will take great pleasure in flinging us into the most inescapable suffering he can find. And I can't do anything about it.

But someone else can.

There's no flash of lightning, no Houdini-style puff of smoke. No stage-craft without the need for mirrors and trapdoors. Just one moment, the White Lady isn't there, the next, she is.

She's still as awesomely strange as when we saw her between worlds, when she took the kids with the promise of saving them. Her featureless, expressive face beams on us all. Nicetas scowls, and I can see him reevaluating, no doubt trying to calculate his power, if he carries enough to strike back should she attack him.

She doesn't though. Instead, she waits, a pressurised silence that builds like the front of a storm before it breaks and the heavens wash the world away.

Now we're getting a reaction other than bored nonchalance from Nicetas. A muscle under his right eye starts ticking, tiny little spasms outside of his control. He's not the master of this situation, and he hates it. Good. Fuck him.

It does my heart good when he snaps. He's been so damned deadly, so unflappably awe-inspiring that seeing any sign of fallibility brings me back a touch of hope. If he has flaws, they can be exploited.

'What do you want, hag?' he barks, his eyes fixed on her while overhead, his spiritual luchador part shuffles uneasily, as far as it can without losing its grip on the two angels. She remains silent, benevolent, observant. 'I've paid the price for the openings. The gates are mine.'

A noise like the exhale of a throat-slit opera singer as they leave the stage a final time comes from the Lady. Then her voice rings through our heads. 'Not if I wish otherwise, *egin-haragi*. You've paid the price to open it. But another could pay me to enter and close it. Keep all from being taken. After all, this is my gate.'

'Except you're owed no debts here, milady. There's none to pay the price you'd need to counter mine.' I can hear that cocky confidence starting to creep back into the shitheel's voice at the same time as I feel the blood drain away from my face as realisation strikes me.

Fuck. There is one here who owes the Lady a debt. Three debts, in fact.

Resignation is etched in Aicha's face as she looks at me. The regret and the sorrow and the fucking apology there breaks me. Aicha Kandicha doesn't apologise. She doesn't have to. She gets it right every Good God damned time. But not this time. This time...

This time, there's a price to pay.

I'm already striding towards her before I even know it, ready to stop this, to take her place, to keep her safe, Good God damn it, anything. Anything for her.

Of course, there's nothing I can do. She shakes her head, and I stop, my foot half-frozen in taking another step. Not by magic. Just that tearing-in-half sensation of wanting to respect her, respect her decisions, her right to pay for her choices. But I want to tear down the universe fundamentally brick by brick, to make reality a place where she doesn't have to do this. Where she doesn't have to go.

But she does. I know it in my heart. I can't take her place. There are rules to this sort of thing. Stupid, concocted-on-a-whim, utterly ludicrous rules but rules nonetheless. It's like the universe forgot about magic until the last moment, when it pulled a rabbit out of its hat and a line of hankies out of its nose, and suddenly wrote some haphazard dashed-together restrictions on it so it couldn't break everything the first time it threw its magic wand out of the pram. Nicetas or De Montfort on his behalf has made some sort of deal or sacrifice on this neutral ground to open the gates. Only a greater debt can outweigh that.

Only a greater sacrifice.

So she turns her face away from me, set to the portal. As she does so, she scratches her nose, the side closest to me. I choke back a sob. She scratches it with her middle finger, pointed right at me. Softly mutters, 'You're a dickhead, *saabi*. Make this right.' Then steps into the portal.

Have you ever watched a sunbeam strike a piece of glass and break up into a rainbow, all the options of colours making up that one invisible streak of illumination? It's something similar and yet entirely different to watch a person, especially a person you love, refract.

Aicha splits apart. I see her potentials, her pasts, her promises, and possibilities mapped out through infinite spatial beads that pitter patter down her soul; I watch them spread wide across the gateway. All of her elements, her energy, her damage, and her devotion displays itself, written in a love letter to a humanity that never deserved her, that was never as good as she was. She paints a pathway through the dimensions with her essence.

It stabilises it, slows the whirling myriad of pathways, of infinite options, of different hells that Nicetas might hurl us into. She's gained some control. But it's not enough.

Nicetas looks on, triumphant as the gateway starts to drag at us. I can feel my feet slipping towards it, pulling us in. Next to me, Isaac scrabbles backwards, trying to stay in place, but it's not working. I can see he's closing on me, closing on the mouth to another dimension. The two angels are diminishing, shrinking down, pulled in like genies back to their lamps no matter how much they long to stay free.

Them. But not Jakob.

I see the moment he decides. Isaac does too, and now it's his turn to deny, to try and reason, to mewl unintelligible but heartfelt pleas to not go. Because Jak is streaking for the gate, leading the charge in a last heroic step. Perhaps he sees it as a chance to make amends for the suffering Ben caused, using him and Nanael when he had them trapped in the skull or for how close they came because of it to helping him destroy the world. Or perhaps he does it because it's the right thing to do.

Either way, Jakob streaks towards that portal. And Nanael...lets go.

There's a moment when they collide into the gate, master magician spirit and Bene Elohim angel, when it solidifies. Their souls wrap around Aicha, their power infusing into her, adding their inconceivable *talent* to the Lady's will, all bound up in her deal with the woman who's saved me over and over again. The way is fully opened, and there's a doorway through the stars, through a million, million Earths, through firmament and foundations standing on a mountaintop in the French Pyrenees. An army could march through. A god could return.

A friend could leave.

I see her for a moment, standing whole again in that frame, looking at me. I see all the thoughts she's kept held tight. I see her love for me, her unbreakable bonds. My sister. My best friend. My saviour over and over. The one who makes this whole world worth it. The one who gave me back the part of my heart that broke that first time I saw Ben die, who helped me learn to heal the rest of it that shattered on finding Susane's broken corpse. She smiles sadly and tips me a salute with her fingertips. Then she turns to go.

As she does so, half-way round, her eyes widen, and she turns back to me.

'Paul!' Her voice edges on panic, so unlike her, it fills every bone with ice in the place of marrow. 'Paul, the other skeleton! Remember the other..'

And then like that, the doorway to an unknown location, somewhere across the realms of every reality that ever existed...

Closes.

And Aicha Kandicha, the gentle genius Jakob, and the angel Nanael are gone with it.

I want to sob, to scream, to rage, rage against the dying of the light. It isn't fair. It's not right. I should have been the one to pay the price. Me. Eight hundred years, I've been ready. Eight hundred years since I said I'd pay, and yet it's others over and over again who pay in my place. I made the deal, made it clear, and Fate won't honour it. Just takes and takes and leaves me a picked clean empty vessel. A hollow man once again.

But I can't. I have to *do* better, *be* better. For her. For them. So I do the only thing I can think of. I fill my vacant, empty heart with hate and fury, and steel myself anew.

Because Aicha's saved us once again.

Aicha's made me remember the other skeleton.

Chapter Twenty-Five

BUGARACH, 10 JUNE, PRESENT DAY

This must end. Or else, all of this
— all of everything – will end.
Time to write an ending.

Stand on a street corner when the wind whips up from the back alleys and swirls a sweet wrapper round the feet of a gathering crowd. Stand a moment and study the sharp-faced magician spinning cups on the thrown up suitcase table top, all charm and disarming flair. The way they move is a deliberate flow that wraps you up in a narrative, interwoven with the cleverly delivered patter. No magic but magical nonetheless. The art of misdirection.

Now combine it with actual *talent*, and you get the bait-and-switch Papa Nicetas has pulled on us.

There's no way he should have been able to make us forget about the other skeleton. Now that Aicha pointed it out, it's obvious. But he drew us in so well with the conflict — wrestling the angels, swallowing our magic, tearing open the portal — that all our attention was already squarely fixed on him. Pinning it down with some dark form of *talent* was an easy, additional step. None of us saw what was going on there. As I turn my head, part of me wishes I still can't see it.

Perhaps the worst of it is the familiarity. Einstein posited the universe is cyclic, repeating itself ad infinitum throughout eternity. If that's the case, then somehow I've come back to my Big Bang, that single solo second when everything exploded with meaning and magic. When I gave up my soul to stop the unnatural force of evil coming through the Grail to defile our world. The same one now flowing into the set of assembled bones on the other side of the plateau.

I can *see* the energy now, a narrow line of twisted moss-mould green that extends like a tether from Nicetas to the other skeleton. It brings to mind a monstrous aberration of an umbilical cord, pumping life force into newly-become death. I know what force it's being siphoned too. It all goes back to the start, the wheel's full turn. It's the energy that spilled over all of us from the Grail. The life force of the Perfects perverted inside that item of power.

Nicetas has brought us to the heights of Bugarach and is harvesting us all one by one. He swallowed down Almeric first — the bewildered, baffled fool who never knew the truth of his rebirths but just repeated his fanatical errors over and over again, leaving behind a trail of *talent*-infused bones in his wake. It's why De Montfort wizened in an instant too. Nicetas stole his reincarnating power, taking his immortality from him in a way even his fae side couldn't counter or handle.

And me? I handed it to him, wrapped up in a pretty package and tied in a silver bow.

Part of me wonders if De Montfort was somehow behind that caillaech teaching me the death magic in Ireland all those years ago just for this moment. It seems unlikely, but considering the long con they've pulled on us, anything could be true. Honestly, though, I doubt it. It wasn't necessary. They probably just intended to incapacitate me and then pluck it from me at will. Me throwing it down Nicetas' throat must have just been the cherry on top of the cake they're making to celebrate the end of the world. Well, Nicetas is. I don't think Simon is celebrating anything anymore. Small blessings. Or cursings, considering the unspeakable evil now coalescing into our world.

The spirit manifesting around the bones is like nothing I've ever seen or felt — not since that glimpse of it through the warping of reality's walls when it pressed on them in Lavaur so long ago. It drips psychic toxins through the air, tearing the luminosity from the sky, so that even the stars themselves start to dim around it. Life leaches from the ground. I can feel the mountain itself dying, the collective of stones and shrubs and trees withering and wilting, the slightest taste of the arriving force bringing ending to all that grows or moves or dreams. It's not just a destroyer, a consuming invader. It's the antithesis of existence. Anti-life entering our world that will drain it until it crumbles into dust. A conclusion to everything, a last curtain-fall finale over a universe still so cosmically young and full of promise.

It is the unmaking of everything.

Isaac's prostrate on the floor a few metres away, but he's not bowing. He's bent before the forces whipping into him and Nithael. Neither has time to grieve for their lost sibling any more than I do for my soul sister. The two Bene Elohim together were enough to hold Nicetas' power — or at least keep him focused. Now Nithael alone is trying to contend with the reborn mage and an arriving force of inconceivable magnitude. Isaac's drawing on everything he has, every inch of his own *talent*, every trick his incredible brain can come up with, every secret name of his god or the heavenly forces he can inscribe to try to strengthen Nith, to try to weaken the invading, pervasive evil creeping across the top of Bugarach.

And he's failing.

Sky-step by sky-step, Nithael is being forced back. I can see Nicetas' shadow-shape, the power above him linked to the presence clawing its way through. I don't know where it starts and Nicetas ends. Their collective power is growing, and the Bene Elohim is weakening.

We're losing the fight.

I can feel the rage I've fed my system with starting to spoil, to turn like wine into vinegar, tipping into despair. This is what they wanted, and it's what they're getting. Sure, thanks to Aicha's and Jakob's sacrifices, there're still two of us here to oppose him, but it's not enough, and the best of us are gone. We were barely holding our own with all six of us here, and now we're down to half-strength while Nicetas' power amplifies every single second.

I'm trying to push the thought down and away, but there's a fatalistic part of me that recognises we can't win this.

We're going to lose. And, I suspect, that means everyone, everything will die.

And you know what? That should be enough, but in some ways it's too big. It's incomprehensible, impossible to grasp the idea that the whole of existence might reach its conclusion in the next few minutes, that there will be no more life, no more stars or planets, nothing but an empty void. I can put words on it, but I can't really *feel* it, not in my heart. My mind goes into denial, pushes the image away like a toddler throwing their toys out of the pram. It's too impossible, too impersonal.

What does get me up is the thought that Aicha's sacrifice is going to be for nothing. That she's entered a gate to who-knows-where, torn to her base elements once again, and there's no point to it. We could have died back-to-back, side-by-side and at least gone down fighting together. She should be with me, here at the end of all things. Instead, she gave herself up to give us a chance. A chance we don't have, and it's *not fair*. Hell, you'd think after centuries upon centuries of seeing the way the world works, I'd be at peace with the injustice of existence, but I'm not. Not this time. Not for a culmination to it all like this.

Aicha's sacrifice should mean something. It has to. I can't bear it being meaningless after everything we've done. So I turn, and I walk towards the skeleton, towards a forming malevolent force that can swallow existence without a thought, armed with nothing but a sword and some half-understood fae *talent*. No reincarnation in my back pocket, no do-overs, or one-ups. I know perfectly well I'm walking towards my death, but the rage is still holding on even as the fear and certainty of failure eat away at it. If I'm going down, I'll go down swinging.

I'm going to try and stab the end of reality in its face repeatedly. It's not going to work, but it's the best I can think of.

It's hard work. The air is thickening, resistant like Atlantic tides pushing against me, so I'm swimming standing up to make progress. It's a fight against myself as well. I don't want to approach the creature coalescing around the *talent*-lit skeleton. The one place in Middle Earth we don't want to see any closer and all that. This is my Mount Doom moment, except I don't have a ring or a Sam to carry me forward. Not even a Smeagol to bite my finger off and save the day.

Just a sword and the last vestiges of sorrow-laden fury held smouldering in my heart.

So I force my way forward step by step. One foot in front of the other, over and over. It's a thousand times harder than climbing the mountain was. An endless progression of pushing against a force so much greater than my own. I know in my heart it's only been seconds, but it feels like hours. Time being an illusion in evidence again. Sadly, without the time to stop for lunch or even a hearty second breakfast. I have to keep moving. Somehow, I have to come up with a solution, an answer to challenge the letter of immediate termination reality just received. And I only have one life, one shot. *Eight Mile*, eat your heart out.

But, of course, that's still not difficult enough, apparently. Just when I think things can't possibly get worse, there's always one more layer of icing to add to the shit-cake.

Because that's when De Montfort stabs me between the ribs.

CHAPTER TWENTY-SIX

BUGARACH, 10 JUNE, PRESENT DAY

I have no words for how much I fucking hate Simon De Montfort, the cuntbungling wankbugle. Okay, I do. But they still aren't enough.

I feel it punch through my side like a cannonball through the mainmast. It doesn't just take the wind out of my sails; it rips the sails clean off and dumps them overboard.

It also takes the wind out of my left lung. Possibly because it's punctured. I can't be totally sure. I may just be struggling to breathe because of the searing pain sending my nervous system into overdrive.

I can't stay upright. I stagger and go down to a knee. All that last-gasp drive, that anger at the injustice is dripping out of my side. Although, that might just be blood. Might not just be though. Might be some internal organs slipping out along with it.

Looking up isn't easy. Focusing in general is hard, my vision doubling, then merging again like I've been hitting the whisky hard but without any of the delightful numbness alcohol provides. I'd give my right arm for a glass right now. Or at least my left lung. Considering it's totally useless and out of operation.

De Montfort's face looms over me, a maleficent moon superimposed on a draining-away sky. He's more haggard than I realised. The lines on his face are deep and innumerable. It's as if every second he's lived since our first showdown has landed on him simultaneously, a time pile-on. He looks a right state, which is hilarious because the Good God knows what he must think about how I look right now.

Standing's clearly hard for him too. He collapses back onto his haunches, then lowers himself to the floor. 'Got you, Good Man.' There's a mumble to his voice, a creaking like air's creeping up a long abandoned staircase, afraid it'll give way under the pressure any second.

I nod, and all that anger is just going, going, gone, replaced by immeasurable, crushing sadness. 'You got me, Simon. After all these years, you got me.' I look around at the blasted wasteland Bugarach is becoming, a blighted, lifeless heath. At the pool of blood I'm kneeling in. At the wizened shell De Montfort's become. 'Was it worth it?'

I can see he's thinking about it for a minute, casting around his mind for the answer to my question. Then he shrugs. 'Probably not. Seemed like a good idea at the time though.'

I laugh, a bitter burble as rivulets of blood spill down my lips. 'Well, damn. That's a hell of an epitaph for existence. "Seemed like a good idea at the time though." Ha.' I think about it for a moment. 'Having said that, it probably is fitting for humanity. We ever were our own worst enemy. Look at what we've made, Simon. With our pride and our ego and our desperate need to be right. We made it all end. Look at it.'

But he doesn't look at it. His eyes are closed, and his chest moves in larger and larger swells. Then it stops. Like the absolute bastard he was, he's checked out before the grand finale and everything goes totally to shit.

Simon De Montfort is finally, once and for all, dead.

And I'm not far behind him.

To say I'm running on empty is an understatement. I've burned through the fumes, and now I'm totally out of fuel and pushing myself along with the handbrake on.

And I'm leaking oil at a frightening rate of knots.

I'm still kneeling, my head down. I want to get up, but I'm not sure it's possible. The air's so turgid, so oppressive. It's like moving in treacle, and besides, my limbs aren't sure they want to listen to me anymore. There's a general mutiny happening, and they've chosen a shit time to decide to give me the black spot. At least I assume that's why I can see black spots floating around in my vision.

Tears roll down my cheeks. There have been so many times I've wanted to die. So often I cursed this so-called gift of life after unending life. I could have so easily ended up like De Montfort or Ben, twisted by the endless repetition of coming back, never being able to escape.

But there's been such beauty too. Skies afire with clouds caught by the first rays of a new dawn. The dancing shade of a thousand leaves dappling across the face on a summer's day. The gurgling smile of an innocent newborn full of potential and promise, unmarred. Wine and song. Friendship. Love.

And there has been loss, of course. Pain and suffering. Prices paid. Weary, aching hearts and bones. But there has to be. There must always be.

What else would give weight to existence? Light and shade. Hope and hurt.

A start and an end.

I'm ready again. Ready for my end. I know there's no heaven waiting for me, no pearly gates and rousing trumpets, a clarion blast calling me home. I've always been heading to dust and nothingness. This was all just a temporary stay of execution, a few extra lifetimes before my soul came apart.

But my readiness isn't everything. Shakespeare was wrong. The world's not a stage with us each bit-part players in our own tragi-comedies. It's a living thing, the collective energy of everything that's ever walked or crawled or sprouted upon it. Every hope and fear and dream and desolation that played out, that plays out right now around me. It's the real screaming into the void but not in fear, not in despair or dread. It's an assembled shout of defiance, an enclave of existence in the emptiness hurling their rebellion, their non-compliance out into the vacuum and filling it with laughter and tears and hate. And more than anything, with love.

Not always good love. Not always healthy. Sometimes tinged with fear. Fear of loneliness, of abandonment, of unworthiness. Sometimes laced with jealousy's corruption, so it becomes about possessing more than valuing. But sometimes...

Sometimes, it's the most perfect encapsulation of all that's right in the condition of life. A mother's arms or paws or tentacles wrapped round to hold an infant safe in innocence, protected from harsh truths and teeth that lurk on the edges of the dark. Sometimes, it's a second of illumination, of understanding that explains all the years past and lights all the years to come.

And sometimes. Sometimes it's a sacrifice. A willingness to give up of everything to save those loved.

I love this world. I love the rolling hills, the endless oceans. The scintillation of dancing grass, the trapped paper-fire of an autumn leaf's change. I love that perfection of a butterfly's wings in whirling motion that you can't pin down. The dances of each species, one with another. The rhythm that floods and pounds and dances through each stream's caress of the banks, each survive-or-die syncopation of hunter and prey. Each celebration for returning home, to the safety and security of those for whom we braved the dark's claws.

And I love the people. All of them. All of their flaws and failures, their inconsistencies and weaknesses. Their lies and little last lingering regrets that sit inexpressibly on the edges of their thoughts, on the tip of their tongue till time waltzes them away into eternal dreamless sleep. All the petty, pointless grudges and gripes that can vanish under threat and transform into acts of selfless, unrewarded bravery for no reason other than that this is what it means.

What it means to live.

There's value beyond measure in all these things. A value beyond my little pan-flash of elongated living. It carries beyond the individual and wraps up in our communal soul. The thing that makes this planet a bastion of light in a cold, empty vastness.

If I'm to go to dust, then this is where that dust shall fall. And if it remains, then I'm never really gone.

As long as it stays, I'm ready to go.

So I push myself up from that one bent knee, and I pray. Not to a god, an omniscient and all-powerful being and external to all that we are. I pray to life, to existence against all odds, to the tiny and insignificant that stand regardless. I let go of all my own self-importance, my dreams and desires and hopes and hates, my power and protection.

Everything emptied out. But I don't feel hollow, not this time. I feel cleansed.

I can feel the blood leaking out of my side rapidly. My time's running short. But I'm not done, not just yet. I'm about to cease to exist forever, but there's one last roll of the dice I can make.

I'm not entirely sure how I'm still standing. My body doesn't understand it. It keeps insisting that with the gaping hole in my side, I should just lie down and let the grass grow over me. But I'm not ready to do that. My mind still holds sway for now.

The dark force coming through has dismissed me entirely. So has Nicetas. The two of them are lost in the thrall of whatever they're doing to pull him through. I wonder if the opening of the gate was part of it or if it was just a way to distract us and get us gone. It having closed doesn't seem to be slowing them down in terms of the beast piercing through the now paper-thin walls.

One foot. Lift. Waver. Forward. Down.

Contact with the ground is a bright pain-wave, like an echolocation on a submarine's radar, spreading out from my side to touch every atom of my being. I feel it in the tips of my hair.

Other foot. Lift. Wobble. Forward. Down.

Breaths are coming fast and shallow. It's so hard to get air. I can't tell if it's because I've lost a lung, if they're both filling with blood, or if it's just the shock setting in. Can't be the last one; I don't have time for that. There's no time for me to collapse. I don't care about the other two things. I can make it before I drown.

One foot. Lift. Forward. Down.

I have my rhythm now. It's hardly a rumba, not even a sedate waltz. But if this is my last dance, I'll make each step of the choreography count. The pain's no more bearable, but at the same time, it's grounding. It means I'm still alive.

One foot. Lift. Forward. Down.

A few more steps. Just a few more, and I'll be there. Part of me wonders what this foul being that's tearing into our reality is. Whether it was ever, once, human. It certainly shows the same sort of hubris, that arrogant superiority. Nithael is restrained, delaying them, distracting them but losing step-by-step. Isaac is just a tether now for the angel, stripped down to nothing but a link between it and all that exists. And I'm just a gnat, an irritating midge, nothing worth even concerning itself with. I hope I'm a murder hornet in disguise. Probably not, but I'll give it a damn good try.

One foot. Lift. Forward. Down.

I don't know how many steps I've taken. How far I've travelled. I feel like Frodo weighed down by the ring, proving that one can, in fact, simply walk into Mordor.

It's been a strange, dark, marvellous road since I stepped out from my mother's arms and took up the robes of Perfection. Swathed myself in black and tied it off with a leather thong. I miss her again. I'm so glad I got to remember her face before all is done. Maybe, in the end, she would have been proud of the man I've made myself into. Even if it took a while to get here. I hope so. Not that it matters. Not now. Not to anyone but me, at least.

One foot. Lift. Forward. Down.

Songs and scenes from plays and lines from well-worn books scramble across my inner landscape, mixing and jumbling in cacophonous joy. Moments of camaraderie, of uncontrollable laughter that spilled out from the very deepest part of my being. Moments when the candle burned brightest, when it drove the darkness back. I see them all. Ben. Susane. Jakob. Isaac.

Aicha.

One foot. Lift. Forward. Down.

I'm near now, so very close. I can almost taste the corruption, like the spoiling of meat spilling out across all matter. Or maybe that's just the blood filling my throat, choking me, my own body seeking to take me down. It doesn't matter which is true. It only matters that I make this right.

One foot. Lift. Forward. Stop.

It takes three attempts for my fluttering hands, tremor-gripped, to gain purchase on my pocket-edge. They just keep slipping off, dropping away, numb and almost useless. I'd laugh over that —after everything I've done, such a simple task might undo me— if disturbing my lungs wouldn't (probably) instantly kill me.

I slide the two digits of my left hand into the pocket, fumble for what I seek, then pull it out. I come so close to dropping it in the trembling action of getting it clear of my jacket, but I manage to get both hands on it, and slowly, so very, very painfully slowly, I unfold it and hold it stretched out between my two hands.

And then like a mercy killing, like an old man kissing his mind-lost wife's cheek after a lifetime together when she's lost to pain and haze before he picks up the pillow for one last desperate act of love...

I wrap the Veil of Veronica around the skull of Torquemada and hold it tight around the head of a new-born monster with every last drop of my failing strength.

CHAPTER TWENTY-SEVEN
BUGARACH, 10 JUNE, PRESENT DAY

I have this will and
determination. Pray God for me
that he lends me his strength...'
Words of the Consolamentum of
the Good People

'Considering I'm trying to smother a terrifying force of evil, to choke the un-life out of it before it gets a foothold in our reality, it really should feel more like I'm using the veil as a tool of suffocation. Instead, it feels like I'm polishing a bowling ball, ready for the big tournament. It detracts somewhat from the dramatic tension, feeling more like I'm chasing the perfect game with the lads rather than trying to keep reality from being rent asunder by some force of ultimate evil.

Of course, the few times I went bowling, I always went with Aicha. I wrap this sacred veil tighter still, till it feels like the skull itself will surely crumple if it wasn't reinforced with pure-brand, one hundred percent malevolence.

And I'm trying to forgive it.

I'm trying to forgive all the misery this creature's brought into my own existence since it first tried to jimmy the locks to our world. Hundreds of friends and fellow Perfects dead in a campaign I suspect Nicetas orchestrated just to jailbreak this bastard, Ben included. The twisting of his spirit with the soiled Grail magic. Susane's payment twice over at De Montfort's hands. Hell, the price he paid himself, his own son swallowed up by whatever this thing did to the energy of my fellow Cathars. I might hate De Montfort even now he's dead, but a part of me, a part I kept telling to keep quiet, thought about how much the death of my own unborn child had driven me off the rails, a child I'd never known. To wake up in the body of my own beloved infant, well — It would be enough to make most people's brain snap, in my opinion. I'm not sure I would've ended up becoming anything better than him had our positions been reversed.

And somehow, some way, I dig out that deep-rooted hate. I pull it out from where it's clinging tenaciously to my brain, my loathing of a now-departed villain who's cost me so much, and I let it drift away. I forgive De Montfort.

Looking over my shoulder, I can see Nicetas and Nithael still wrestling against a cosmic backdrop. The resurrected priest is holding his own even though the Grail energy is fully transferred across to this skeleton, or near enough, power is still pouring into it. It's that dark-claret red now, and I'm willing to lay money that it's Nicetas' own *talent*. Just as he took from De Montfort and Almeric, so this beast is taking from his own loyal servitor. I wonder what he was promised aeons ago for opening the door to it. What he thought he'd get from the deal. The horrors he lived through that made him take that first faltering step down such a terrible, burdensome road.

But against all my pre-conceptions, all my useless fury and hurt. Against Aicha's loss to eternity...

I forgive Nicetas.

Now it's just me and this creature, and finally, it's aware of me, aware of what I'm doing. It wraps stems of its own power around me, binding us together in this strange embrace, and I know we're tied now. If this works, if it gets forced from this strange, sad, wonderful world of ours...

I'm going with it.

I don't want to. Wherever this thing's been lurking for the past few centuries, for possible millennia or more prior, it's going to be precisely zero fun. I bet there's no decent bars, no wine, women, or song. Best-case scenario, it's going to be about as boring as the traditional Church vision of Heaven. Worst case? It's going to make being back in that cave in Faerie a dream I wish I never left.

It doesn't matter though.

I can feel my own fear, that weakness at my core that's so utterly terrified. It's the child who never left my soul, just hid out in the furthest recesses and whimpered at the enclosing darkness. The little scared boy I never gave the space to heal, just pushed him down and locked him away behind banter and bluster, behind an only half-concealed death wish and foolhardy, ill-conceived actions. I can see him in my mind right now, can hear his cries of anguish at all we've been through, at all that's still to come.

I can't tell him it's going to be all right. It's not. But I pull him close to me, into me, envelop him, and accept him. It's not the time to be divided. It's time to be whole.

While standing here, forcing my own *talent* into the veil while power greater than any I've ever imagined swirls like thorn vines to swaddle me like I do the skull, my lives flash across my mindscape. All the times I got it wrong. The people I failed to save. The situations I made worse. The deaths I caused. The misery I wove with thought or word or deed. When I acted from fear. Or selfishness. Indifference. Anger. Arrogance.

All the prices that were paid when the bill was really mine, yet others had to pick up the tab.

There are a lot of them. More than I imagined, really, or at least more than I've let myself remember. Memory's just another tool to use to fool ourselves, to make it possible to live with our actions, our conceits, and our carelessness. We pick out those prize moments, paint them golden, gild them like tawdry souvenirs to stick up on display. And bury those bad ones in an old sea-chest, locked away from our eyes, only drawn out when every now and then we need to see our truths.

My storage box must have been bursting at the seams.

I watch all those memories, wash myself in them. Live those instances anew, gathering the person I was to myself. I'm not those people now any more than this body I'm wearing is the same one as then. This life I lead is the culmination of all of them, from eight hundred years to eight seconds ago. Change is the only constant, whether we grow or wilt and fail. And it's never a clean exponential curve. More a swinging pendulum arm that we hope reaches longer at one end, climbs higher before inertia pulls it back once more, down into the dark.

I hold each of those thousands of Paul Bonhommes in my mental grip one by one. Study them, see them in truth, weak and wanting, foolish and flawed.

One by one, I forgive them all.

I can feel the weight lifting even as the pressure of this god-level spirit's embrace crushes me tighter and tighter, embedding into me, seeking to tear my being into scraps, to feed me to infinity's winds. And I understand now. It's not just that it's god-level.

It's God.

Or one of them, at least. As the tendrils of *talent* sink deeper into me, I can taste its essence in my own. Amazing, really. I'd have thought something so big, so vast, so other, so external to our understanding of existence would feel incomprehensible. The finite failing to comprehend the infinite.

And sure, there are flashes of that. Moments of the stretching gulfs of time I cannot hold in my head, that make my grey matter feel like it's bleaching to the bone colour of the worlds that have cracked and collapsed to dust in eye-blinks.

But under that...

Underneath it are things as familiar as air in lungs, as tears on cheeks, as aches in hearts. The pain of rejection, the fury of aims thwarted. Doors closed, desires refused. Wants and needs and wasted opportunities. That same little voice of doubt that's been squashed down and silenced, that perhaps the ends don't justify the means, that perhaps things outside of our immediate experiences can also have value.

I think I expected more of a "be not afeared" or, considering there's definitely a strong undercurrent of what I think of as evilness, more "be very afeared". Ineffable seems like a basic condition of being a deity. But I understand all too well the base rage that underpins this god. It's the temper tantrum of a toddler who's had access to their toy box restricted because they keep pulling the heads off their dolls.

And that's enough. Enough to make this supreme world-destroying being relatable. So despite the fact it holds nothing but contempt for humanity, for life, that it'll bring an end to everything if it can...

I forgive it.

I empty myself of every one of my emotions, positive and negative, and now I'm an empty vessel once more. Except, now I'm not a hollow man nor am I just cleansed out.

I'm a prism. I let the power flow through me like light through a sphere of glass, and it refracts out.

I'm pouring magical fucking rainbows into the veil, supercharging it. Pouring my love for life, for Earth, for the galaxies and planets unknown, for everything that has ever existed, that ever could exist into this scrap of supposedly sacred cloth. Because if there's anything in this oft-time, cold-to-the-bone existence that's holy...

It's love.

I feel peace like I've never known. I know it won't last. When we go to the other side, to the plane where this thing came from, I get the feeling it'll just be it and me, and I can't imagine it's going to be best pleased that I blocked it from stepping through into our reality. I wonder whether there's such a thing as death through that particular tarnished looking glass. Whether I'll ever get it. How much I'll long for it.

But that's a worry for another time, another place. For now I get a moment of true serenity, a oneness with everything I'm trying to protect. I'm ready. I'm ready to go. To let it all be. To pay the price that someone needs to pay.

This time, let it be me.

The Veil of Veronica bursts into flames.

It starts in the centre. The middle of it smoulders, then ignites, a pale washed green flame that singes my eyelashes even at a distance. It spreads out, consuming the fabric, devouring it like a hungry glutton before a meagre buffet. A second later, the heat is searing my fingers. Even as I try to cling on, ignoring the sweet scent of flesh roasting, trying to hold on to that previous serenity, to force my forgiveness to banish us both out of this plane, back to where the being in front of me came from...

It disintegrates into nothing, the last scrap of material turning to ash in my now charred, useless fingers.

And I'm staring into the grinning skull of the Evil God, wrapped up in its planet-devouring *talent*. Unarmed. Alone and afraid.

Here. At the end of all things.

CHAPTER TWENTY-EIGHT

BUGARACH, 10 JUNE, PRESENT DAY

Fear might be the little death. But I'm afraid. Afraid my death will be anything but little. And mean even less.

I'm not sure I ever really knew fear before. Not like this.

Funny thing to say. In some ways, I've never not known fear. I've been afraid since the moment I was born, since that last vestige of innocent safety got stripped away from me, and air filled my bawling lungs and gave me something to cry about. Gave me uncertainty and doubt and incomprehension to permeate my tiny little being.

Fear's been a boon companion from that first second.

There've been times it's nipped at my heels, hounding me forward. Times it's wrapped me up, so I fled to a pipe or bottle to hide. Times it's led me to greatness, and times it's provoked me into plumbing the depths of depravity, of the worst that humanity has to offer.

But this. Staring down into eye sockets that contain an ancientness only outweighed by its malice, glee dancing in unfathomable black holes ready to swallow whole universes without a second thought. This is a level of fear I've never conceived of.

It's not fear for myself. I'm done. Any form of ending now for me will only be a mercy. I've gone over my allotted time by such a huge margin. There's no sadness in me for that.

This is terror that runs right down to a molecular level. I can feel it in my individual atoms. This is an end to everything. I am here, right here, at the moment where life itself stands on a knife-edge, and I've given my all. And it isn't enough.

I can't. I can't fail. Please.

I feel like Westley standing before the Dread Pirate Roberts. Please. What reason do I have to live? True love.

I can feel it. That love. Love for existence, for life. For the chances it gives, for the mistakes it punishes. For a cycle we all thought endless that is about to be broken.

Please.

Not for me. Not for those I love. Isaac's failing. Aicha's gone. Everyone else is dust and memory-ghosts about to be exorcised as I crumble. But for love itself. For every creature that ever cared for another, every plant that spread its pollen into the sky, seeking continuation. The embrace of continents that reshape the world as they cling or rub against the other. For every sensation, every separation, every rejoining, every rejoicing.

Please. For true love for Life.

Please.

Somehow, in the face of the culmination of all that ever was, in a broken once-man's last plea, there comes an answer.

As so often as is the case, it's an answer in the form of a question. Will you accept? I can feel it in my bones, in my brain, in my whole being. If I do accept this, if I become host, it'll most likely tear me into infinitesimal pieces, lost across eternity.

There's no hesitation. There's only one possible answer to it.

Please.

I step back, hand over control of my very anima itself.

And the Good God roars in, filling up the empty, reforged vessel that once was Paul Bonhomme.

Now we're firmly into the realms of the indescribable. All those connections I sought out to forgive the Evil God in front of me? They're gone, with the being now wearing me like Marilyn Monroe shucking on a stained-old raincoat. It's pure and perfect, love incarnate, and those are still just *words*. How can you describe perfection to a species flawed by design, our obsolescence built in as a part of the condition of existing? For a moment, I get to ride shotgun with the limitless, and if I still controlled my tear ducts, I'd be weeping uncontrollably.

All those primal emotions of the Evil God crash into us like tidal waves from an enraged ocean. We're way beyond words, of course, but I can pick out all the intent. The sensations of abandonment, of outrageous denial, the entitlement that peppers my flesh with burning holes, my pores clogging and igniting, my skin cells swelling, cancerous, eating themselves down towards the bone.

The answer washes out of us — regret, empathic pain, sadness. *Necessity.* The years smooth away from my face, each wrinkle worn in by a thousand years of Maeve's reign deleting itself. My cheeks glow so radiant, I can see them reflecting in the bone-mirror in front of us.

The reply is a soundless scream of indignation. I want to tear myself into non-existence over the knowledge it brings. This realm always belonged to it. What right does the created have in the face of its creator? None. I feel despair settle in my soul as my fingers curl up, brittling, blackening — a mirror of the frostbite in my soul as they drop like frozen dew-tears from a weeping willow's hunched up form.

But under it, underneath the agony of the maker's wrath boiling my brain till I can feel my synapses popping one by one, cool waters ripple. That ripple spreads outwards, a calming balm; it carries away every regret, every marring mark on my being where I failed or fell. My lungs expand and drink in that sense of freedom, of independence. I breathe out the distilled essence of choice, so that it swirls in and out of the void, threading through sockets and nose-holes, a dragon-dance of self-determination. It doesn't follow a path we've set for it. It chooses its own, autonomous.

The skull inhales, an intake that pulls like the desert winds, implacable and razor-like, swallowing down the gifted breath to nothingness. It's a denial, a refusal. A straight no. A rejection of options in the certainty of ultimate and utter control. The coiling inhalation is more than a wind now; it's a gale, a cyclone, and I can feel it stripping the flesh from my face, eating away at the tendons and muscles to leave nothing but a reflection of the grinning death's-head in front of me.

I feel the sadness in the Good God possessing me. And I feel afraid.

Because we're not winning here. It's not enough. My sacrifice alone, it's not enough to stop the Evil God from coming through, from reclaiming what was once theirs. I'm still just a mortal, still marked by a beginning and an ending. And the latter is arriving fast.

I can feel the Good God burning through my essence to stay here, to entreat their sibling, to beg for a chance for our realm. It's a distraction, an interesting debate but not enough to block the Evil God from what it wants.

I may have reached a state of Perfection again, but one Perfect's sacrifice isn't enough.

The void looms large on what may well be the last ever starlit night.

Bugarach is where the end of the world starts. And that's only the prologue. The end of everything follows closely behind.

I'm no longer limited by my flesh, which considering the way it bubbles and rots in places, bursting pustulant buboes and gangrenous gaping wounds, is probably a good thing. I imagine the pain I feel would be overwhelming if so. As it is, the physical seems to be nothing but a distraction. I push it aside. There are no answers to be found there.

Instead, I seek outwards, projecting myself through the Good God's karma like an amplifier, launching my plea to the four corners of Earth, into the firmament, the foundations, across the expanses.

Please. Please.

One ear pricks up. One who saved us once already. Who gave my best friend the way to save me more than once and then took her away from me as a price I never would have paid. One who's outside of space and time and understanding just as much as the two entities locked in a conversation writing itself in ravages over my mortal frame. One whose doorstep we stand upon like a bunch of bobbing, blue-hooded dwarves.

The White Lady.

I can feel her, the state she's in. She's been waiting. Only waiting for that last plea to reach out into the ether, that SOS for help. Some things can't be given unless they're asked for. And sometimes?

Sometimes all you need to do? Say *please*.

Her answer comes like a thread woven by a leaf's dance down from a branch, like a chime struck by a glacier's passage through sediment and season. I feel it, but I could never verbalise it, never nail it down into the mould that languages cast. But if I had to? If I really needed to break it down to such a basic form of communication?

I think the closest thing I could come up with would be, "*As you wish.*"

The earth to the side of me cracks as though in a sudden tectonic shift, opening up a shaft that seems to extend down all the way to the heart of the mountain. A vein, not of gold but of life, traces from tip to root, from sky to soil.

It feels like a well's spring bubbling over with existence, like Spring breaking from Winter's grasp to rejuvenate the lands anew. Out of it rises what looks like a dove reimagined as a phoenix, the white of its feathers caused by unimaginable heat blazing out, hot enough to consume the sun. It illuminates the world so I'm sure I can pick out the walls of Carcassonne far below, till I'd swear I could see all the way to Toulouse itself.

Then that light coalesces, concentrates, and streams forth across the crags and peaks.

To strike the peak of Montsegur.

The ruins of a fallen castle built on the last remnants of a broken dream light up, a golden ghost in a summer night made midday. And along that luminous pathway, like a new Bifrost formed just for this moment, comes marching a small army.

An army made of Perfect souls.

Two hundred and ten. Two hundred and ten people. Good Men and Women. Two hundred and ten walk out of the ruins of the gates of Montsegur, across the light-streaked sky, to the summit of Bugarach.

Two hundred and ten who sacrificed themselves to be true to their beliefs rather than taking the easy way out. Who died with honour rather than living without.

And a voice whispers in my ear, 'She was right. I did see you again, Paul. Afore the end of it all.'

It's a voice I've not heard in eight centuries near enough. A woman who turned down my offer of escape, who walked with those who looked to her for guidance onto the pyres of the Crusaders. Who discovered *talent* of her own when I tried to ride to the rescue armed with mine. Who answered me with frustrating riddles as to why she would die when I could help her and the faith now known as Catharism to live.

Esclarmonde of Foix.

Now I realise where she got her *talent* from. Who the mysterious "she" was that she bargained with. Exactly who told her that we'd meet again before the end.

Looks like Aicha wasn't the only one of my friends over the years to make a bargain with the White Lady.

Now the first of the Perfects steps onto the mountaintop. They join where I stand bound up with a grinning undead god and the incarnation of Goodness simultaneously. The first Cathar spirit enters into me, passes through me. For a moment I feel them, a honeydew on my tongue, a scent like rosebuds and cherry blossom in my nose, a feathered touch on the last of my blistering skin. Then they pass through, out, and into the skeleton in front of me.

One rib bone dims and fades from that putrescent flesh-rot green. It fades back to the off-white of nothing but simple bone. The sacrifice of one Perfect soul annulling that stolen from another.

Then another passes through me and another, and bone after bone relinquishes its glow. The Evil God's fury is here, present in diseases that wrack my body, cancerous aches in the marrow of my own frame. He sucks down the last of the bordeaux-coloured essence of Nicetas, so that the battle behind us comes to an end, the reformed flesh dissipating and the skeleton's animation ceasing, collapsing back into a lifeless pile. Nithael is free, but they don't move. They watch, only observing. This one is humanity's battle to win. A Perfect sacrifice paying off.

The addition of Nicetas' energy is nowhere near enough to keep off the assault of the pure spirits pouring through me. One, two, three essences wink out as the creature burns through what was once the man who opened up the way for him to come through, but then the kernel of that strange madman is used up, snuffed out.

Papa Nicetas is gone forever.

And it's not enough.

There are two hundred and six bones in the human body.

One by one, the *talent* infused in the skeleton extinguishes, flaring away into non-existence. Step by step, as more and more of the fallen Perfects fling themselves through my prism, through the symbiote I've formed with the Good God; the Evil God's hold on our world is undone.

Until at last, all that's left is a glowing skull and one tiny pinky finger bone. Then that, too, is snuffed out. And now, it's just that one place, that prison Ben once wielded to threaten Isaac and Nithael, hoping to tear a hole into our world, a hole that I now understand was to bring the Evil God back in.

There's not much more of me left, mind. I'm falling apart. Literally. I guess this is what being a zombie must feel like, only I don't have a craving for brains. I've always managed without any; no point wanting them now. I can't see, can't look down anymore, can't move this fleshless skull of mine. I'm not sure if it means I'm paralysed or if there's nothing left below the neck. Whichever it is, I'm on my way out. I'm not just burned out; I've poured paraffin over myself and chain-smoked a packet of sticks of dynamite. I've nothing left.

'You've done your part.' Esclarmonde's whisper is a cool compress to my fevered brow. I open my mouth to respond, to insist I can still carry on, that I'll go march the bastard back through the gates of hell...

The last Perfect spirit, apart from Lady Esclarmonde, leaps from the blackened stump that was once my tongue and barrels full force into the face of the Evil God itself.

Maybe it's a tender kiss goodnight. I prefer to think of it as the Good People proving their worth, spitting in the Devil's malignant eye.

Esclarmonde passes through me, her wings spread wide, carried on the crest of Perfect love. She grows, expanding to the size of a rook, a raptor. A roc. She passes through the walls of the worlds and carries away the skull in her claws. Gone from our lives. The door the Evil God was forcing his way through is locked once more. And my work is done here.

So I die.

Again.

One last, final time.

CHAPTER TWENTY-NINE
HASTINGUES, 8 APRIL, SEVERAL MONTHS AGO

The thudding of tentacles on my hastily thrown-up shield sounds like hail hammering down on an old tin roof. Peculiarly slimy, hairy hail. With sucker pads.

'Lou, chill the fuck out! It's me!' My voice reverberates around the enormous underground chamber, echoing back off the smooth surface that amplifies it naturally. At least it means the words carry to the gigantic monster on the floor below me.

'Oh, Mister Thnack! What a pleasant surprithe! I thought you'd be dead for sure!' The cheery, bright tones of the giga-cephlopod are at odds with the drab surrounding us. Shafts of light do penetrate, but they're washed out, wearied by their journeying down the myriad of angled tunnels Lou Carcoilh uses to send his tentacle-ears out into the world, hunting prey but mainly eavesdropping on TV shows.

I do love it when people sound cheerful about me being alive. Although it's equally possible he's pleased at the thought of my possible death. I know practically nothing about the implausible, impossibly enormous hairy snail-dragon below.

Lou's eye-stalks hover into view, popping over the rim of the tunnel, the sheer drop plunging thirty or forty metres to the compact soil below. They waggle back and forth like slightly drunk punching balls. 'Did you bring me back my treasure then? Fabulouth!'

I drop the shield. Now Lou's recognised me, the immediate threat of getting torn to pieces has reduced significantly. Of course, with my new friend, the chances of him accidentally killing me with some form of puppy-like enthusiasm is still relatively high.

Not that it matters too much. Main thing is to hand off the goods. 'Here you go. As promised. Not only the Veil of Veronica' —I hand him the relic, which is not unlike a particularly used dish cloth if you look at it and a terrifying beacon of fuck-off power if you *look* at it— 'but also these twofers.'

Drawing back the mouth of the canvas tote bag, I let him see the gleam of the two skulls inside. Even without opening my *sight*, these look like they're straight out of a horror film or a dark magic ritual. There's something about real human skulls that is both instantly recognisable and deeply unsettling. Combine that with the *talent* each is radiating, the magical equivalent of a couple of rods of weaponised plutonium, and they're obviously not something to be messed around with.

Unless, of course, you're Lou Carcoilh. A pair of tentacles whip out to pick up the skulls and hold them up, one to each eye-stalk to inspect the polished bone. A low whistle emanates from his mouth far below. 'Ooh, that'th really impressive. Jutht packed full of tathty magic. And the aesthetic! All "I am the prinnntthhhhhhe of darknnnneeeettthhhhhhh". Going to make my shell look so gothic. I don't suppothe you could bring me some black candleth next time, could you? The dribblier the better!'

I'm about to give him a warning about the danger of playing with flames in an enclosed environment. Then I remember that Lou's shell is considerably larger than most middle-class homes and is also impervious to fire. Guess I'll add black candles to the shopping list. Maybe I'll get him something really metal, like some silver candlesticks shaped like demons. Although, knowing my luck, Lou'll probably use them to summon some unspeakable Lovecraftian horror by accident. Think I'll give that one a miss.

The gigantic snail looks curiously at the three objects I've brought him, each wrapped in a different sucker pad. Then the eyes swivel back to me. 'Hey, look at this!' And then, with three of the most powerful magical items I've ever encountered, Lou Carcoilh, the giant snail, starts juggling.

I can only be glad that Isaac's not here to witness this. I think he'd drop dead of a coronary on the spot. Either that or smite him for sacrilege. Luckily, it doesn't last too long. I've no idea quite how his sucker pads work, but while he manages to throw each of them once, when he catches them again, they stick fast. He stares, bemused, at the skull of Arnaud Almeric, recent prison of an angel and master magician, and starts shaking his tentacle like a polaroid picture. The tentacle moves faster and faster, and suddenly the terrifyingly powerful and incredibly rare magic skull is sailing through the air at a speed just below supersonic. My heart's in my mouth, and I'm sure the skull's about to either get pulverised into dust on contact or bury its way back out to the surface and keep going till it reaches orbit.

Instead, another of Lou's tendrils whips out and snatches it out of the air. 'Interception!' he yells, a terrible American accent added on. 'Denied! EA Sporth! It'th in the game!' I'm terrified for a moment he's going to slam dunk it through an imaginary hoop, probably ending up with it burrowing through to the earth's core —and won't an awesomely *talent*-imbued skull be an interesting contribution to add to the molten lava keeping our planet alive and warm— but he pulls back at the last moment, and the tentacles all shoot back inside his impermeable shell. I stifle an audible sigh of relief but only just. I can feel the sweat dribbling down my back.

Right, anyhow, that's job done. 'Thanks then, Lou. I'll come see you when we need to borrow the skulls back or if I come across any other terrifying objects of unknowable power you can use to hone your circus skills.'

I turn to head back, but one of the creature's tentacles is stuck to the wall on the way, hanging loosely down. For a moment, I think it's a threat, a double-cross, that now he has the objects, Lou's going to finally crack and eat Mister Thnack. Instead, his voice comes up from behind me.

'Really? So soon? Don't you have time for a quick beer before you go?'

A thought hits me like a clap of thunder. The tentacle isn't hanging there threateningly. It's like the guy at a party trying to lean casually against the wall as he fruitlessly seeks to engage everyone in awkward conversation even as his inner introvert is overloading at a rate of knots and screaming at him to run away. Lou Carcoilh is trying to make *small talk* with me.

I turn back around disbelievingly, peering down to where the monster is. Scanning the multitude of tunnels and pathways arriving into the walls and ceiling, I can't see what I'm looking for. 'Unless I'm much mistaken, I don't think you've got a pub hidden away down here.'

'Ahh.' The chirpiness is back in Lou's voice. 'Don't worry about that.'

One of his appendages rockets off down a tunnel about ten metres to my left. When it pops back, it's curled around the handle of a no-brand blue plastic carrier bag. The familiar *clink* speaks of bottles huddled together. The tentacle swings closer, and another pad dips in and pulls out one of those oversized beer bottles that've become all the rage in recent years, what Americans call forties. With only a minor amount of subtle tugging, I liberate it from the sucker, scoop the worst of the deposited snail gunk off, and then pop the top off with a thought. Magic has its uses.

By the time I've opened it, the tentacle's back, waving another bottle that would look gigantic in my hand but only looks like a child's dollhouse accessory for Alcoholic Barbie™ in Lou's. The tendril wiggles the bottle back and forth. At first I think he's trying to hypnotise me as the follow up to his shitty juggling act before I realise he wants me to clink. I do so, surreptitiously wiping the other hand on my trousers. Lou goo is some sticky shit.

'*Tchin*!' The voice carries brightly up as the bottle goes shooting down. The enormous snail empties the alcohol into a mouth the size of an industrial trash compactor in a second. The empty bottle's left stuck to a sucker, so Lou just scrapes it off with his teeth and chomps that down too. I settle for slowly sipping at mine once I make sure none of Lou's slime is on the bottle top. Getting any of that in my mouth is the stuff nightmares and soapy mouth-washing sessions are made of.

There's a communion to be found in drinking. I wonder if that's why alcohol's been accepted for so long when so many less harmful substances have got banned. There's no need for words. It's just a moment shared in silence.

'Thankth, Mister Thnack.' Lou's voice is quieter than usual, albeit still louder than a town-crier with a loud-hailer. The tone catches me off guard though. There's a real warmth, a genuine gratitude there.

I was planning to knock the bottle back as quickly as manners allow and then hustle off. I still need to get back to Toulouse today, and after all the bullshit I've been through in the last week, I just want to go home and fall over in bed for a month. But that "thanks" catches me. I sit myself down on the lip of the tunnel, my legs dangling over the abyss, and savour my drink while Lou crunches his way through another couple of bottles.

'How do you manage it, Lou?' I shouldn't really ask. The question doesn't just border on Rude; it mounts a heavily armed incursion claiming large swathes of territory as its own into Rude. But I want to know.

'Manage what, Mister Thnack?' The chirpy brightness is still there, but he doesn't fool me. I can hear the wavering to his tone. He knows what I mean.

'Manage this.' I wave my hand expansively at the cave. 'No matter how big this is, you're still stuck here. Locked away underground. How do you stay upbeat? How do you stay sane?'

The last sentence might be stretching it a bit, but I have no other gigantic monstrous snail-dragons to compare against. All I can do is wonder how well I'd do if I were stuck for eternity in a cave, never able to leave. Considerably less well, I suspect.

'Oh, it'th fine!' Again, I can't help feeling like the breezy voice carries a hidden edge. 'It'th true, it would be lovely to go outside sometimeth. To smell the fresh cut hay, feel the sun on my stalkth, sure. Maybe munch a cow or three and really stretch out all the kinkth in my muscleth, you know?' As the words go on, the wistfulness builds, that forced sparkle dropping back and the truth coming out. 'It'th not alwayth eathy, you're right, being down here on my own. Away from the daylight. Away from all the people, all the vibrant life.' His eye-stalks perk, the saucer-like globes popping back up to be level with my head. 'Apart from Thteve, Thteve, Thteven, and Thtephan, of course!'

I almost dread to ask, but I can recognise a cue when I'm given one. 'And they are…'

'My petth. Hold on. Let me find them…'

Various tentacles detach themselves from their hooked-on perches against the walls and start scrabbling around on the dusty floor. It's like watching Audrey Two have a seizure mid-song. Eventually, one swooshes up towards me and triumphantly brandishes a very still earthworm attached to a sucker. It's either dead or petrified with fear. I can't help wondering if it's possible to give an earthworm a heart attack. Do they have hearts? Can you make an earthworm cry? Shaking my head, I focus on the one in front of me. Those are questions for another time.

'Thith ith Thteve.' The chirpy tone falters slightly. 'I think.'

'Nice to meet you, Tht... Steve.' I manage to correct myself just in time. Poor old Lou has it hard enough. He doesn't need to be mocked for his lisp on top of everything else.

'He'th such a good boy. Alwayth there when I need him.' As he speaks, Lou's tentacle whips around wildly, giving Steve the worm equivalent of a ride on the Formula Rossa, the world's fastest rollercoaster. Do worms have brains? Surely they don't have skulls that they can be crushed against from snail-dragon induced whiplash? I resolve to read some books about worms when I get out of here. Then swiftly correct myself. I resolve to try to read some books about worms when I get out of here but will almost certainly fall asleep on the first paragraph. Be honest in your resolutions, people.

After his white-knuckle sucker-pad adventure, Steve gets deposited gently while another tentacle brings me another beer.

'Where are you getting these from, Lou? I don't see a convenient bar or off-license stashed down one of those tunnels, unless you're holding out on me about your nightlife?'

The roar of laughter that booms from the oversized cephalopod shakes the whole cavernous space. I'm forced to anchor myself to the floor with *talent* so I don't get dislodged by the resultant tremors. The locals must get confused as to why they keep getting minor earthquakes each time they're watching stand-up comedy on the telly.

'Oh, Mister Thnack, you're a laugh a minute!' The chuckles echo back and forth, building as they bounce off angled walkways, back into the main space. 'There'th no barth I can get to. The doorth would have to be enormouth! No, silly, thethe are beerth people have forgotten when they're drunk or what they've left outside. If they're too drunk to notice a gigantic tentacle stealing their boxeth of beerth, they don't need any more, am I right?'

Well, I can't really argue with that. In fact, thinking about times I've been that drunk myself, Lou was probably doing them a solid favour, getting rid of any further temptation.

Cracking open our beers, we sit in a silence that, if not companionable, is peaceful, at least. The Good God knows I can do with a little bit of peace. It's a resource I've never been high on. Not for a very long time, at least.

Eventually, a thought starts building in my brain. One that destroys any possible peace, an itching powder thought that insists on making its way to my tongue, that's determined to escape the confines of my brain and make itself heard even if I don't really want to say it. 'Lou, are you happy? Haven't you ever been tempted to, y'know, throw a fight? Call it a day and have done with the whole thing?' Fuck me, it's such a horrible, rude thing to ask, but I can't help it. The life this jovial oddball of a monstrosity beneath me lives? Well, it doesn't seem like much of a life to me. I hate myself for having asked it, but I couldn't resist. There's a part of me, that part buried down deep inside in the dark and pain, that needs to know.

Lou Carcoilh, to his credit, doesn't react badly. He doesn't slap me off the ledge with a tentacle as he'd be well within his right. Hell, he doesn't even correct me for calling him Lou instead of Lou Carcoilh. Instead, he rubs at the back of his left eye-stalk with a tentacle, so I can hear the tiny hairs rasping against his sucker pad like a kid strumming a tooth-comb. Silence reigns for a while.

'Honethtly, Mister Thnack?' When the words come, they're slow, thought out, measured. 'I can't lie. There are timeth, timeth sitting here in the dark for monthth alone, no voiceth except thothe I hear from the TV. No kind wordth. No laugth shared. No meaningful momentth. Jutht time ticking away, disappearing back where it came from while I stay ever the same, when I've asked myself, "Lou Carcoilh, what'th the point?" I may be here for another thousand yearth, ten thousand. A million, for all I know. Ith it worth it, really?'

Quiet settles on the cavern again, so heavy it feels like anti-sound, like anything said will be swallowed up by the silence. It's almost unbearable. So I don't bear it. I break it.

'So is it?' I have to know. 'Is it worth it?'

The eye-stalks come back up, widen, shock clear in them despite their alien nature. 'Oh, yeth! Oh, yeth, Mister Thnack! It'th so worth it. Sure, I might be stuck in thith cave, but I still *live*. To hear the songth of birdth, to feel the morning'th dew on the glistening grath even if I can't see it... It'th a miracle, a moment of communion. Even in the dark, there are dreamth. And while there're dreamth, there'th hope.

'Maybe one day, my deal will be done, and I'll stroll once more among the meadowth. Until then, I've storieth I've heard, songth I remember. There're friendth in the voitheth from the TV screenth. And more than that, I've dreamth. I've hope.' Lou's voice changes, warmth infecting it as a thought hits him. 'And I've Thteve, Thteve, Thteven, and Thtephan. So I'm never really alone, am I? Pluth... well, pluth there'th you now, isn't there, Mister Thnack?'

The hesitation in his voice makes my breath hitch. The hopefulness there. I can feel my eyes stinging, a certain wetness. Must be all the damn dust in this cave.

I raise my bottle up. 'Yeah, there's me, Lou. Here's to dreams and future freedom, my friend.'

Lou's tentacle whips over but slows just in time to delicately clink another bottle with mine. 'To dreamth and friendship. That'th freedom, right there, Mister Thnack.'

I take a long pull on the bottle, enjoying the feeling as the sour bubbles burst down my throat, revelling in just the simplicity of sensation. 'I guess it is, Lou. I guess it is.'

'Lou Carcoilh, not Lou, Mister Thnack. Lou Carcoilh.'

'Right you are, Lou Carcoilh.' I tilt my bottle to salute the giant snail, then down the rest in the honour of the impossibly weird and implausibly wise creature hidden under the ancient hill of Hastingues. Then I stand and head back up the passageway, leaving him to his dreams of brighter days and futures, holding on to his hope, down there in the primeval dark.

CHAPTER THIRTY

SOMEWHERE ELSE, SOMEWHEN ELSE. MAYBE. I HAVE NO IDEA, HONESTLY.

Non-existence is surprisingly comfortable. I mean, I could have imagined it might feel a bit like slipping into a warm bath of acid, my head falling under the surface, dissolving away, at peace with the decisions made.

I didn't expect it to feel like a well-upholstered wingback chair by a roaring, radiant fireplace well stocked with neatly chopped logs.

Nor did I expect a healthy measure of whisky in a cut-crystal tumbler that smells, well...

They call whisky the water of life. Aicha might have got pissed off with that under the Fair Trade Descriptions Act, but there you are. That's what the name means in Celtic.

This doesn't smell like just the water of life. This smells like the *juices* of Life, if you get what I mean. And it tastes even better.

I take a moment to savour it, my eyes closed. It's ambrosia, the nectar of the gods, the distillation of the very essence of whisky personified. You could buy a ten thousand euro bottle back on Earth, and it wouldn't taste this good.

I think it's my reward for a job well done. Probably a commiseration prize too. If that's the case, I've certainly had worse over the years.

Eventually, I can't justify relishing it any longer. I'm bordering on rude, even if it's understandable considering just how perfect this most perfect of drinks is.

So I open my eyes and look at the woman in front of me.

Of course, she's not really a woman no matter how much she looks like that right now any more than I was when I sat in Maeve's body. I've mingled with their essence. I know who's sitting in front of me. *What's* sitting in front of me. A wise woman with traces of the ones who guided my steps — a flicker of the Mother of the Sistren of Bordeaux here, a quirking trait of Gwendolyne there, the safety in the compassionate eyes of my mother's unending embrace. I's just a way for me to comprehend the incomprehensible again. For a moment, at least.

I sigh and swirl my glass, which is still just as full. Having a one-on-one chat with your god definitely has its perks, even if it involves you being dead.

'I take it this is just a brief pit stop?' I take a healthy swig. Hell, if it's replenishing automatically, I might as well try to get a buzz on while I'm at it. Bit of Dutch courage for what's to come.

The matronly figure in the chair across from me smiles, though it doesn't quite drive the sadness from her eyes. 'Of course, Paul. But then, all of this was never anything more than that.'

That...that actually annoys me. Quite a bit. I can feel my hackles rising. 'Hold on. All right, I get it. Compared to you, we're nothing but gadding mayflies popping in for a moment, then popping our clogs the next. Doesn't make it meaningless.'

She looks at me with such compassion that I can't really take in anything but her eyes, glittering gems that they are. It's only as I realise my own ones are bouncing up and down, trying to track hers, that I realise she's shaking. I blink and then clock that it's because she's laughing, her shoulders shaking with a mirth carried across on the most melodious laughter I've ever heard. Trust me. Get a recording of it, put it on Spotify — guaranteed triple-platinum hit the next day.

'Oh, my Good Man, my poor, long-suffering Cathar,' she murmurs, wiping at her eyes. 'That's the very reason why it's so meaningful. You burn so bright, my little magnesium spark in the deepest of nights.' She leans forward and rests her hand on my cheek — soft, supportive, comforting. 'What could matter more than a light in the darkness?'

Oh, right. She's the good one. Of course we matter to her. I feel abashed, ashamed considering she just went in to bat on our behalf.

'Is he...' I don't know what to say, quite how to phrase it. I felt the connection between them back on the mountaintop. They're siblings of a sort. Friends once upon a galaxy. Asking, 'Did we kill your bro?' or 'Have we ruined your chance for reconciliation with your former BFF?' both seem like pretty tactless questions, considering.

'Gone. Is it forever?' She strokes my cheek, a gesture so loving, so reassuring, I could be back in that old straw bed at the family shack, huddled down by my mother's side. 'What is? But long enough for this world to grow old and be gone before the next time, I should think.'

I can't help myself. I breathe a huge sigh of relief. If that's the case, then it's all been worth it. Every single thing along the way, all the suffering and misery. All the losses. I can live with paying the prices demanded in that case.

I sort of feel like I should be using this conversation to unravel the mysteries of existence, to demand the answer to Life, the Universe, and

Everything, but, honestly, none of them are burning a hole in my central cortex at this particular moment. I guess I'm finally at peace. Maybe it's part of knowing what's coming next.

'The comment before — the pit stop thing?' I take her hand off my face gently, hold it in mine. I don't want to let go of her. Not ever, really, but especially not now. If this is to be my last sensation of touch, my last contact with another, well — again, there're worse choices. 'I assume this was just a momentary grace period before I head off into the dust?'

I see the quirk of her lips as she purses them, and I think she's having to try very hard to be serious, to not laugh. This time it doesn't put my back up though. It's that sort of indulgent humour when someone you love is making an obstinately endearing fool of themselves, saying all the wrong things but for all the right reasons. 'Is that what you want, Good Man?'

'No, I...' I start to say it's what I deserve. I mean, in terms of the offer I made, the deal I struck in order to be the conduit to force the Evil God back out of our plane of existence. The subtext, though, is that it's what I deserve for all the bad decisions I've made, the mistakes and mess-ups. Except, I forgave myself for those, didn't I? I must have done; otherwise, none of this would have worked, wouldn't have made me pure enough to be the conduit, and we'd not be here, right as not.

In the end, I find that it's not just that the cat has my tongue, but the feline swine has run off with it and played with it until it's a bloody mess. Then buried it underneath the prize petunias. So I settle for shaking my head instead.

The almost-grin disappears, although the amusement still lingers in the twinkle of her eyes. 'You've done me a great service today, Cathar, a hard and heavy burden that you shouldered without complaint. And not just this day. You've had to wait for this for eight hundred years. But you don't have to wait any longer.'

I'm confused, trying to work it out. Then it clicks. I'm Perfect again. I'm not going to dissolve into dust, collapse into nothingness. This is it. I'm finished. This is where I get to step off the wheel of Dharma, call it a day, dust myself off after a job well done, and go have a sneaky peek at what comes next.

I'm not going to lie; it's a relief. I wasn't looking forward to ceasing to exist even if I resigned myself to it. Another set of adventures, jumping on board the boat to sail to the Farthest Shore? I can get down with that. Except, of course, there're a couple of those damned hopped-up, crack-head bumblebee questions buzzing round my cortex again, demanding answers.

So instead of taking my "not having your soul obliterated" extension of grace as a gift horse, I don't just look it in the mouth; I knock all of its teeth out one after another with a sledgehammer to have a real good peer in there, see what I can see. 'What about Isaac? What about Jakob?' It takes some doing to shape the next question. In the end, it comes out as an inquisitive croak, like it burns to let it out. I blame the whisky. 'Aicha?'

Apparently, saving existence buys you some amount of goodwill because instead of smiting me, as would be well within her purview for my cheekiness in asking for answers rather than expressing gratitude for my continued existence, she gives me an indulgent smile. It's the sort a parent might give to a child who's gorged themselves on a whole packet of sweets and is crying now because their tummy hurts. It's a real "I love you, but you brought this on yourself" kind of smile, which doesn't really match with the info she gives me next.

'Isaac is fine. Nithael replenished him while the Perfect energy drove my sibling away. He's on the top of Bugarach right now.'

No doubt searching for me, any trace of me. Phone in hand, hoping desperately that I'm going to call, tell him where to come and pick me up from in my new body.

Ah, that's what she meant by the "brought it on yourself" look. Because now I can see him. I can see the pain in his face, the desolation at having lost his brother, lost Aicha, and now lost me. The loneliness that he's the only one left, a loneliness that's going to etch itself deeper and deeper into his face, into the panes of his soul till one day they shatter and break.

I'm not feeling at all at peace now, not even slightly. The radioactive itchy ants are marching through my brain again. I think they might be doing a conga line. And there's still the other part of the question to get an answer to.

She doesn't, the Good God bless her, keep me waiting. Which, considering she is the Good God, means I've just asked her to bless herself. Bit weird, but whatever. 'Aicha and Jakob are alive. Gone but alive.'

I could melt through the gaps in the seat cushion and pool into a puddle of relief on the floor. A terrible pressure, the held-back tides of consuming sadness, dissipates, and it's like I can breathe properly for the first time since that portal closed. Now, though, there's another question.

'Where?' And then even more importantly. 'Can I get there? Can we get them back?'

A little sadness interweaves with that benevolent smile now. 'Outside of my purview. As for getting there and getting back? Well, there're two aspects to why I can't answer that. First, no spoilers, right?' It's a motive to live by, so I can't criticise her too much for that one. 'Second, I hate to break this to you, Paul Bonhomme, but you're Perfect and dead. It's time to move on.'

The electric ants are now doing relay sprints around my brain that'd make Usain Bolt jealous. 'But if I wasn't, if I could get back, would it be at least possible?' I have to know.

She nods. 'Possible? Yes. But very difficult. So endlessly hard, poor Cathar. Don't you want to rest? And again, you've reached Perfection once more.'

I go to wave her off in an "I get it, I get it" kind of way when something about the way she twitches her eyebrow makes me pause. It's like she's trying to give me a nudge, a little tip to help me out if I don't want to move on. And I don't; I really don't. Fuck the whole sailing peacefully off into the West bullshit now. I'm about to kick Gandalf in the private parts and commandeer the boat to sail straight back for Middle Earth.

And that — that gives me an idea.

I take a real good long chug on the whisky. It's not a classy way to drink single malt distilled from the goddess' own wild oats by the taste of it, but damn it's so delicious, it works, and I have no idea when, if ever I'll get to taste this again. So I swallow down as much as I can, savouring the burn all the way down, like drinking dragon fire straight from the source.

Then I stare hard at the Good God herself. I'm studying her for tells, but I don't think I want to take her on in a poker tournament anytime soon.

'So,' I start slowly, thoughtfully, rolling each word around on my tongue like a really, exaggeratedly pretentious sommelier. 'I can't go back because I'm Perfect, right?'

The divine being in front of me nods, and I'd swear she's trying not to smirk.

'But if I wasn't Perfect, I could go back?'

Again the almost-smirk with the nod.

I digest this, running it around my brain, which is easy. It can just follow the grooves worn by the electric brain ants. It's a doozy of a problem, but

I think I might just — *just* be able to work out a solution. However, I need to know a couple of other answers before I put it into action.

'If I go back, will I get my *talent* back?' Maeve's body is gone, and getting my hands on a fae human-like enough for me to hijack isn't likely to be an easy task even outside of the whole moral conundrum of stealing a body just to get their power.

The god-in-woman-form waves her hand magnanimously, like a visiting queen cruising past the adoring masses from the window of a Rolls Royce. 'I think, all being considered, if you can make it back, I can make sure you get your *talent* back.'

Well, that's one big concern done. Now that just leaves one other. 'What about the whole "continuous reincarnation" thing? Do I get to keep that even though Nicetas swallowed it down?'

She beams, the smile more wondrous than the dawn of the sun after an endless night, its rays spreading out to warm and wake the land. 'I couldn't possibly comment on that. After all, that's private between the two of you. It's not my business whether he spits or swallows.'

Well, we might not have the answer to that question about Nicetas, but we do in relation to "what does Paul Bonhomme do with a mouthful of heavenly whisky when a divine entity makes a dirty joke?"

I angle my head towards the fireplace so as I don't at least *discharge said mouthful over God herself*, but it's a pretty close thing. Instead, the flames roar up for a minute in a way that suggests that this whisky must be a much higher percentage proof than I'd have guessed from the taste. Makes me wonder if the Good God doesn't have a little still set up out the back, and I'm basically drinking her moonshine.

Once I stop coughing long enough to remember how to breathe again, I manage to knock back a good restorative measure of the homebrew I spat everywhere. She's stopped laughing, though mischief dances behind her irises. I suppose I shouldn't be surprised God has a weird sense of humour. Have you seen duck billed platypuses? That takes a pretty twisted imagination.

I get the feeling I've received all the answers I'm going to. If I can undo the whole Perfection thing, I can head back. I'll get my *talent* back. I may or may not get my reincarnation magic back, so I'll just have to do my best to avoid finding out for as long as humanly or even inhumanly possible. And then...

Then getting Aicha and Jakob back is possible.

I'm not glossing over the whole "endlessly hard" comment that she made, which, considering what we've just been through, doesn't exactly fill me with confidence. But that's a worry for later. One thing at a time. I finish mulling over what I was thinking about and take another hard slug of what I have decided is the real holy spirit. This time, though, I finish the glass. I guess that's a subtle hint that it's time to make a decision. You don't have to go home, but you can't stay here.

'So,' I say, ruminating on each word as I shape it, really taking it as slowly as I can. First, to make sure I get it right, and second, because this is the most safe and comforting environment I've ever been in, even discounting the perfect liquor. I allow myself to savour a last few moments of peace. 'I've got a few things to say.'

The Good God cocks her head, an invitation to carry on. That she's listening.

'Well, to start with, thank you. Thanks for stepping in and, well, saving everything.'

She nods, amusement still doing a can-can across her expression.

'Seriously, I know you're probably going to say something like, "I only help those who help themselves," but I get it. You're big on that whole "hands off" approach, right? That's what the whole argument between you and the other one stemmed from. You leave us to our own devices —free will, zero destiny, et cetera— while he wants to control everything, micro-managing reality, am I right?'

There's no amusement with the nod this time. Not that she's angered by what I've said. But it's hard to hold humour and sorrow in the same regard.

'So getting involved at all: the messages in the sand, breaking the rune on my finger in Ben's lair, any of it, not even mentioning the whole "manifesting on Earth to go toe-to-toe with the BBEG". You went above and beyond, seriously. I'm guessing not many people get to say thank you to you face-to-face, so on behalf of everyone who has no idea how close they came to ceasing breathing last night, thank you. Seriously.'

There's a wetness around her eyes. I think I might have made the supreme being, at least for our corner of reality, cry. She leans forward, wraps her arms around my shoulders, and presses her lips to my forehead. It's a priceless gift, the benediction of God herself, and I'm pretty sure I'll feel the presence of her kiss for whatever slice of eternity is given to me before I'm done once and for all.

She pulls back and looks at me. She knows the answer, but she's happy to humour me. 'And what's the last thing you'd like to say to me, Good Man Bonhomme?'

I smile — no, I grin, a wide-mouthed, shit-eating grin that'd give the fucking Tarrasque a run for his money. 'I just wanted to tell you to go fuck yourself repeatedly, you absolute dickhead.' Then I give her a two-fingered salute.

Her eyes go wide in mock horror and disbelief. 'Paul Bonhomme! Swearing at the Good God themselves. Telling us to go fuck ourselves? That —' She smiles a lazy, happy smile like the cat who got the cream...and a plump cushion to sit on and all the belly scratches she could ever dream of. 'That's a mortal sin. You can't be Perfect saying things like that.'

The glass is gone from my hand, and the walls of the room start to wobble and waver like a *Star Trek* teleportation scene, everything blurring and fading, with just her face still clear for one moment. She touches her fingers to her lips and blows me a kiss that I feel brush against my cheek like butterfly wings.

Then she's gone.

And so am I.

CHAPTER THIRTY-ONE
BUGARACH, 10 JUNE, PRESENT DAY
Like tears in the rain.

I open my eyes to see the stars.

It sounds like such a simple thing to say. But it's two things I never expected again.

To see the stars. To open my eyes.

So I really see them. I drink in their scintillation, the waning as high-level cloud wisps dim their brilliance. The return to exuberant lustre as they pass. The ghost-cloud swirl of the Milky Way's phantom embrace, impossibly far, inconceivably vast.

Cracked soil crumbs press into the crick of my neck. The previously soft earth was baked to a texture akin to granite in the blazing heat of the battle fought up here. Every time I breathe, it feels like I'm getting a massage with a cheese grater. And I love it. Who knew it was possible to take such comfort in discomfort?

I should get up, really, but to say the past experience has been a bit overwhelming is sort of like saying fae are a bit tricksy or politicians probably shouldn't be taken at their word all the time. There's a massive, complicated, tangled skein of problems and decisions to deal with once I start moving again. There always is. That's what being alive means.

The famous philosopher Ferris Bueller once said, 'Life moves pretty fast. If you don't stop and look around once in a while, you could miss it.' It works whether it's life or lives. Sometimes, days stretch off like endless childlike dreams of summers. And sometimes, I wake up, and I forget I'm not still wearing those black robes, still ministering through Occitane, coming to from a strange, vivid dream of impossible futures. Times when I forget Susane died. Times when it seems only a moment ago — present and pressing down on my chest till I can hardly breathe.

Lives move pretty fast. I just want to appreciate the moment for a while.

So I lie here, my back pressed against a thousand soil pebbles of differing shapes, and I accept the discomfort, embrace it, welcome it. I stare at galaxies and universes as impossibly distant as I am from where I started from, places I'll never see, journeys beyond my reach except in my dreams. And that's okay. Limits are inevitable. They give us something to push against, to try to overcome. Our dreams are what allow us to test those, to surpass what was believed possible.

And I live. Nothing more. Nothing less. I live. In one single instant, without expectation or demand, I simply exist. I let time dance unobserved for a moment, let life move inexorably onwards without my direct involvement.

I live.

Of course, there's a limit to it. Eventually, that uncomfortable pressure across the majority of my body in contact with the ground passes from "oh, the wonder of sensation" to "fuck me, that's quite irritatingly uncomfortable", and time comes crashing back in, asking me if I'd like to take the next dance. Why yes, I guess I would.

So I sit up, brushing away the fragments of the ground that have worked their way down the collar of the T-shirt I'm wearing despite the faux leather of my bulky jacket having kept a fair bit of it out. I didn't even realise I was wearing clothes. So much for being totally in tune with all my senses and sensations. The comfortable heft of the Avirex is matched by the jeans, plus a pair of roll top Timberlands, suitable both for walking down mountains and breaking kneecaps.

Apparently, God has good taste in clothes.

There's a whole world of theological discussions to be had there, of course. Was that really God I met? What about their sibling we drove out of our reality? Did they create this world, this existence, really? Or did they find it like a discarded play toy? Or more like an ant farm, maybe, and one of them kept the other from setting them all on fire with a magnifying glass rather than actually making the ants themselves. In a set of dimensions where angels aren't really angels and demons love where they live and just want to have a good time, I'm not sure I can really get on board with the ideas of supreme beings even if one did bring me back to life.

It's a conversation we can have when the time is right. The right time being when we've a whole stack of bottles of single malt, even if none of them are ever going to live up to the taste of that sweet nectar I got to taste in the possibly-God's shack. I'm sure 'Zac'll have a few thoughts on the...

I practically jump upright. Fucking hell — Isaac! Whipping my head back and forth, I search. There. He's over there.

About twenty metres away is the man who saved my life, who, along with his angel-half, battled the dark energy of a god, who's been there for me every time I ever needed him for hundreds of years. He's kneeling with his back to me, and by the moonlight, I see the bones scattered around him like a clumsy archaeologist has knocked a display down and is now staring in horror at the mess he's made. Except it's not horror. Even without seeing his face, I can feel the pain from here. It's grief. Pure and utter grief. He's not searching. He's mourning.

"Zac.' I try to shout, but my voice is half-hoarse. I swallow a couple of times, getting some moisture into it. "Zac!'

His head whips round, and he staggers to his feet. By the time I've taken the first two steps towards him, he's covered the rest of the distance. He throws his arms around me, burying his head against my shoulder, holding me tight. Wracking, gasping sobs shake his frame. I hold him, let him get them out. He's earned those, every single one of them.

Eventually, he calms, his breathing returning to something like normal, and he's able to speak without his voice hitching. 'How? How are you here, my boy? I thought... I thought you were gone...forever...'

There's the tiniest break back in his tone, and I wrap him back up in a hug to reassure him I'm here. Isaac the Blind, my second father, loves me deeply, and I show him it's entirely reciprocated.

'Apparently,' I say once he's back under control again, 'saving existence from ultimate evil buys you a bit of latitude.' I can see the myriad of questions starting to form on his lips, his inquisitive mind whirring into action at such a statement, so I hastily add on, 'I'll tell you all about it later, when we can get a drink, promise?'

He nods, not exactly appeased but accepting the answer at the very least. There's one thing, though, he needs to know right now.

'Listen.' I pull back so he can see me, can read how serious I am in my eyes, know that I'm not playing with him or building his hopes up unfairly. 'Jakob? Aicha? They're both still alive.'

I can see the disbelief writ large in his expression, the doubt. It's not that he doesn't have confidence in me, I know that. It's the price he paid last time. The centuries he spent hurting, hoping that his brother was alive. It cost him so much, and to have got Jak back only to lose him again after a short few weeks must be eating him alive. Me popping back up from the dead? Well, this might be a more unusual scenario than normal, but still, it's hardly outside the realms of possibility.

I nod gently but repetitively, insistently. 'They're both alive, 'Zac. I swear it. And we're going to find them. We're going to get them back.'

Tears trace down now-well-trod pathways worn by those that ran down his cheeks before, but he doesn't crumble this time. Instead, he pulls himself up, his lips pursing, his brow furrowing. Resolution writes itself through his posture and through his core. 'Aye, my lad. If they're alive, then we bloody well will.'

A thought occurs to me regarding that. 'The White Lady — she's not still about, is she?'

Isaac shakes his head. 'As soon as you were gone, after the pyrotechnic show she put on, and that was a bloody sight to behold, lad, I can tell you, there was neither sight nor sound of anyone left. Just the scattered bones and Nith and I. I... I thought we were the only ones left...'

The tears flow again, more freely even, but he brushes himself off, perhaps shaking the last of those dark thoughts away along with the few morsels of dirt clinging to his blazer sleeves. He looks back up, resolute. 'I've looked through everything here. There's nowt — of value anyhow. All the magic's gone. Just empty, hollow bones and these.' He waves a hand at the two operating tables that De Montfort brought here to hold the assembled skeletons.

The bones are easy. I just stash them in my etheric storage to get rid of at some convenient location later on. Leaving two whole human skeletons on top of Bugarach would be a pretty unkind surprise for the next hiker to come up here, plus might raise questions we could do without. As for the tables?

'This one's for you,' I murmur under my breath, then pull together a ball of fire in the palm of my hand. It's not as easy for me as it is for her, and I can feel it scorching my skin slightly, but eventually, I can feel it has formed sufficiently. Then I lob it at the two tables and watch them burst into flame.

I set them burning like a beacon for Aicha Kandicha. A message from the mountaintop. That we're going to find them.

That we're going to light the way home.

AUTHOR'S NOTES

We're here — not at the end of all things, but simply at the end of the first story arc. It's been an honour and a privilege to share this first part of the imPerfect Cathar story with you, and I thank you from the bottom of my heart for walking this first leg of the journey with me.

But remember — this is only the first leg. We're less than halfway through the whole story. There's a long way still to go, and some hard roads left to walk for Paul Bonhomme and his crew before we get to the end.

This is the end of the historical flashback sections for now — though you can expect some novellas and short stories still to come in between the main stories. In fact — surprise! — there's a special Halloween novella coming very soon called An imPerfect Samhain which follows Paul and Aicha investigating missing children on the Cote D'Azur in the 1950s. It seemed poignant to finish them on these three moments of self-reflection or realisation for Paul.

De Morieve really lived, and was one of the few noblemen to survive the bloody guillotine during the French Revolution. He was an extraordinary looking man, with sharp protruding teeth, known for his cruelty. After his death and burial, children in the area started turning up dead with vampiric marks on their necks. Seventy years later, when his tomb was disturbed, it started up again. His descendent — according to legend — took it so seriously he summoned a priest, staked the remains — which were supposedly entirely intact and looked as fresh as when he had first been buried — then burned them to ashes and scattered them on the sea. De Morieve — combined with Vlad the Impaler — was arguably the inspiration for Bram Stoker himself.

The First World War, of course, was precisely as horror-filled and traumatic as Paul described it. What a stain it must have left upon a generation.

My thanks as always go to my family for their love and support; my editor Miranda for her incredible work at bringing out the best in every single word; my beta readers Becca, Becky and Lauretta who helped me to discover what really needed to be said; my ARC readers who do sensational work in not only giving their honest reviews but spotting typos that slipped through the net — special mention to Leigh and Brenda for their detailed notes and Mardie for the audio spots! — and for all their support and encouragement; Athena for her sensational work proofreading the audiobooks; Mel-Mel and Jimmy who keep sense and order in the imPerfect imPs group on Facebook; the FAKA authors whose advice and friendship have been invaluable throughout this process with special mention to Heather G Harris for her pearls of wisdom that have helped me arrive at this point; and every one of my friends, old and new, who have walked with me thus far in the adventure. The road ahead is bright and shining and the next twists and turns are calling to me!

The novella 'An imPerfect Samhain' will come out before the end of October '23 and then book 7 — 'imPerfect Blood' — will come out, along with the rest of the next trilogy, in Spring '24. Paul's travails are only just beginning...

Read on for a sneak peek at the first chapter of 'imPerfect Blood'...

REMEMBER

Do please consider leaving a review, or clicking a star rating on Amazon. If you can click follow too, that'd be fantabulous. It keeps the terrible hungry demon Sozeb from clawing chunks from my very soul.

Just remember. Never say his name backwards. Especially when you're still in your Prime.

ABOUT THE AUTHOR

It's been a strange, unbelievable journey to arrive at the point where these books are going to be released into the wild, like rare, near-extinct animals being returned to their natural habitat, already wondering where they're going to nick cigarettes from on the plains of Africa, the way they used to from the zookeeper's overalls. C.N. Rowan ("Call me C.N., Mr. Rowan was my father") came originally from Leicester, England. Somehow escaping its terrible, terrible clutches (only joking, he's a proud Midlander really), he has wound up living in the South-West of France for his sins. Only, not for his sins. Otherwise, he'd have ended up living somewhere really dreadful. Like Leicester. (Again – joking, he really does love Leicester. He knows Leicester can take a joke. Unlike some of those other cities. Looking at you, Slough.) With multiple weird strings to his bow, all of which are made of tooth-floss and liable to snap if you tried to use them to do anything as adventurous as shooting an arrow, he's done all sorts of odd things, from running a hiphop record label (including featuring himself as rapper) to hustling disability living aids on the mean streets of Syston. He's particularly proud of the work he's done managing and recording several French hiphop acts, and is currently awaiting confirmation of wild rumours he might get a Gold Disc for a song he recorded and mixed.

He'd always love to hear from you so please drop him an email here - chris@cnrowan.com

f   facebook.com/cnrowan

a   amazon.com/author/cnrowan

g   goodreads.com/author/show/23093361.C_N_Rowan

⊙   instagram.com/cnrowanauthor

TURN THE PAGE FOR THE FIRST CHAPTER OF THE IMPER-FECT CATHAR BOOK 7

'IMPERFECT BLOOD'

CHAPTER 1 - THE MOTORWAY TOWARDS TOULOUSE, OCTOBER 26TH, PRESENT DAY

I'm missing my drive. On this drive. Heading for Isaac's drive. Drive, drive, drive, drive. Funny how words lose all meaning. Just the same way meaning can.

It's weird, not knowing what's going to happen to me when I die.

I don't mean in the religious sense, where I used to think I'd head off to join the great big rave up in the sky. Break out the glow sticks and the electric harps. No, my faith got lost a long time ago. It probably got left in the pockets of one of my bodies when I died.

Because that's the point. Before, when I kicked the bucket, a second later it'd be righted, full back up to the brim, ready for me to take another swing at it. Reincarnation magic is handy stuff, allowing me to just pop another coin in life's arcade machine. Continuous 1 Ups every time I got killed gratuitously. Which was most days with a Y in them. Now, though?

Now, I'm not sure. See, my reincarnation magic definitely got torn away from me, woven into a spell to allow the evil prick - who may or may not have made this reality - back into it. I sacrificed myself to stop it happening, and as a pat on the head from the not-evil-but-still-a-bit-sus other being who might be God, or a god, or at least the creator of this tiny corner of life, I got to come back, *talent* and all. Problem is, when I asked them whether I got my reincarnating magic as well, they just smiled. Enigmatically. Which is, in my professional opinion, a bit of a dick move.

So, what happens when I die? Will I pop back up like the proverbial penny, bad or otherwise? Will there be a choir robe with my name on it, or a pitchfork ready to be inserted into my unmentionables? Or will it be what I expected when I broke my Perfection, centuries ago, to stop the Evil Prick God the first time round? Will I dissolve off into nothingness, ceasing to be?

It's weird, not knowing what's going to happen to me when I die.

I'm not going to lie, there's a part of me that's deeply worried by the whole thing, that wants to just go and bury my head in the sand until mortality gets the message, does the decent thing and goes away. My whole method for success in the Talented world hasn't even been brute force and ignorance. More brashness and idiocy, all underlined by picking up another nearly-new body each time I pop my clogs. Foul-tempered hydra eating people in the subway system? No problem, I'd just go and feed myself to it over and over until it got indigestion and had to take a post-meal nap. Then lop off all the heads in one fell swoop.

Which brings me to the other major problem. The problemest problem of all. It wouldn't normally be me doing the lopping. It'd be Aicha, the all-round badass immortal Moroccan warrior princess who's saved my bacon so often, I should probably start making people some bacon sandwiches before it all goes off. Although, being a vegetarian, I'd rather not. Perhaps we could say she saved my veggie bacon-substitute so often. Or perhaps I could not get so tangled up in making nearly as much of a mess of this metaphor as I do of most situations when she's not there to give me a clip round the earhole.

Because she isn't here. Not anymore. She's not dead. Maybe-God already confirmed that much to me. It was the main reason I came back to life when I could have cashed in my chips for an eternity with my feet up by the pool side, drinking ambrosia pina coladas. No, she's definitely still alive. She's just not alive *here*, in this world. She fell through a portal, saving us all, sacrificing herself once again. And I'm not going to rest until I find a way to pay back all the times she's pulled me back from the edge. Until I can get to that other reality and bring Aicha Kandicha home.

The whole 'pledging not to rest' is mainly an image, but I'd be the first to admit I'm not getting enough shut-eye. Sadly, finding creatures *powerful* enough to pull a Jim Morrison and break on through to the other side is about as easy as it sounds. Even when my other best friend slash mentor slash father figure body-shares with an angel.

That'd been my first thought, of course. Nithael came down from the higher dimensions. Surely if he can go up and down, going sideways is easier, right? Apparently wrong. Neither of them can explain it to me, at least not in words of sufficiently few syllables for a Bear of Little Brain such as myself to understand, but Nith can't or won't help. I'm going to go with 'can't' so I don't end up trying to pick a fist-fight with an angel. That's never going to end well.

Instead, I've spent the last few months scouring the Pyrenees, hiking back up to Bugarach, where the big showdown with Team Evil Dick God went down; hanging around Montsegur and Rennes-Le-Château and anywhere else rumoured to be a place of *power* in the mountains. Which is more than a few locales, thus why it's taken me months. I even went back to Lourdes, which is hardly packed full of happy memories for me after I got most of my *talent* eaten by Melusine there. But I know the being I'm seeking helped Aicha out when I got myself stuck knee-deep in the shit. Again. It's part of the reason she ended up getting sucked into the portal. All part of the deal she made with the White Lady.

So I'd really like to get hold of said Lady, and find out what the deal was, and see if I can't strike one of my own. Except she's nowhere to be found. Normally sightings of the Lady spring up more often than UFO sightings in the drunken backwaters of the US. Not at the moment, though. Neither sight nor sound to be heard or found. Whether it's a consequence of her assist to beat back Papa Nicetas and his attempt to bring through Pant-Shittingly-Terrifying-Evil™ into our world, or just because mysterious hella *powerful* beings gonna mysterious, I have no idea. I do know that it's massively annoying though.

At the same time as going up the rocky mountain and down the rushy glen, I've also been a-hunting for a certain little man. One who looks like the sort of plastic monster that came in cereal packets at the end of last century, if they were over-sized and malicious. The Nain Rouge. There's two good reasons why I'm looking for him. First, because he helped Aicha find the White Lady last time. Second, 'cos he spectacularly screwed the pooch when he was supposed to help us get into the Winter Realm in Fairie undetected. Far as I'm concerned, he owes me. And, like most people, when you need to call a debt in, he's gone into hiding and is nowhere to be found.

So, after enough fell walking to mean I'm actually feeling in peak physical form for once, and enough frustration that I'm ready to drown myself in a bath of whisky till I feel better, I'm coming back home. Back to Toulouse.

I mean, I've been back a few times – popping in to grab a change of clothes, a quick nap in a real bed. Thing is, when you've lived for as long as I have, you accrue a healthy bank balance, unless you splurge it all up the wall getting out of your gourd for years on end. Trust me, I've done it. Luckily, long enough ago I've rebuilt my fortunes since.

Trouble is, Toulouse doesn't hold any real appeal until I find Aicha. So, I've mainly been crashing in bed-and-breakfasts, or even the huts set throughout the mountains for hikers to sleep. As most sightings of the Lady happen at night, I've wanted to be there when the opportunity comes to pick up the scent. Problem is, it's not that the trail is cold. It's that it doesn't even seem to exist.

And, if I'm honest, I've been avoiding Isaac. Him and Nithael. Because it wasn't just Aicha who was lost. Jakob, his brother, and Nanael, Nith's kin, both got sucked into the portal too. Except they'd already become disembodied. So, we have no idea what will have happened to them – if they will have survived, or in what form. The pair are devastated, having only recently got them back after centuries of absence. Now, they're lost once more. And I'm not helping Isaac in his search. I'm off doing my own one. And, if I'm honest, as much as I love Jakob, Aicha's my priority. That feels like a betrayal of my oldest friend, and is the reason why I'm finding it hard to look him straight in the eye right now.

Of course, there's a name for acting like that. And that name is cowardice. Which doesn't seem to be the right way to honour Aicha in her absence. Were she here, she'd slap me round the back of the head till I could feel my brains poking out of my tear-ducts and then drag me by my twisted ear round to see Isaac. So that's what I'm going to do. After several weeks away, and months since I called round, it's time to stop being a cowardy cowardy custard.

Driving back up the motorway from the South of Toulouse towards the ring road is a silent affair. I've not been able to bring myself to listen to music on any of my drives. Tunes aren't bringing me any solace at this time. It's something we did together, driving towards unimaginable danger, blaring out some banging beats, taking the piss out of each other. Plus, it makes me remember her insistence on us getting our own theme music. Until we make that happen, I'm not in the mood for getting my groove on.

As I get closer and closer, an uneasy feeling starts to grow. It's one of those ones where you know you've forgotten something, where you keep looking at the clock, part of your brain pointing out the position of the hands, insisting it means something, but you can't remember. Not until it's too late.

So it is with me now. It's only when I get onto the ring-road itself, only as I'm driving round towards the motorway off towards Auch, that the realisation of what's been missing sinks in, because suddenly, finally, I feel it.

The wards. The wards I gave to Isaac. The wards Nithael supercharged so they extended all the way down to the south of Auterive. The wards that should have been thrumming on my skin like static electricity for the past seventy kilometres or so. The wards that are only evident in their absence.

The wards. The wards are down.

ALSO BY C.N. ROWAN

The imPerfect Cathar Series

imPerfect Magic

imPerfect Curse

imPerfect Fae

imPerfect Bones

imPerfect Hunt

imPerfect Gods

An imPerfect Trap (prequel novella to imPerfect Magic)
An imPerfect Samhain (out 28th Oct 23)

Printed in Great Britain
by Amazon

44968523R00148